Rounding the corner of his house cautiously, Wally saw a naked man in his alleyway. He was surrounded by a roughly circular patch of scorched grass.

The naked man saw Wally, sprang at him and grabbed the lapels of his coat. "*What year is it?*" he snapped.

Unused to naked men taking him by the lapels in his own yard, Wally answered automatically, and very quickly, "1995, it's 1995, I swear to God!"

The stranger released Wally and, for just a moment, began to panic utterly, just totally lose it . . . then pull himself back from the edge. "Crot!" he snarled. "Total snowcrash! Blood for this, my chop!" The date clearly displeased him greatly.

On Wally the light began to dawn. This was the moment he had been waiting for since the age of six—here—now!

"Look, cousin," Wally said, "it's cool out here. Come on inside. Get some hot coffee in you—you drink coffee? We got *real* good coffee—"

The naked man looked up at him and instantly, visibly, became devious. "Sure, yes, hot caffy would be optimal. I can . . . uh . . . I can explain all this—"

Wally watched the stranger carefully on the way into the house. They hung the right into the study and the naked man froze in his tracks, staring horrorstruck at a painting on the wall. A Jack Gaughan *Analog* cover. "Oh crash," he moaned. "It's worse than I thought! You're science fiction fans, aren't you?"

Wally took a deep breath and drew himself up. "Sir, I'm afraid it is worse even than that. My wife and I are Secret Masters Of Fandom."

The stranger fainted dead away.

BOOKS BY SPIDER ROBINSON

LIFEHOUSE

SPIDER ROBINSON

A Baen Books Original

Baen Publishing Enterprises
P.O. Box 1403
Riverdale, NY 10471

ISBN: 0-671-87777-1

Cover art by David Lee Anderson

First printing, April 1997

Distributed by Simon & Schuster
1230 Avenue of the Americas
New York, NY 10020

Typeset by Windhaven Press, Auburn, NH
Printed in the United States of America

For
the two Evelyns

. . . may we meet again in The Mind . . .

We come spinning out of nothingness,
Scattering stars like dust.

Look at these worlds spinning out of
        nothingness:
This is within your power.

Out beyond ideas of right-doing
        and wrong-doing,
There is a field.
I'll meet you there...

—Rumi,
a thousand years ago in Lebanon

If the Eternal Return is not allowed
        by modern physics,
and if the Heat Death can also
        be avoided,
then eternal progress is possible.

—Prof. Frank Tipler,
PHYSICS OF IMMORTALITY, 1993

Prologue

The Tar Baby's alarm caught them making love, or the whole emergency might never have happened.

It might seem odd that they let something as frivolous as sex distract them even momentarily from their responsibilities. They were as dedicated, motivated and committed to their work as any guardians in history, as responsible as it was possible to be. And they had, after all, been married to each other for over nine centuries at that point.

But then, theirs was—even for their kind—one of the Great Marriages. They had mutually agreed on their five hundredth anniversary that in their opinion, things were just getting really good, and as their millennial approached, both still felt the same. And perhaps even we mortals can dimly understand that any hobby which endures over such a span of time must have within it certain elements of obsession. They had long since taken into their lovemaking, as into their marriage itself, the spirit of the Biblical injunction, "Whatsoever thy hand findeth to do, do it with all thy might," and they were good at finding things to do.

The precise timing of the alarm, moreover, was

1

more than diabolical: it was Murphian. For several hours they had been constructing a complex and beautiful choreography of ecstasy together, a four-dimensional structure of pleasure and joy extending through space and time. A DNA double-helix would actually be a fairly accurate three-dimensional model of it. It was itself part of a larger, more complicated structure that had been under creation for nearly a week, a sort of interwoven pattern of patterns of pleasure and joy, of which this particular movement was meant to be the capstone. The tocsin sounded in both their skulls *just* as, in the words of Jake Thackray, "They were getting to a very important bit . . ." and for two whole seconds, both honestly mistook it for a hyperbole of their imaginations. By the time they understood it was real, a necessity at once emotional, biological and artistic urged them to ignore it—just for a moment.

This, in their defense, they did not do. Their responsibility was too much a part of who they were. Orgasm may be the source of all meaning—but it needs a universe in which to mean. The instant they realized the alarm was not a shared hallucination they stopped doing what they were doing (or more precisely, stopped paying attention to the fact that they were doing it), queried the Tar Baby, downloaded a detailed report of the situation, and studied it, fully prepared to leap out of bed and hit the ground running if the emergency seemed to warrant it.

It did not. Indeed, it seemed to be practically over. Only one sophont appeared to be involved—and not a sophisticated one. It carried only a single (pathetic) weapon, and no data transmission gear of any kind. The Tar Baby reported no difficulty at all in investing it, and was even now reprogramming it. There was another higher lifeform of some kind present, about fifty meters away from the Egg, but it did not display sentience signatures and thus could not be a significant threat. To top it all off, the whole nonevent was taking place less than two thousand meters away, a distance they could cover in seconds.

Yes, doctrine did mandate a suspenders-and-belt physical visit to the site to obtain eyeball confirmation of all data. But doctrine did not (quite) say that it absolutely had to be done *this instant* . . . not unless there were complicating factors present. They both double-checked, and there were not. They very nearly triple-checked. They concluded, first separately and then in rapport, that a delay of as much as fifteen minutes in the on-site follow-up inspection could not reasonably pose a serious or even a significant risk. They ran their logic past the Tar Baby, which concurred. It agreed to notify them at once if the situation were to degenerate, and to preserve all data.

This whole process had taken perhaps three seconds, a total of five seconds since the alarm had gone off. The weeklong work of art was still salvageable. Sighing happily, they returned to their erotic choreography, and in under ten minutes brought it to a conclusion satisfactory in every sense of the word, the brief hiatus actually improving it trivially, both as sensation and as art. They spent an additional five minutes on breath recovery and afterglow, and were *just* about to get up, less than fifteen minutes after the Tar Baby's first call—when suddenly it called again.

And this time it *shrieked*.

✧   ✧   ✧

They came that close to being vigilant enough. Less than fifteen minutes late on a pointless backup. Less than one minute *too* late.

Unfortunately, they were not playing horseshoes.

And so the whole universe very nearly ceased to ever have existed. . . .

Chapter 1
A Walk in the Park

June Bellamy was walking in the woods, listening to FM on dedicated headphones and thinking deep thoughts about mortality and love—or perhaps about love and mortality—the first time she came close to annihilating upwards of twenty billion people.

It was definitely the mook's fault, not June's—the whole thing. That is quite clear. All she wanted to do, at the start, was to grieve, and she had gone out of her way to do so privately. Nonetheless she was—thanks to the mook, and the headphones—the one who ended up personally endangering some twenty billion lives. Repeatedly. Whereas he was out of the story almost at once, never had more than a moment's worry over it, and would not even remember that for nearly a century.

It is almost enough to make one suspect God of a sense of irony.

It was a splendid Fall afternoon in Vancouver. June was thirty-three years old and in excellent health. The woods she walked through were part of the former University Endowment Lands now called Pacific Spirit Regional Park, adjoining the sprawling campus of the University of British Columbia: about the only land on the Vancouver peninsula that had never been settled by white people or developed, and at least in theory never would be. The trail she had chosen had good drainage; despite the fact that it had rained for twelve of the past fourteen days—excessive even for Vancouver—leaves that had been lying in sunshine today *crunch*ed under her walking shoes. There was just enough crispness in the air to encourage activity, and the trapped ozone of several thunderstorms to add alertness. Traffic and houses and bustling human activity were no more than a kilometer or so away in any direction—but no trace of them reached here, into the forest sanctum. There were surely other hikers in the woods—but not many, and few June was likely to meet. It was a wonderful place in which to be conflicted.

The only death she knew to be on her personal horizon was the impending death of her mother, in San Francisco, of colon cancer. She thought it more than enough reason to be conflicted.

She had just that day returned from what she knew would be her last visit with her mother. She had known since the first phone call from her father, the previous week, that Laura Bellamy had at best a matter of days left. The cancer had come out of nowhere and gutted her without warning or mercy: by the time she was symptomatic she was, as June's father put it on the phone, a dead woman walking.

And by the time June had arrived at her hospital bedside she was clearly done walking. She had looked shrunken and—the pun made June tremble the instant it occurred to her, because she could never ever share it with anyone—and *cured*, like leather: she had looked like someone who *ought* to have that many wires and tubes coming out of her. She was fifty-four, and looked ninety. June knew exactly the phrase her lover/partner Paul would have used to describe his almost-mother-in-law's condition if he'd been there: "circling the drain." She'd looked like a crude, ill-thought-out parody of Laura Bellamy, one that was not intended to be sustained for long.

But she had also looked—this was the part June could not get out of her mind, as she walked through the forest—fearless. June's mother had, to the best of her recollection, always had the usual human allotment of fears, doubts, and uncertainties. Now she had none. It was clear in her sunken, shining eyes. June had wanted mightily to ask her about that, to discuss it with her. But it had proven almost completely impossible.

That had been the very worst part of the whole depressing experience. Everyone in the room, including the Alzheimer's patient in the next bed, had known perfectly well that Laura Bellamy was terminal. But June's father, Frank, suffered from— clutched like a drowner—the illusion that his wife did not suspect anything of the sort. The notion that even a doctor who was trying to could have concealed such news from Laura Bellamy was ridiculous, but Frank was in deep denial—and, as always, needed his wife's help with it. He needed to believe he was protecting her from *something*, even if it was only knowledge of her doom. He had met June in the hospital lobby and explained solemnly that they must be very very careful not to let Laura suspect the Awful Truth. By the time June had realized he was serious, it was too late to protest; they were on their way in the door of her mother's room.

Where she found, to her horror, that Laura Bellamy would rather have died than admit in her husband's presence that she knew she was dying. Unlike most men of his generation, Frank Bellamy had not often needed his wife to simulate ignorance or stupidity; she was willing to indulge him, this once.

And therefore June, who had abandoned her partner in the middle of an important project and traveled thirteen hundred kilometers for the specific purpose of having her Last Conversation with her mother, who had rehearsed it in her mind for several tight-lipped dry-eyed days because she knew this was her one and only window, had been unable to have it . . . had been forced to smile and chatter cheery inanities about how everything was back home in Canada these days and even help, herself, to shore up the grotesque illusion that her mother was soon going to recover and resume her interrupted life.

Horror.

They'd held a wordless conversation with their eyes, of course, while the rest of their faces spoke hollow lines for Frank's benefit. But eye contact lacks bandwidth; the communication had been ambiguous, fragmentary, profoundly unsatisfactory for June.

Once—once—she had succeeded in inventing an errand that would require her father to leave the room for five minutes. And then she had gone and dithered away three of them, finishing up the useless surface conversational thread they'd been chewing when he left, too nervous to begin. Finally she'd said, "Mom—we *have* to talk."

"Yes, dear," her mother had said at once. "But if we take it out of the box now, there's no way we can have it all tucked back in again in two minutes . . . and that's when he'll be back."

She'd made the words come out calmly. "There probably isn't going to be another chance. I've gotta get back to Canada, and I can't risk coming back."

"Yes, there will."

"Phone? He can't stay here twenty-four hours a day—"

Her mother had smiled at that. They had never had the clichéd mother-daughter phone relationship; Laura Bellamy felt that talking on the telephone was unsatisfactory, and that talking long-distance was like hemorrhaging: something to be done in brief bursts if absolutely necessary. "They won't let you have a cell phone around all this medical gear, and I'm afraid I'm just too lazy to hobble down the hall these days. Don't worry, dear: we'll talk."

"*When*? How?" Her voice had risen in pitch, and she was furious with herself for losing control. She was *not* here to add her own emotional burdens to her mother's obviously overfull agenda.

But her mother's serenity had only increased. "Do you know, I don't have the faintest idea? And I don't know how I know. But I'm quite certain—so don't worry, June. All the things we need to say to each other will be said . . . in time."

June's eyes had narrowed suspiciously. "What, are you going religious on me, Ma? Now?"

Laura had smiled. "I don't think so. I'm still just as fundamentally ignorant as I ever was, about all the important things. I have no Answers; I've had no revelations. But somehow . . ." Her face had changed subtly, in a way June could not classify. "Somehow, I'm not . . . not quite as *clueless* as I was. Just . . . just trust me. All right? We *will* get it all said, one day—and we'll probably find out that we already knew most of it. And meanwhile, it's all going to be alright."

And with theatrical timing, her father had reentered the room just then.

The next hour or so of their discourse had been transmitted by eye contact, with its terrible signal-to-noise ratio (was that a punctuation mark? or just a blink?), and hampered by the need to keep a plausible surface conversation going with an inarticulate man. Shortly June had found herself unable to decide whom she resented more: her father, who had the nerve to find his beloved wife's brutal dying too much to bear, or her mother, who, faced with a choice between her daughter's needs and her husband's, had the nerve to make the only choice she possibly could. And of course, awareness of her own irrational selfish resentment had made June despise herself, so she had resented them both for that, too.

And then, as visiting hours were drawing to a close, her mother had said, "You know, I read a book once, I forget who wrote it, but he said the most beautiful thing. He said—let me see if I can get this right—he said, 'There is really only one sense. It is the sense of touch. All of the other senses are merely other ways of touching.'"

And she had held out her hand—her shrunken, IV-trailing hand—and of course June had taken it, and—

❖   ❖   ❖

—and something had happened. Even now, walking through the woods of Pacific Spirit Park back home in British Columbia with Coltrane whispering in her ears, June was not sure just what. But information exchange had taken place. Data of some kind had come surging up her arm from her mother's feeble grip, and data of some other and different kind had flowed in the other direction.

It had *not* been the "getting it all said" that her mother had spoken of earlier. The questions June had walked into that hospital room with were still unanswered; the words she had gone there to say were yet unspoken. But *some* kind of profound communication had taken place, something just as far *beyond* talking as talking was beyond eye contact. (And something, therefore, just as unsatisfying as eye contact had been—if for different reasons.) June did not have a mystical bone in her body . . . but she was quite certain that her mother had taken something from her in that brief physical contact, and imparted something important to her in return. Something almost tangible, in the form of an energy almost palpable. Some kind of change had occurred in June. She just wished she knew what, so she could explain it to Paul when she finally saw him again.

She was still trying to analyze it, as she wandered heedless through the woods, jazz saxophone playing softly in her FM headphones. *How*, she thought, *am I different?*

I am different in some way that I cannot define. Changed. I sense that the change is, or probably will be, temporary. Nonetheless it is important. And it reminds me of something . . .

The memory surfaced. It had taken awhile

because it was a memory not of a real event but of an imagined one.

This is what I used to imagine it was like to have a magic spell put on you!

When she was a little girl, a voracious consumer of Tolkien and his disciples, she had often acted out fantasy scenarios of her own devising in her solitary play hours. This was what it had felt like just after the wizard had placed his enchantment upon her, and just before it was fully activated by the inevitable appearance of the handsome warrior. It had something to do with the inevitability of that appearance, and the certainty that they would recognize each other at once. It was, now that she thought of it, probably one of her earliest gropings, in imagination, toward the concept of empowerment.

Well, she already had a handsome warrior in inventory, thank you very much. She *had* recognized her Tall Paul on sight . . . and had basically won him in combat and directed that he be scrubbed and brought to her tent. Even better, he had a tent of his own now. She was as empowered in that area as she felt any need to be.

But she did, now that she thought of it, feel more than usually empowered today, in a strange sort of way. Usually when she was in raw nature like this, she felt like a stranger, who must be careful not to offend through thoughtlessness; like a visitor to the zoo, whose gawking curiosity is a kind of impertinence; like a tourist. Today she felt, for once, at home here in the woods. And the woods seemed to agree.

She saw more wildlife than usual, for instance. Several squirrels. A raccoon. Something she took to be a weasel, that browsed her with his eyes, like a penny-pinching shopper, and decided she was too expensive. Birds—June *never* saw birds in the woods, even when she was right underneath the chirping things and the branches were bare, but so far she had seen at least half a dozen, without even thinking about it. All of these wild things noticed her in return, and were wary of her—but none of them seemed to feel any need to flee. Perhaps they were all under the influence of the magic spell.

Between her light head and her heavy heart, she felt no alarm at all when she became aware of the man ahead of her on the trail, even though he was clearly a sleazebag.

She reached up to switch off her radio headphones, succeeded only in turning the volume all the way off, and settled for that.

She did not even momentarily wish she had her handsome warrior with her for backup. She was armed and competent—and more than that: somehow she knew that on this day of days, she could face down a mugger with impunity, calm a psycho with her gaze, unman any rapist. Death— not the concept but the grim reality, up close and personal, ravaging one of her loved ones—had in some odd way given her power, and she could sense it. She mistook an electric tingling in her earlobes for a symptom of it. She studied the sleazebag carefully, but her pulse remained steady.

Caucasian male, about her age. He looked like when he was five Santa had asked him what he wanted to be when he grew up, and he'd chirped, "A perpetrator." In the distant neighborhood where her lover had grown up, in a country adjoining America called The Bronx, he would have been termed a mook. He could not possibly have passed within a thousand meters of a cop in thick fog without instant radar lock taking place. At the moment, even in the middle of nowhere and believing himself unobserved, he was managing to skulk, mope, loiter, creep and look furtive, all at the same time—a virtuoso performance. He reminded her of a man she knew called Hopeless Harry.

He was well over two meters tall, and seemed to mass well under fifty kilos. He wore clothes meant for other people, who unless they were color-blind were not missing them, and a jailhouse haircut. On his back was a large designer backpack. Its designers had intended it to say *behold me: I am rich, stylish and fit* but on him it had the look of a false mustache, making him look, impossibly, even more suspicious.

June had been moving quietly, one with the forest, even before she saw him; now she became a Shao-Lin monk walking the rice paper, leaving no trace. Her first instinct had been to change course and avoid him . . . but that backpack intrigued her. An instinct only slightly younger on the evolutionary scale told her it contained treasure. June Bellamy liked treasure. And she was in the mood for a distraction from her thoughts.

She left the path and shadowed him for a little less than a hundred meters, paralleling the meandering trail. He was the kind of mook who could have been tailed through the French Quarter during Mardi Gras; for someone with a magic spell on her in a forest this damp he was candy. Twice, he spun craftily on his heel in the hope of surprising someone following him; both times his gaze passed right over her without stopping. *Call me Chingachcook*, she thought smugly.

He kept staring from side to side as he walked, looking for something. Occasionally he would leave the path, pick a spot at apparent random, paw at the earth briefly with his sneakered foot (it was probably the name that had first attracted him to sneakers), and then move on.

Finally his eye was caught by a large, freshly toppled tree about twenty meters from the trail. The bank on which it stood had been undercut by centuries of Vancouver rain, and the days of sustained downpour just ended had finished the job. The huge elm had fallen to a 45-degree angle before being caught like a drunk by its neighbors; roots clawed at the sky like tentacles frozen in spasm, bearded with brown glistening tendrils that made her think of shit tinsel. He looked around one last time, failed again to see her fifty meters away, and unslung his stylish backpack.

She began to understand when he removed a collapsible entrenching tool and assembled it. The earth the tree had lately protected was freshly turned, easy to dig. There was indeed treasure in that bag, and Captain Kidd there proposed to bury it. June smiled.

And almost instantly felt a stab of sadness. A week ago, such a gift from God would have been a blessing and a pure joy. Now it was a consolation prize. A prize booby.

Still, she was forced to admit to some interest in just *how much* consolation; she took a position of vantage and dropped into a squat as the mook began digging.

The longer he dug, the better she felt. The deeper he wanted his plunder buried, the more likely it was to console her. But when he began approaching a depth and dimensions which would have served for the grave of a child, nearly waist-deep in the hole he was making, she entertained a brief Pythonesque fantasy in which, having buried his treasure, he would protect its secret by shooting the guy who'd dug the hole. That way she wouldn't have to wait for him to pass out of earshot to uncover the swag, and there'd be that nice handy entrenching tool.

Come to think of it, digging up a grave wasn't something she was really in the mood for, just now—even one with treasure in it. She'd settle for marking the spot, and coming back with Paul sometime. Let him do the grunt work; that was what handsome warriors were for. Well, one of the things.

The mook's shovel, which had been saying *chuff—shrrrp . . . chuff—shrrrp . . . chuff—shrrrp* with decreasing rhythm like an asthmatic slowly recovering from an attack, suddenly said *chuff—shrrrp . . . clack!*

Not *clank!* as if it had hit a rock. Not *chup!* as if it had hit a root. *Clack!* As if it had struck . . . she didn't know, plastic or plexiglass or formica or something. Something manmade.

He made a muttered sound of irritation that, if it had become a word, would have been "Naturally," set that shovelful of dirt aside carefully, without any *shrrp*, then offset his point of attack slightly and tried again.

Clack!

"Aw, fuck!" he groaned.

No, no, she wanted to say. *"Fuck!" is the sound of an axe sinking into a tree. That was "Clack!"*

As if insisting on his point of view, he said "Fuck!" again, louder. But this time, the way he said it was so different, and so incongruous, so full of an almost religious awe, that it caused her to focus her attention on him. Because of that—remarkably—she actually recognized what happened to him next. It was a thing she had never expected to see in quite that context, but if you were looking right at it and paying close attention, it was unmistakable.

Standing up, hip-deep in an unfinished grave, fully dressed, shovel still held in both hands, the mook threw back his head, keened like a forlorn kitten, and had an orgasm.

It might even have been the orgasm of his life. As she stared, marveling but never doubting, June was impressed. Thanks to her mother, she had been confident in her own sexuality since the age of fourteen, but she had to admit that in a varied life she had never received applause quite as enthusiastic and sincere as the mook was now awarding to . . . no one at all. It was more than vocal: his body language was so emphatic and so explicit that she decided he might well have found work as a male erotic dancer, even with that body.

I've heard the expression "Fuck the world" countless times, of course, she thought, *but I'd never actually seen it done before.*

He was not even rubbing his groin against the wall of the pit in which he stood, though he could have. Instead he simply thrust, violently, at the air itself, and seemed to find it a more than adequate lover.

For all its intensity, the event seemed to take somewhat less time than usual, at least in her experience, and when it was over, he simply let go of the shovel and sat down in the hole, his head disappearing almost completely from view. As the top of it bobbed up and down with his slowing respiration, its coconut-husk hair made it resemble a hedgehog trying to frighten off an intruder with a display of puffing bristles.

Something in that hole, June thought, *causes men to have instant orgasms, of higher than usual quality. I might just find a use for such a thing. God help me: I* am *starting to feel consoled.* . . .

She waited, and watched, her vision so narrowed and focused that she seemed to see him in the crosshairs of a periscope, her hearing so acute she became aware of a mosquito hovering near her left wrist (the silenced headphones passed ambient sound so well, she had forgotten she was wearing them), her attention so concentrated she ignored the mosquito.

"Angel Gerhardt," he said aloud, his voice hoarse but happy.

Of course. After you have sex with the universe, it is polite to offer your name. He must be a nonsmoker.

"Heinz," he said, "but everybody calls me Angel."

I see, she thought. *And your address?*

"Nine four seven four Williams Street. Two two two, fourteen hundred. Frosty at eWorld dot com." Despite their prosaic nature, he spoke each of these factoids blissfully, as though they were special joys to be shared in afterglow. "No, there's my old lady and another couple and a dog and three cats. Linda Wu. Tony Solideri and Mary Carry-the-Kettle."

There were short pauses between each sentence. By now she understood that something silent in that hole was interrogating him, somehow, and she memorized every syllable. Whatever it was, was a potential enemy, and she did not want it better informed than her.

"I was looking to bury a couple o's of flake till it cooled off a little," he said, still lazily ecstatic. "Yeah. No. Yeah, they do. No, they don't. Yeah, I'm sure. I don't trust them. Well, Linda, a little." Even those last two sentences sounded happy.

The next pause was long enough to give her time to work that out. Yes, his lover and house-mates knew he was out burying cocaine. No, they didn't know, or even suspect, just where. This suited June. She was much less interested in even two ounces of coke than in whatever the *hell* was in that hole . . . but either way it would be nice never to have to meet anyone who would have Angel Gerhardt for a friend.

Then she caught herself, remembering the e-mail handle he had revealed: Frosty. Admittedly, it was more energy-efficient than walking around wearing a sandwich sign that read, "I deal cocaine in felony weight"—but not much smarter. Angel could not be considered a reliable judge of *what* his lover and housemates did or didn't know. Worse, all the neighborhoods that bordered on Pacific Spirit Park were upscale: he had probably attracted attention on his way into the woods. She did not believe anyone could have tailed her the way she had tailed him; nonetheless it came to her that it might be well to complete her business here and be gone quickly.

Angel seemed to agree. He said only one more word—"Okay"—then stood up in the hole, set down the shovel and began taking off his pants. A strange dread clutched at her, though she could not have explained why undressing was weirder than having a spontaneous orgasm dressed—but all he did was remove his threadbare boxer shorts, wipe himself off with them, drop them into the hole and put his pants back on. He was so skinny that he seemed to have no difficulty getting the pants off and on without removing his sneakers. Then he hoisted himself out of the hole and began hastily filling it back in. He did it more intelligently than she would have expected. When he was done, he collected underbrush and sprinkled it over the fresh-turned earth—again, more artistically than she'd have predicted. Then he put his backpack back on, picked up his shovel and walked away.

His course, apparently randomly chosen, brought him rather near to June before he reached the path again, but somehow she knew he was going to walk right by without seeing her, and he did. He wore a vague, fatuous smile, and his eyes were unfocused.

She glanced briefly toward the huge drunken tree. Whatever was down there under its uprooted base would probably stay there awhile. In any case she was not ready to confront it. She followed the backpack.

She was tempted at first to just stroll along beside Angel, since he seemed oblivious, but she resisted, and took up stealthy station fifty meters behind him again. She was glad when, a few hundred meters later, he stopped and shook himself like a man coming out of a deep reverie. She had plenty of time to become invisible before he turned and scanned his surroundings. His expression was inhabited now, but still serene. For an instant he reminded her absurdly of her mother in her hospital bed. He checked his watch then, muttered something she couldn't hear, and resumed walking.

Shortly he found another exposed bank, took out his shovel and began digging again.

As she watched, she noticed something subtle. He was not digging like a man who had already dug one hole this size this afternoon. Something seemed to have returned to him the energy he had expended earlier.

This time his task was accomplished without incident. She was not much surprised when he buried the entire backpack: now anyone who had noticed him enter the woods and saw him leave would know he had left something behind. The trick in finding it would then be to go to the only dry trail in the forest, and proceed as far as the *second* easy place to dig. The world had lost a great rocket scientist when Angel Gerhardt decided to go into the crystal trade. Sure enough, when he was done he left the shovel about five meters away (concealed by a mound of leaves that would stay there for at least an hour, unless a breeze came up), both to mark the spot and to make it easy for anyone who found the stash to dig it up.

Then he went away. He no longer looked serene; now he looked pooped. He dragged his feet. But he moved.

After she was certain he was out of earshot, June took her cell phone from her hip holster and dialed Paul's number, irritably removing her forgotten FM headphones when she hit them with the phone. Self-contained, with no wires to a Walkman or CD player on her person, they fell to the forest floor. She expected to get his machine and did; she suffered through the outgoing message with even more than her usual impatience, wishing for the thousandth time that he'd get a modern machine, which allowed your friends to cut off the message by pushing the proper key. The moment she heard the beep she began talking quickly and quietly.

"Honey, I'm into something heavy here. I'm walking in the Endowment Lands, and I ran across a mook looking to bury something nice just off the Lowrie Trail, Dorothy twice, but that's not the good part. He was digging away at the base of a huge old toppled elm tree, and he hit something with his shovel that made a sound like *clack*, something like plywood or plastic. And then—" She knew how all this was going to sound, but didn't want to edit it. "—I know this is nuts, but then he had an orgasm, all by himself, standing up. And then he started to talk out loud, as if somebody was grilling him—only I was only fifty meters away and I swear there was no one else there. He said his name was Angel Gerhardt and he lived over in the East End on William Street and his e-mail handle, God help us all, was 'Frosty,' and he named his girlfriend Linda Wu and his two housemates and said none of them knew where he planned to bury the . . . the thing . . . and the weird part was, he didn't say any of this like a mope giving information to the heat, he said it like a guy opening his soul to his new lover, happy as a clam. Then he filled the hole back in and buried the package in another spot. He's gone now. I'm going to put the package somewhere else—but I'm not going near that goddam fallen elm without you, and maybe Rosco. I don't know what we've got ahold of here, but whatever it is is very very big. Call me as soon as you get in, okay? I hope everything went okay."

She put the phone away and squatted there in

the woods, thinking hard, for a minute—almost but not quite long enough. Then she got to her feet, went to the shovel and picked it up.

If she had thought just a little longer, it might have occurred to her that in fantasy stories, it is generally unwise to tamper with the belongings of one on whom a geas has been placed. The moment her fingers touched the shovel, she came.

Chapter 2
Silent Light, Holy Light

Wally and Moira had, in a sense, spent most of their adult lives training for the advent of the naked bald man. That didn't help them much.

Happy round people in their mid-forties, they were hard at work at 11 P.M. on Halloween night, side by side at their respective computers in the study of their Vancouver home—popularly known as The Only Dump In Point Grey—when a short sharp silent blast of very bright light burst in the big window behind them and momentarily washed out their screens. As it faded, they saw that they were both hung, their mice impotent; each rebooted at once, then used the brief interval of startup to adjust their blood-sugar levels, Wally with a bird's nest cookie and Moira with coffee.

"More Halloween nonsense?" Wally suggested as he chewed.

Moira frowned. "Thought we paid off the last of the little thugs hours ago."

"Maybe we should have given that Ace Ventura chocolate instead of rice cakes."

"It was instinctive. I see Ace Ventura: I think bowel movements: I reach for the fiber." She gulped coffee and glared at her monitor. "No, a smart-aleck kid going to that much trouble would pick something with bang, not flash. Why waste that much magnesium to not annoy somebody very much?"

"Right. Got to be a fan or fen, then. Dr. Techno, or one of the Latex Goddesses."

She shook her head. "Any other time of the year, I'd say sure. But this close to VanCon, all the fans bright enough are too *busy*. Like us. At least, they'd better be."

Wally finished his cookie hurriedly; his system was back up. "Maybe we should duck and cover," he suggested, typing furiously.

"Eh?"

"Maybe somebody just nuked Coquitlam. Or points east."

"Huh." She gave it half her attention; her own desktop had finally come up and typing with a coffee cup in one hand took some care. "Nah," she decided, reopening her application, "if the sound wave hasn't gotten here by now, we're okay. I gotta get this thing uploaded."

"Damn," he said. "It didn't save." He poked futilely at his own keyboard. "I lost the whole flippin' file."

Moira smirked and kept working. "You should get a Mac."

"I hate obsequious machines," he said automatically, and let it go. Mixed marriages can work, with enough good will. "You're right: if it was a nuke, it was way out in the Okanagan somewhere. Come Spring we'll have peaches the size of pumpkins."

"And use them for lawn lanterns," she agreed. "Seriously, what the hell do you suppose that was?"

Wally typed twelve lines before her question

caught up with him, then shrugged. (She saw it; they knew each other's rhythms.) "Bright. Short. Sharp; no perceptible waxing or waning. No sound at all that I heard. Magnesium . . . big laser . . . searchlight, maybe. None likely in our alley, even on Halloween." He typed some more, then cycled back again. "No, I don't come up with *anything* that makes sense. Except fannish humor, and you're right: there's no punchline to this one."

Moira finished a flurry of her own, played back his answer, and frowned. "So . . . what? Elvis has just entered the building?"

"No, he was here four hours ago—and *he* got a Mars Bar. Seriously, hon, my honest best guess is that Captain Kirk just beamed down to ask for directions." He resumed typing at top speed.

Moira frowned fiercely now, and actually stopped typing for several seconds, even though she was paying connect time again by now. This was a perfect example of one of the Great Differences on which her twenty-year marriage to Wally was founded. He found the irrational, the inexplicable, amusing. She found it barely tolerable. "We ought to take a look out the window, at least," she muttered, and resumed netsurfing.

"Sure thing," he said, and kept typing. "Just as soon as I upload my column for the LMSFSazine, finish that web-page upgrade for the SCA, answer all the e-mail rumors on the new Beatles stuff, and—oh, yes—download about twenty megs of current VanCon traffic and route it to the proper serfs, I'll join you there at the window. Save me a seat."

She didn't bother to recite her own litany of tasks; she had already dismissed the matter and was deeply engaged in a rather tricky attempt to hack her way into NASA and sniff out information regarding the first live guitar jam—the first musical interaction—ever to be performed in space (scheduled, according to rumor, to occur aboard Mir, during the next visit by the shuttle *Atlantis*; a Canadian and a Russian trading off on acoustic and electric). It was her intention to obtain the best possible recording of the event, and play it at VanCon, the annual Vancouver science fiction convention she and Wally helped run.

He was editing his column, and she had just settled on a promising line of attack, when they heard the wail.

It came clearly through the window behind them: the unformed sound of a baby in distress. Odd that they both thought "baby" the instant they heard it—for both the volume and pitch of the sound were unmistakably adult (though the gender was indeterminate). But that cry was not even an attempt at a word.

"There is a baby the size of a football player in our alley," Wally said calmly, fingers poised over his keyboard, "on Halloween night."

Moira caught herself trying to use her own keyboard as a breed of Ouija board. "One of us should really look out the window."

He began to tap his keys without quite typing them, a nervous mannerism she was sure she would learn to accept in no more than another decade at most. "That's the requisite number," he agreed, and poked a key tentatively.

Her face clouded up . . . then smoothed over. "And babies are my department. I see." She disconnected from the net, treating her mouse with elaborate gentleness, and rose from her seat.

Although their workstation was large by most home standards, so were Wally and Moira; she could not move her chair out of her way unless he got up too, so the only way she could get a look out the window was to kneel up on the chair and lean forward until her cheek pressed against the chilly pane. She did so.

Several seconds passed. Wally typed, but his heart clearly wasn't in it.

"What do you see?" he asked finally.

"Bad news," she replied slowly. "I think I'm getting a zit."

"Oh, for—" He got hold of himself, and saved his changes. "Right. Sorry. You're quite right: we *do* have to take up the tacks before we can take up the carpet." He darkened both monitor screens, extinguished both gooseneck lamps, levered himself up out of his own chair and went to dial the overhead light down. He waited there by the rheostat, in near darkness, watching his wife look out the window and down into the alley. "It's Captain Kirk, right?" he said.

More seconds passed.

He was beginning to become irritated by the time she stirred slightly and spoke his name; but then his irritation vanished at once, for there was something wrong with her voice. "Yes, Moira?"

"We've spoken of my ongoing ambiguity with regard to certain of the so-called assigned gender roles, right?"

"Yes, dear. And I am sworn not to break your stones about it."

"Thank you. With all due respect to sisterhood, I think this is one of those times when a Y chromosome is called for. He's naked, and he looks dead, and he's bald—so for all I know he *is* Captain Kirk, but this is definitely not my department, okay?"

"Our side of the fence, or Gorsky's?"

"Our side."

His pidgin, then. He sighed. "Wait here in the cave. Now, where did I leave that stone ax . . . ?"

She turned away from the window. "Wally, seriously—"

He halted in the doorway. "Woman, you have invoked the Y chromosome—now run for cover and get the bandages ready. No, better yet, go to the phone, dial nine one, and wait for my scream." He grinned and left the room, feeling like a Heinlein hero. A Secret Master of Fandom and Permanent Secretary of the Lower Mainland Science Fiction Society had, after all, certain standards to maintain. And how tough could a nude bald corpse be?

She turned her Mac into a voicephone and did just as he had suggested, then went back to the window—moving both chairs out of the way this time—telling herself that at the first sign of funny business she would punch that last digit into the phone and then put a chair through that window and . . . and . . . and rain coffee cups and lava lamps on the naked bald man until he surrendered, that's what.

Wally did take the time to change to better footgear, put on a light jacket, and slide a short length of rebar up one sleeve before leaving the house by the back door. It was a typical Vancouver October night, save that it was not raining; the jacket was useful only as camouflage for the weapon. He rounded the corner of the house cautiously, staying far from the building and crouching slightly. Even with his own den lights extinguished, there was still enough light from the streetlights out front, the moon overhead, and spilling over the fence from the detestable frosted windows of the Gorskys (Gorskies? Gorski?) next door, to illuminate the alleyway with reasonable clarity.

There was unquestionably and no shit a naked bald Caucasian male lying there on his back, just below the den window.

Dead, however, he was not. He was in the slow process of trying to lever himself up from complete spread-eagled sprawl to a sort of sitting fetal position. Wally had plenty of time to see clearly that the naked man was not merely bald but completely hairless . . . and uncircumsized. Wally guessed him to be about twenty-five, and in excellent shape, well muscled and trim. He noted absently that the nude intruder was surrounded by a roughly circular patch of scorched grass, and that the circle of scorching was wide enough to mark both Wally's own house and the fence as well. He further noted, and filed, the depth of the impression the stranger had left in the soggy earth; as if he were made of lead . . . or had somehow *fallen* onto his back from . . . ah, doubtless from the top of the fence: that explained it. Considering that the fence was made of chain link topped by savage little twists of jagged steel, and that the stranger was nude right down to his soles, he must have wanted to leave the Gorsky property quite badly. For the first time Wally warmed to him slightly. (Like nearly everyone else in the district except Wally and Moira, the Gorsky clan lived in a million-dollar stucco-and-plaster steroid monstrosity that looked like the box a real home had come in—and did not trouble to hide their disgust at the property-value-lowering presence of Wally and Moira's shabby human dwelling in their midst. In retaliation, Wally had befriended his crabgrass.)

The naked man saw Wally for the first time. His eyes widened comically, and he gasped, a sound so loud and sibilant it was nearly a shriek. He drew up his knees, buried his head between them, and wrapped his arms around them to keep them secure, like a turtle withdrawing into his shell.

Wally moved, cautiously, to try and get a glimpse of Moira in the study window, thought he saw her wave a hand. He let the chunk of rebar slip out of his sleeve and into his palm, and tapped the stranger with it.

As a lifetime science fiction fan, Wally feared little so much as the prospect of appearing stupid in retrospect. He chose his words with care, and was rather proud of them. "Excuse me," he said gently, "but do I correctly understand that you are Blanched Du Boy, and you have always depended on the blahndness of stranguhs?"

The stranger poked his head back out, and stared fixedly—not at Wally, but at the house . . . or more properly, at the portion of its foundation nearest him, about a meter away. His eyes seemed to be bulging out of his head—or was that just the lack of eyelashes? No . . . no, he was genuinely terrified . . . not of the large homeowner poking him with a piece of rebar, but of a cement wall. He scuttled involuntarily away from it, until he fetched up against the fence.

"John!" he muttered. "Unsnuffingbelievable! One more hackin' meter west, and—" He shivered violently.

Wally thought it was about time; it wasn't terribly chilly out here, this was after all Vancouver, but it shouldn't take much to chill a naked man. "I say—" he began again.

The stranger whirled on him—not easy to do from a sitting position. "*What year is it?*" he snapped.

Wally blinked. "The same one it was when you decided to get drunk," he said.

The man was on his feet so suddenly he seemed to have levitated; he sprang at Wally and took him by the lapels of his coat. "*What year?*" he thundered.

Unused to naked men taking him by the lapels in his own yard while he held a piece of rebar, Wally answered automatically, and very quickly, "1995, it's 1995, I swear to God!"

The stranger released him as quickly as he'd seized him, and the strangest thing happened. For just a moment Wally saw him begin to panic utterly, just totally lose it . . . then, confoundingly, he felt his own naked arms with his hands, felt his cheeks, and pulled himself back from the edge. Terror gave way at once to towering rage: he smote himself mightily on the thighs. "Crot!" he snarled. "Total snowcrash! Blood for this, my chop . . . grotty wannabes!" The date clearly displeased him greatly.

On Wally, the light had just begun, dimly, to dawn. This was the moment he had been waiting for since the age of six—here—now! He opened his mouth . . . then glanced up at the window and closed it again.

"Look, cousin," he said after some thought, "it's cool out here. Come on inside like I said, okay? Get some hot coffee in you—you drink coffee? We got *real* good coffee—"

The naked man looked up at him and instantly,

visibly, became devious. "Sure, yes, hot caffy, very kind of you, caffy would be optimal. I can . . . uh . . . I can explain all this—"

"Yes, I'm sure you can," said Wally. "I'm looking forward to it." He gestured. "If you'll just walk this . . . uh, in this direction." And then he waved and gestured for Moira's benefit, before leading the way.

Wally watched the stranger carefully on the way into the house. He was one of those people who looks good with his head shaved—in fact, now that Wally noticed, he looked a little like a younger version of Captain Picard from *Star Trek: The Next Generation*. He seemed alert, but some of the things that interested him were interesting. He paid close attention, for instance, to the process by which Wally opened, and then closed, the back door—but did not attempt to hide his interest, as would a burglar casing the joint. He shielded his eyes with his hand from the meager 40-watt bulb in Wally and Moira's back hall. He noticed the stack of newspapers and the recycle blue-box full of waste glass and metal waiting for Garbage Night, and for some reason they seemed to amuse him. The stove in the kitchen made him snort. Then they hung the right into the study, and the stranger froze in his tracks, gaping.

Wally was aware that not everyone admired large women as much as he; nonetheless this behavior seemed rude for a guest. Then he realized that the stranger had not yet noticed Moira. He was staring horrorstruck at . . .

. . . a painting on the study wall. The Jack Gaughan *Analog* cover, for a story called "By Any Other Name"—a simple crouched figure seen from behind, brandishing a futuristic weapon at a number of translucent fireballs. Wally owned many scarier paintings.

But the stranger had clearly never seen anything so utterly terrifying in his life—not even the cement wall of Wally's foundation. "Oh *crash*," he moaned. "It's worse than I thought! You're science fiction fans, aren't you?"

Wally took a deep breath, and drew himself up. "Sir, I'm afraid it is worse than that. My wife and I are SMOFs."

The stranger fainted dead away.

Wally gave Moira a meaningful look. "The first thing he wanted to know was what year it was."

She stared down at the inert stranger, then back up at her husband. "Oh, Wally, *really*?"

He nodded, unable to suppress the grin any longer.

Her own eyes became large and round, and for just a moment it looked as though she might pass out herself. Then she got control, and smiled. "And the con's only a few weeks away!" she cried.

The two Secret Masters Of Fandom raced to each other, joined hands, and began to dance.

When the hairless man opened his eyes, it was in a *white* room which had no windows and only one door. The door had no knob or handle or keypad or other obvious means of causing it to open, nor did it appear to slide on tracks. There was a bare lightbulb in the ceiling, but its switch appeared to be elsewhere.

The room contained no furniture or decorations of any kind.

The balance of its contents were all sentient beings. Specifically, the hairless man himself,

Wally, Moira and the Buddha . . . represented in this specific instance by a football-sized and -shaped bronze statue of him which was, ironically, the only purely material object present. Everyone but the hairless man looked generally the same: short, round and smiling beatifically.

He sat up slowly, took in his surroundings, and the fact that he was no longer naked. He now wore an old grey sweatshirt shrunken almost to normal-range size, a pair of sweatpants cinched tight at the waist but with adequate room to store a pup tent and an inflatable raft in the legs, and odd foot coverings that Wally was accustomed to refer to as "sockasins." He seemed to find the coverings tolerable.

"This is my meditation room," Moira said.

He nodded.

"If the beginning of this conversation goes well," Wally said, "we can continue it in more congenial surroundings. Over 'caffy.' But you *did* drop in without an appointment."

The stranger said nothing.

"We caught a burglar once," Wally said. "We left him in here for a week. Took the Buddha out, left him an empty wastebasket. He was very very contrite when we let him go. We had to help him to the sidewalk. Nothing much but solids in the basket by that point . . ."

"I understand," the hairless man said. "Come, let us reason together."

"When are you from?" Wally asked. "Originally, I mean."

The hairless man did a creditable imitation of puzzlement. "What do you mean, '*when*' am I from, Daddy-o? I'm from Frisco; I'm part of a team of long-hairs hacking on a matter transporter at the University of Frisco, and while I was there after hours there was this terrible—"

"It's possible to pipe sound in here," Moira said. "Are you by any chance familiar with the work of the Gyuto Monks?"

Beside her, Wally visibly shuddered. The Gyuto Monks, chanting, sound very much like a sustained short in the circuit that powers the world. Like the Grand Canyon: anyone will be impressed by them, but few can endure them at any length.

The hairless man sighed, and his shoulders drooped. He might not have known the Gyuto Monks, but he knew a threat when he heard it. "In your reckoning it would be the year 2287."

Wally and Moira each outsmiled the Buddha.

"I'm Wallace Kemp, and this is my wife Moira Rogers," Wally said.

"I am Jude," the time traveler said.

Wally and Moira exchanged a glance. "Hey," Wally said softly, making his Paul McCartney face, and she glared at him. To Wally's surprise, Jude seemed to catch the reference too, and looked suddenly wary.

"What was your purpose in time-traveling, Jude?" Wally went on, louder.

"The information would be of no value to you."

"Let us decide that. Unless you're in a hurry to get started meditating? We could get you a wastebasket—"

"I came back in order to drive a taxicab, one time," Jude said. "There. That is the complete truth. Satisfied?"

Wally digested that. "You know how to drive a car?" Moira asked.

Jude sneered. "Primitive mobile—myocontrol— how hard can it be?"

"Does it have to be a cab?" Wally asked.

Jude's face fell. "The discussion is pointless," he said. "My mission is a failure."

"Why?" they asked together.

He rubbed his forehead, where his eyebrows ought to have been. "Because there was a major snowcrash—" He glanced suddenly at Moira. "—pardon me, madam, a fuckup, and I undershot. This is the *wrong ficton*."

Wally nodded, pleased to have confirmed that Robert Heinlein's term for a place-and-time, "ficton," would one day pass into the language. "Yes, I got that. So it was necessary that your cab ride take place in a ficton earlier in history than this?"

"Yes, by several years."

"What year?"

Jude looked stubborn.

"Look," Wally said reasonably. "You must see our problem. I told you we are Secret Masters of Fandom. You are obviously a time traveler. There can only be four kinds of time traveler: idiots, fanatics, criminals and very careful historians—which last does not seem to describe you. Anyone else would know it's too risky. Before we can let you go, we need to know which kind you are."

Jude frowned. "In your terms, I suppose I am a fanatic. I would call myself a religious martyr."

Wally nodded. "And you plan to alter history, for theological reasons. By driving a taxicab. Even though that will annihilate reality."

"*My* reality," Jude pointed out. "Not yours. If I had succeeded, *my* ficton would have vanished utterly, yes—but yours would merely have turned out somewhat differently."

"True," Wally agreed. "Still, you're going to have to tell us about it, if you want to leave this room."

Jude looked distinctly uncomfortable. "May I first ask you a question? Matters of religion can be volatile. I know it is a little early in history for this question to be truly meaningful, but . . . may I ask both of you your views regarding . . . Elvis?"

Looking back on all this in years to come, one of the small things Wally and Moira would be proud of was the fact that neither of them cracked a smile at this juncture. They did exchange a momentary glance which was a promissory note for a shared belly-laugh later, but Wally answered seriously, after only a second's hesitation, "He *has* left the building. If he were alive, he'd have stopped his daughter's wedding."

"And while he was here," Moira said, "he was a relatively talentless nutbar who happened to get struck by lightning, and didn't do anything important with the energy. Why?"

"Praise John!" Jude said fervently. "Are you, then, by any chance . . . Fab?"

Wally and Moira exchanged another glance. It was getting harder and harder not to grin. The idea that there would be a Church of Elvis in the not-too-distant future had become something of a cliché in recent science fiction—but until now only Wally, in on-line forums and in his column in LMSFSazine, had ever suggested that it might and should be countered by an equally fervent cult that worshipped the Beatles.

"I think you could say that," Wally agreed slowly. "Washed in the Juice of the Apple, you mean? I wouldn't call us devout, strictly speaking—we're **fen;** we must remain skeptical on all matters of religion, by policy—but I own the Black Album, and all the Christmas Fan Club Messages." He saw that register. "And I was at Shea Stadium in '65, if that helps."

"Twenty-three August, yeah yeah yeah!" Jude cried excitedly. "Oh, thank The Four, some gear luck at last! You *must* help me—*it may yet be accomplished!*"

"What may?" Wally asked, but his eyes were already starting to gleam.

"The Reunification!" Jude said. "The Healing . . . the Reforging of the Bond . . . the utter destruction of the forces of Elvis!"

Suddenly Wally *knew* what he was talking about. It all . . . well, came together, over him. "Oh my *God*," he breathed, thunderstruck. For the third time he met his wife's eyes, and was startled to see that she hadn't caught up yet. "Don't you get it, love? In the future, there's a major showdown between the Church of Elvis and the Church of The Beatles—the anti-Asian Christians versus the pro-Asian Pagans—and we're looking at a kamikaze samurai. God, the most awful Beatles anecdote of all—and Jude here came back through time to change it!"

Moira was lost, but game. "' . . . most awful Beatles anecdote . . .' John's death? Or something to do with Stu Sutcliffe?"

"No, no—you've heard this one, I'm sure; I've told it a hundred times. John and Paul have buried the hatchet; they're sitting around in the Dakota one night in '79, getting stoned and watching telly while the wives chat in the kitchen. Lorne Michaels comes on the tube: it's the Saturday after Bernstein offered the Beatles a million to reunite, and Michaels makes a counter-offer on the air, live: if the Beatles will come down and play on *Saturday Night Live*, now, he's prepared to pay them . . . union scale, a thousand bucks or so apiece. Rim shot. And across town at the Dakota, John looks at Paul and Paul looks at John and they both start to grin—"

"Oh my God, I remember now," Moira said, "And they called a cab—*but it never showed up* . . ." She turned pale.

"One of the great Lost Moments of history," Wally said, his voice trembling.

Jude broke the silence which followed. "It's plaintext, right? If the cab had arrived, John and Paul would have appeared on *Saturday Night Live* that night. The planet would have convulsed in its orbit, a generation gone mad with joy. George and Ringo both would have been on the phone before the credits rolled—and sooner or later, *The Four would have gotten together again*! John would have gone back home to England, and that Presleyan crot would *never* have gotten a shot at him *there*." His voice was rising. "And sooner or later, they'd have learned the truth about Eppy's death, and in their holy wrath crashed the forces of Elvis forever—"

Wally couldn't help interrupting. "Wait a minute—are you saying that *Elvis Presley* was behind Brian Epstein's—"

"Indisputable proof will be uncovered in another eight years," Jude said, "but isn't it obvious? Faggot Jew Commie . . . creator of the Anti-Elvis . . . *pills* as the instrument of death . . . did you think it coincidence that Eppy died *just* as The Four were communing publicly with an Eastern, non-Christian religious figure in India?"

"Elvis *did* approach J. Edgar Hoover, and volunteer to spy on the Beatles for the DEA, that's documented," Wally said softly. He was talking to himself. "And his daughter's flaky husband is the guy who stole the Beatles' publishing rights out from under his mentor, Paul McCartney—"

"Elvis Presley made his evil plans in full, the day he read John's Jesus Quote . . . and from beyond the grave, he triumphed," Jude said in a vaguely chanting tone, clearly quoting from scripture.

Moira noticed that her hand hurt, from crushing Wally's hand, but forgot it almost at once, distracted by horror. "You mean . . . you mean He Whose Name We Must Never Mention really shot John as an agent of—of—"

Jude nodded solemnly. "It will be the chance discovery of his secret memoirs by a prison guard in 2003 that blows the story. I meant to undo all of that—and with your help, *I still can.*"

As unconsciously as they had mangled them, Wally and Moira let go of each other's hands, and sat up straighter, hearts hammering.

"You've got the time machine *on* you," Wally suggested. "Or in you. Implanted, or something."

Jude shook his ironically bald head. "All the assets I have, you see."

"So you're going to automatically slingshot back to the future, or something, and try again."

Another headshake. "Return to my ficton is fundamentally impossible. Time travel only works backwards. Even if I had another machine, I could not travel to the future—it isn't *there* yet."

"You're stuck in this ficton, then? But then it's too late, right? John's been dead for fifteen years!"

Jude looked sly. "But there is another time machine—in this ficton—and in this city."

"No *shit*," Wally and Moira chorused. "I mean," Wally went on, "'speak on, sir, omitting no detail however slight.' Where? And why?"

"Let me table the question of its location for

a moment," Jude temporized, "and address your last input first. Authorized time travelers—as opposed to myself—are naturally hyperconscious of the danger of corrupting history. Therefore a clandestine machine is maintained throughout all periods of historical interest—so that if a researcher's cover story should collapse, at worst they can make their way there and escape to an earlier ficton, aborting the hang."

"Smart," Wally said. "So all you really need is a ride across town somewhere?"

Jude sighed. "Well, no. I am not an *authorized* time traveler."

Slowly, Wally nodded. "So then, what you need is . . . ?"

Jude hesitated . . . then took the plunge. "A substantial bribe."

"In what form?" Wally asked.

"Cash. Small bills would be best. . . ."

Wally boggled, shamelessly. He had been very good for a long time, but this just didn't seem *logical*. "Cash? You mean, 1995 dollars? What the hell would time travelers want with *cash*?"

"Think it through," Jude suggested.

Wally frowned fiercely. That one stung: a science fiction fan should never need to be told to think it through. "Apparently I lack data," he said stiffly.

"Okay. You're the guardian of the time machine, stuck in this primitive ficton forever, and if The Fabs are good you will have very little actual work to do: the need for your services had better be rare. Sooner or later you go native. Now: what can I bribe you with? Money in 2287 dollars, that you can bury for your descendants? Unnameable futuristic comforts and delights that you may never even risk letting any local observe you enjoying?

Or the means to render this Stone Age existence as tolerable as possible?"

"But why can't I generate as much cash as I want?" Wally said, falling into the Socratic spirit of the thing. "If I'm from the future, surely I was smart enough to pack some market tips, memorize some important dates—"

"—which you could only capitalize on at the cost of altering history," Jude pointed out. "Calling that kind of attention to yourself is precisely what you must *not* do. You must be a kind of invisible man—yet you must earn a living, in a ficton with all the privacy of a large bedroom, for altruism's sake. This is a recipe for bribery."

"Ah," Wally said. "I get it. And you're willing to take the risk they aren't, to get money to bribe them with. If you show up with a barrel of cash, they'll think it over and decide what's done is done, and the smartest thing to do with that money is quietly slip it back into the system— by spending it themselves. I guess if I were tending a time machine in the Court of Herod, I might take a hundred goats to bend a rule. You might pull it off."

"If you will help me," Jude agreed. "I need valid financial entities of this ficton to act as my agents. If you will let me give you market advice, I will make us . . . let me see, '95, '95 . . . say, two hundred thousand Canadian dollars, and give you half. And—Julia willing!—the joy of having undone the anagrammatic Evils of Elvis and saved Saint Jock. Will you help?"

Wally's heart was beating very fast. "Hold the phone. Check me out on this: you go back in time sixteen-odd years. You show up at the Dakota in a Yellow cab. Johnny and Paulie make the curtain, and history changes. And *this* ficton—here, now, sixteen years later—ceases to exist, right? Moira and I and everybody we know all disappear like Boojums?"

Jude did not hesitate. "These avatars of you, yes. But there will still be a Wally and a Moira. Have your lives been so good since John's Murder that you would not have them different? In a world with four strong Beatles to inspire it? Stack all the music recorded since 1972 against *Rubber Soul* . . ."

Husband and wife both started to answer, and fell silent. They *had* met, fallen in love and married well before the date in question. It wasn't as though the proposed alteration in history would cost them their marriage. Merely some dispiriting shared history . . . which would be replaced with—

"You live here; I don't. Is this ficton, in your opinions, gear? Or grotty? When do you believe the Sixties died, and why? Would you not see that undone, the Yellow Submarine relaunched?"

Wally found that tears were trickling, silently and unobtrusively, down his cheeks.

"Please help me," Jude said softly. "It is my destiny. I was born and named to do as Paul commanded: to make the sad song better."

"We'll do it," Wally and Moira both said at once, and took each other's hands again. They shared a grin that began as a promissory note for a kiss, and began inflating in value almost at once. Perhaps they had not been so happy since the day Moira proposed.

Jude, for his part, appeared to go into something like religious ecstasy. He shivered all over, smiled hugely, and began rocking gently from side to side, seeming to glow. "Then you shall live out the year," he said happily.

Through his own warm glow, those words reached Wally. He stopped grinning long enough to say, "Beg pardon?"

Jude waved his hands in the air, as one who would say, *no, no, it's nothing.* "Vancouver will be destroyed later this year. Not a problem."

"The *Big One?*" Moira squealed. "Juan de Fuca Fault? *This year?*"

"Yes, yes—but you will have a hundred thousand dollars with which to flee. And I will tell you when. Save as many friends as you like—as long as they are absolutely discreet."

An extraordinary cascade of thoughts went though Wally's brain in a short time.

Jesus, they do *say it's overdue—the whole Pacific Rim's going up lately—*

—Our home here in Point Grey sits on the only rock around: the only part of the greater Vancouver area that would not *immediately liquefy and submerge in the event of a quake. Of course, we'd get some thirsty by and by—*

—After we *agree to help Jude, he gets around to mentioning cataclysmic earthquakes in the near future?—*

Oh no, I see: he wanted us to be able to know and honestly say that our choice was pure, wasn't based on selfish motives—

—except for a piddling hundred grand—

—ohmyGod, to have the Beatles back! How many albums would they have put out between 1979 and now? Oh Jesus . . . imagine hearing Tug of War *without "Here Today"—but with John himself! Hell, those new tracks we're supposed to hear next month could have been out fifteen years ago—*

—get a grip, boy. Now which, if any, of my friends can I trust to keep their mouth shut about this? Oh, shit—

—can I condemn the rest to death for being gabby? Justice, perhaps, but rather harsh—

—is there some way to get them a warning at the last possible moment? Or can I come up with some alternate explanation for how I know for sure a quake is coming? A prediction I got from the Internet, maybe? Or—

—I'll miss this soggy town—

—where the hell will we go? Will Vancouver Island survive? Go-to-the-States or tolerate-Canadian-weather is a choice it's been nice not to have to make—

—no wonder Jude freaked when he learned what year it is—

—that's funny . . . why did he calm down, though, almost at once? He didn't even ask me the exact date: he just thought for a second, and relaxed—

—oh my dear God, he's not from Vancouver! And there's not much of 1995 left anymore—

"Jude," he said, enunciating carefully, feeling his lips and tongue starting to go numb, "what is the date of the earthquake?"

Jude was still ecstatic. "Oh, we'll have more than enough time, I should think, assuming you have any reasonable amount of capital. Point two megabucks shouldn't take more than a few weeks. You *do* know . . . um . . . a flexible broker?"

Moira started to answer, would doubtless have expressed amusement at the notion that there could be any difficulty locating a shady broker in the city which held the Vancouver Stock Exchange, but Wally overrode her: "*Tell me the date, Jude.*"

"Really, don't worry," Jude assured him. "It's not until Fall."

Wally groaned.

"Wally, what is it?" Moira said.

He turned to her. "I told him it was 1995, and he freaked," he said. "And then he felt the air with his skin, and relaxed . . . because it couldn't possibly be later in the year than late Summer. Don't you get it, love? Either he isn't from Vancouver—or in his ficton, Vancouver is as cold as the rest of Canada."

Moira's eyes grew round. "Oh my stars and garters. Jude!"

"Yes, Moira?"

"This is Halloween Night."

He nodded. "I have read of it. Anti-Christian ritual holiday, yes? Dress up, like Sergeant Pepper, take Magical Mystery Tour. We have a similar ritual in late October. And your point is—"

"Halloween Night falls on 31 October."

Jude grasped the floor on either side of him to keep from falling through it. "WHAT?" Gravity reversed itself; suddenly he rose like a launched missile, clutching at the floor with his soles to keep from flying away. "This is *October*?" Even internal gravity failed him: his trunk repelled his hands, and they flew out to either side. "The *end* of October?" He forced them to his will, brought them back in and beat them on his thighs. "The LAST FUCKING *DAY* of October?"

"It almost never gets cold here," Wally said apologetically.

Physics restored itself in Jude's vicinity: he went inert, *fell* back into his seat, with a thud, and kept collapsing, like a dropped dummy.

They gave him a moment with his despair. They wanted to ask, but the question was too obvious. To ask it would have insulted all three of them. Finally, Wally cleared his throat as discreetly as he could.

"Less than forty-eight hours," Jude said hollowly.

They both sat perfectly still. How appropriate a place in which to receive the news, Wally thought. Except the clothes on their backs, a statue of Siddhartha and a forty-watt lightbulb, there was not a single material possession in the room.

All right, then: it was a good place to think. Wally thought, as hard and fast as he ever had in his life. This time, even a summary of the resulting cascade of cogitation would be impossible, but he was through within a matter of perhaps ten seconds.

"All is not lost," he said then.

Jude nodded dispiritedly. "There is time to save ourselves, yes. With your help, perhaps I can establish a cover identity that will hold. I suppose it is possible that later, when things settle down and you rebuild your credit standing, we might try to . . . but then the problem becomes vastly more complex, you see. *This* time machine will be destroyed by the quake—and since its replacement in Halifax will just be entering operation, enforcement of regulations will be at its strictest: it'll be *years* before I'll even dare try to . . . oh *crot*, if only I'd arrived even a *week* earlier—" He was near tears in his frustration.

Wally turned and caught Moira's eyes. "Tomorrow morning we can put eighty-seven thousand dollars in cash into your hands," he said. Moira's eyes widened—and then slowly, she nodded. They turned back to Jude.

Burned once, he was reluctant to let hope back. "That . . . thank you, but I don't think that would quite be enough to—"

"You were always lousy at math, love," Moira said to Wally. "The correct figure is ninety-six thousand, seven hundred and fourteen dollars and fifty-two cents."

Wally nodded, mortified. In his haste, he had neglected to include their own personal net liquidity in the equation. The figure he had named represented only every penny presently in the Lower Mainland Science Fiction Society's VanCon account, entrusted to him and Moira by a couple of thousand Pacific Northwest science fiction fans. In his heart, Wally did not feel there was anything really dishonorable about offering that money. There was not going to *be* a VanCon in two weeks . . . and only a handful of chronic pains in the ass were ever even going to *ask* for a refund. Nonetheless, he knew the moment Moira spoke that, having pledged both his life and his sacred honor, he really should have thought to include his fortune as well. He excused himself on the grounds that the sum was so negligible it might have escaped anyone's attention. "Actually, darling," he said, anxious to redeem himself, "we could hit a few cash machines, and get another two grand before we max out. So the correct figure is ninety-*eight*-seven and change."

"Well," she said, "I thought we might—"

"We can charge our plane tickets out of town," he pointed out. "We can even put movers on plastic, to ship the books and music to a safe place. There's enough walking-around money in the house." He turned back to Jude. "Can you pull it off with ninety-eight-seven?"

Jude frowned in concentration—then all at once, shockingly, he giggled. "I'll tell them I have to charge them G.S.T.," he said puckishly.

Wally and Moira dissolved a lot of tension in that burst of laughter. (Canadians in 1995 regarded the Goods and Services Tax with all the affection Bostonians in 1776 had held for a similar levy on tea.) Each felt rather as though they had gnawed a leg off to escape a trap—but there was a sort of dizzy calm in that . . . and a quiet joy that the sacrifice would be sufficient after all. For think of the prize! New Beatles songs—not a lousy pair of them, but albums and albums—conceivably even some kind of *tours* again, with a living John Lennon, and stage technology the Beatles had never dreamed of in their touring days. *A world healed of disco.* A reconsolidation of the hopes and aspirations of the Sixties, tempered by experience—

—and it would be Wallace Kemp and Moira Rogers, Secret Masters Of Fandom, Secretary and Treasurer of LMSFS, who had helped to accomplish it! (Even if they never got to remember that . . . talk about your selfless sacrifices . . .)

In less than an hour, Jude had been fed, taken on a tour of the house and the hard drives, shown to a guest bedroom, taught to use a primitive contemporary cable-TV remote and a flush toilet, and left alone to sleep. Wally and Moira talked for another half an hour in bed, making plans, but they knew they needed rest and it had been a long night; they put out the light at around midnight, and were both asleep in a matter of minutes. Wally's last fleeting thought, before he slipped over the edge and into Strawberry Fields, was the bemused recollection from a Catholic childhood that, in that myth-structure, Jude was the patron saint of the impossible.

Realizing their total liquidity in small bills the next day required some ingenuity as well as effort; fortunately Wally, a professional hacker, had "social engineering" skills which proved useful. He and Moira left Jude alone with the TV and Moira's Mac (to Wally's disgust, he was told that the basic Mac interface would triumph in the future—as indeed it had already begun to do in his own ficton), and Wally spent the day stalking money while Moira worked the phone. By nightfall, just as movers were arriving to ship their most precious possessions to Toronto at outrageously padded emergency rates, he was able to hand Jude a large Tourister suitcase stuffed with cash.

"How does it feel," he asked as he passed it across, "to be one of the beautiful people?"

Jude grinned. "Baby, you're a rich man, too."

Wally handed over a bulky envelope. "Just in case you fail—in case they won't take the bribe—here's a plane ticket to Halifax, and cab fare to the airport. You can always sit on that cash until it's safe to try again." He smiled. "Keep it in a big brown bag, inside the zoo."

Jude's eyes were misting. "What a thing to do. Thank you, brother."

"Driving a cab is a little harder than it sounds. Try and arrive a week or so early, give yourself time to practice. Watch it done a few times, first. I typed out some tips; you'll find them on a sheet headed 'Baby, You Can Drive Their Car.' There's a tube of pepper spray in the envelope with it: don't use it until he's stopped, on a dark street, then reach past him fast and turn the key counterclockwise. Our temporary new number in Toronto is in that envelope, too. If we don't hear from you in a few days, we'll assume you were successful." He caught himself. "Excuse me. Dumb: if you succeed, we'll never know it. Never have known it. Boy, that's a hard concept to get my mind around. And I'm going to hate to lose the memory of the last twenty hours or so."

"I know it seems paradoxical," Jude said, taking his hand, "but I feel in my heart that if I succeed in my mission, somehow, in some way, you will remember your part in it for all the days of your life."

Wally did not agree, but it was a pretty thought; he let it pass unchallenged.

Moira looked up from her sorting and packing. "Get a move on, Jude. John and Paul are waiting. Give our love to Yoko and Linda."

Jude nodded and left without another word, threading his way through the movers.

"Have you noticed?" Moira said. "He has a passing resemblance to Jean-Luc Picard. . . ."

His last words came back to them both with great vividness and force . . . on the very next evening, as they sat up late into the night, in the guest bedroom of a friend and fellow SMOF in Toronto, listening in growing horror to a television and a radio and an Internet Reuters feed that all doggedly *refused* to report anything whatsoever about an earthquake in the Pacific Northwest. They tried desperately for hours to persuade each other that Jude had merely made some small error in the date, or that the authorities were censoring the news to prevent panic, or . . .

But they were not stupid people, only silly ones.

By dawn, shortly after Wally realized and pointed out that only in the unlikely event it finally provoked Canadians to open Boston-Tea-Party-style insurrection could the G.S.T. reasonably have been remembered in history long enough for someone from the year 2287 to have heard of it, they had both finally conceded that love is not all you need.

Wally gave Moira the chore of booking transport back home, while he went down to Bathurst Street and, with some difficulty, bought a handgun.

Chapter 3
What'd I Say

Jude ceased to exist about a hundred meters from Wally and Moira's house. Operation of his physical plant was taken over then by Paul Throtmanian, who made a point of existing whenever it was not inconvenient. It was he who conveyed the bag of swag a kilometer or two, from one end of Point Grey to the other (passing within a block of the edge of Pacific Spirit Park), softly and triumphantly singing John Lennon songs every step of the way. When he got within two blocks of his current home—just as he got to the words, "I don't believe . . . in Beatles"—Paul too ceased to exist, and became Ralph Metkiewicz, programmer, solid citizen, and tenant-of-record for that address.

Ralph was the only safe person to be in this particular neighborhood—was a considerably safer identity altogether than either of the other two. (Though there were no warrants outstanding for him under any of those names.) Nonetheless he kept the lowest possible profile, walking in shadow whenever possible, and using every trick he knew to make himself unobtrusive when he could not. He knew it would not be safe to openly enter his home tonight, even in darkness. Moira's sweatshirt and Wally's parachute pants and sockasins were just too weird for his persona, too memorable should certain questions ever be asked. Not that they would be, but he was an artist . . . and a professional pessimist, besides.

Happily, Ralph's home had been chosen specifically because one could leave it without being seen, even if it were surrounded by many policemen . . . and the process worked just as well in reverse. He entered the underground parking garage of an apartment building on West Fourteenth, used a key to open a knobless maintenance door on its far wall, let himself thereby into a long concrete corridor that led past the building's boiler room, and then turned left. Halfway along this corridor, which ran the width of the building, he bent and picked up a small unobtrusive piece of articulated wire from the filthy floor, about the length and strength of a paper clip and bent at six places. At the corridor's end he came to a blank wall, seemingly made of particle board sealed somehow to the raw concrete. There was a heavy-duty electrical outlet set in it at about chest height, inset perhaps a quarter of an inch as if sloppily installed. He inserted the bit of wire into the right-hand slot of the socket in a certain way, rotated it clockwise, twice, and heard a small *clack!* sound. Then he repeated the procedure, counterclockwise, with the left slot. He removed the lockpick and tossed it behind him toward the spot on the floor where he'd found it. He set down his bag, put his fingertips into the shallow space formed by the wall socket's inset, braced himself, and heaved sideways. The wall slid away smoothly and noiselessly to the left. He reclaimed his satchel of swag, stepped through the resulting opening into a tunnel, turned and slid the false wall back into place, and continued on without troubling to turn on the lights. At the end of the tunnel he found the keypad in the dark, tapped the combination, and was admitted into his own basement.

The moment the door locked behind him, Ralph was tempted to become Paul again. But he waited until he had queried the security system and confirmed that his was the only entry, authorized or otherwise, since his departure. *Then* he morphed back to himself, losing Ralph's slouch and outthrust jaw, and emitted a sustained whoop of triumph and glee that made the basement ring.

It was more than the ninety-eight large. His place in the annals of the great was assured. As of this moment, Paul Throtmanian was legend. He had detected, perfected, and just now effected *the first new con in at least a hundred years*.

With any luck, the bulk of the fame—the on-the-record portion—would be posthumous. Ideally his achievement would not reach the ears of anyone who wasn't bent until Paul was comfortably in the ground, or at least past the statutes of limitations. But the players would all know, well before then. In the bucket-shops of Vancouver and Melbourne and Markham, at all the major stock exchanges, in the great seine of Times Square, in the cabs of Florida pickup trucks painted with the names of hurricane-repair contractors, backstage at alien-abductee conferences, after hours in Alternative AIDS clinics and Stop Smoking clinics and Facilitated Communication clinics and Cure Cancer clinics, on cruise ships and in revival tents and in Vegas and Key West and along Bourbon Street, in between dropping wallets or recovering memories of fetal rape or pretending to treat frozen shoulder or dispensing market or other psychic advice, the grifter elite of the English-speaking world would sooner or later speak of Paul Throtmanian with respect, and even admiration. The beauty of the sting, the sheer joy of it, the thing that would sell it, was that the higher the mark's IQ, the *more* likely he was to bite. Pleasure without guilt, like Pepperidge Farm cookies. You could almost use MENSA's mailing list for a hit sheet. It was possible that his fame would become planetary, for the gag would work in any culture which had been exposed to science fiction. It was even conceivable that the gambit might come to be known as *a Throtmanian* . . . the way Murphy's and Vesco's and Rockford's names had entered the language. Today, Paul had become one of the immortals.

For *once*, he would outshine his partner.

That thought came close to derailing his joy, for he loved her and respected her professionally and did not *want* to envy her, and besides there was darkness in her life just now. But he also knew that she would not begrudge him his triumph—she would probably take some of the credit for it, and probably deserved it—and perhaps his glow would brighten her present darkness just a bit. If not, perhaps ninety-eight large in cash would. And he had to share the news or burst.

She must be back from California by now, was probably at her own apartment waiting for his call. (They had learned, early on in the five years they'd been a team so far, that both their personal and professional relationships went better if they maintained separate addresses. Aside from that they were practically married.) So: check in with her at once. Or nearly . . .

He left the cash in a place even the building's architect could not have found without deep radar, and set demons to guard it. He stripped off Wally's and Moira's clothing and fed it to the furnace, along with the air ticket to Halifax, the Toronto phone number, the cab-driving tips and the envelope that had contained them. The pepper spray and the cab fare he took with him as he padded naked up the stairs. He went straight to the phone machine, which greeted him with four blinks. The first call was a hangup—no manners left in the world. The second was an infant or small child, happily pushing buttons at random—no parents left in the world. The third caller warned him that the opportunity to buy into lucrative lottery ticket syndicates in other, tax-free nations was about to slip through his fingers—Paul recognized the voice, and grinned. The fourth, at last, was his lady love, who said:

"Honey, I'm into something heavy here. I'm walking in the Endowment Lands, and I ran across a mook looking to bury something nice just off the Lowrie Trail, Dorothy twice, but that's not the good part. He was digging away at the base of a huge old toppled elm tree, and he hit something with his shovel that made a sound like clack, *something like plywood or plastic. And then . . . I know this is nuts, but then he had an orgasm, all by himself, standing up. And then he started to talk out loud, as if somebody was grilling him— only I was only fifty meters away and I swear there was no one else there. He said his name was Angel Gerhardt and he lived over in the East End on William Street and his e-mail handle, God help*

us all, was 'Frosty,' and he named his girlfriend Linda Wu and his two housemates and said none of them knew where he planned to bury the . . . the thing . . . and the weird part was, he didn't say any of this like a mope giving information to the heat, he said it like a guy opening his soul to his new lover, happy as a clam. Then he filled the hole back in and buried the package in another spot. He's gone now. I'm going to put the package somewhere else—but I'm not going near that goddam fallen elm without you, and maybe Rosco. I don't know what we've got ahold of here, but whatever it is is very very big. Call me as soon as you get in, okay? I hope everything went okay."

Paul frowned. It was a good thing for her, he reflected, that he loved her. . . .

His phone had no redial button (it was barely a touch-tone), and he had a mental block against remembering her cell phone number. So it was necessary to go consult the tackboard in the kitchen, again. Along the way he stopped in his bedroom and threw casual clothes on, chiefly to give him time to deal with his irritation.

Even for God, this seemed low comedy.

He didn't have the slightest idea what the hell June had stumbled onto—any more than she seemed to. But it never entered his mind to doubt for an instant that *whatever* it was, was of greater and more lasting significance than ninety-eight large in small bills. Or even maybe the first new con of the century. That much was obvious. This was his punishment for being a male chauvinist pig—penance, for the sin of Pride.

Most infuriating of all, the mystery fascinated him.

It seemed clear that her mook had triggered some kind of security system light-years beyond anything Paul had ever heard of—and security was a field he had given diligent study. Whoever had designed the system possessed technology the RCMP or American NSA would unquestionably kill, maim and/or torture for. Paul's most plausible first-hypothesis was aliens, and he emphatically did not believe in flying saucers.

What that system was meant to protect, he could not even begin to guess. He did not waste time trying. It would be more efficient to just go find out. He was already scheming ways to beat the system as he returned to the kitchen.

There he made and drank Ghimbi coffee while he replayed the relevant tape, twice. At the third mention of Rosco's name, he went to the bedroom and got him. Then he sat in the kitchen again and thought hard for several minutes, occupying his hands and eyes by cleaning and oiling Rosco and practicing with the speed-loader.

Maybe he was looking at this the wrong way. Just backwards, even. Maybe he was going to become *twice* as immortal as he had thought. How many players had ever hit two world-class jackpots on the same day?

He read June's number off the wall and dialed it. She answered at once. "Hi, hon."

She sounded depressed—more accurately, chipper: the way she sounded when she didn't want you to know she was depressed. June said depression was like farting: that all humans are subject to it, but it is not done in polite company. He knew it ran deeper than that, for they had long since reached that point of intimacy at which they could fart unself-consciously in each other's presence. But he respected her need to suffer in silence, and tried not to be insulted by it. "After considerable reflection, I've decided to let you live," he said.

"That's nice."

"I will, of course, do my best to ensure that your every moment is infinite agony—but it just seems to me Hell doesn't deserve you."

"It never will. What'd I do?"

"What did you *do*? Only you could have done this to me, bitch. I pull off the triumph of my career, dead bang perfect the first time—and you top me before I can even tell you the news. It's fucking typical, I tell you. You're a menace."

"Paul, what the hell are you talking about?"

At once he inferred that she was not alone. Something had gone horribly wrong since she'd left her message. It was now imperative to know whether the third party could hear Paul's end of the conversation too, or only June's. "I see. Good as a nod, is it?" he said, hoping to hear an "Uh huh," that would mean they could communicate safely as long as he could phrase his questions to require yes/no or similarly cryptic answers.

Instead she said, "What?"

Confused, he tried, "You're alone?"

"Yeah, I'm out for a walk, over in the Endowment Lands. Why?"

He had to nail it down. "Where did we first meet?"

This should do it. If someone were listening, she would answer with the Official Version: the one they gave to strangers, straight acquaintances, and casual friends.

But she answered accurately. "Fogerty's. I'm

really me, okay? So what's going on? Did something go sour with your thing, or what?"

Now he was baffled. "No. No, it went just great . . . right up until I got home heavy and found your message."

"What message?"

"—," Paul said, and then repeated it for emphasis.

"I just got out of Customs three—no, four . . . that's funny—four hours ago. It didn't go real great down in San Francisco, so I dropped my stuff at my place and came out here to think. Did this message actually sound like me? What did I say?"

The one thing he was certain of was that the phone message was from June. Not an impressionist, not a computer-assembled matchup of voice recordings: June. In speech pattern, emotional nuance, it was unmistakably his lover. He knew he might be wrong, but he was positive.

She was an amnesiac or a zombie. There was no third choice.

"Look," he said slowly, "I think it would be best if we discussed this in person. I really really do."

Brief pause. "Okay. My place or yours?"

Paul thought quickly. They had long since agreed and arranged that, for reasons of professional risk hygiene, neither should be able to enter the other's home in its owner's absence— the stated theory being that what you do not know, you cannot babble if drugged or otherwise coerced. Paul had never quite been certain that security was the only reason for this arrangement, but had never pushed to find out. June was the senior partner of the team; it was enough that she always let him in when he knocked, and usually came when he called. But now he was seeing things through new eyes. If someone else *were* operating her now, the tactical advantage for him lay on his own turf.

"Come in the front way, okay?"

Longer pause than before. "Paul?"

"Yeah, love."

"What *time* did we meet at Fogerty's?"

He blinked. Okay, fair enough. "Twenty minutes after closing."

Her relief was audible. "I'll be there in about fifteen minutes."

He hung up the phone and glowered at Rosco, so frightened and angry that holding him did not make Paul feel as ridiculous as it usually did. Dammit, he had not expected to have to be this paranoid again for months, yet! A man deserved a break after a big job.

Mess with my *woman's head, will you? I'm coming for you, pal. I don't care* who *you are: I'm bringing it to you. You just bought the whole package. Batteries* are *included.*

The living room projected out four feet from the rest of the house, with a big bay window facing north that wrapped at east and west ends. Someone sitting in the rocker by the window could see a pedestrian or motorist approaching the house, from either direction, from at least a block away. So could someone crouching beneath the window with a toy periscope in one hand and Rosco in the other.

She came from the right direction. It was for sure her. She was alone. She did not appear to be under any kind of duress or constraint, did not look drugged or at gunpoint. She looked totally serene, in fact, until she was within a few feet of the door, at which time she allowed an expression of mingled curiosity and weariness to cross her face. It was still there as she let herself in the unlocked door and locked it behind her. Then it was gone, for you cannot look curious and weary and hoot with helpless laughter at the same time.

"I'm sorry," she said when she could. "I know you told me, but I guess I didn't—I hadn't—" She lost it again, and sat in a nearby chair.

Under other circumstances he might have been irritated—but he was too relieved. So far as he understood, zombies did not giggle. Or break their lover's balls. "Issss," he said in a hokey baritone, and rubbed his free hand across his bald scalp, "a pozzlement!" The hand she could not see put the safety back on and put Rosco away in his small-of-the-back holster.

She got the *King and I* reference, and giggled even harder. "Thanks," she said when she was done. "I needed that. You look like that guy from Star Trek, the one without the wrinkles. 'Make it so!'—that one."

"It'll grow back," he said in his own voice. "And it was worth it, believe me." He got up from his crouch, went to the door and rearmed the security system.

"The scam worked? Oh, that's great, honey—you're a genius! A bald genius. How big?"

"Ninety-eight kay," he said smugly, buffing his nails on his chest. "Perfect blowoff. They won't even know they've been stung for hours yet." He admired his manicure. "I'm so smart I make myself sick."

Suddenly she was serious. "You're not wrong. I take my hat off. Do you have any idea how many people spent their whole *lives* trying to think up a new bit?"

He had not meant to be sidetracked by this,

but he couldn't help himself. "Aw hell," he said, "it's really just a refinement of the Horse Wire."

By this he referred to the classic con outlined in the film *The Sting*, in which the mark is led to believe the player has secret advance access to telegraphed racing results. It is indeed the historical grandfather of most "insider-information" cons, and a case could be made that Paul's creation was merely another, admittedly highly refined, variant.

But June answered as if he had primed her. "The hell it is. It looks a little like a Horse Wire, but it's fundamentally different. It's about the only con I ever heard of *that doesn't require the mark to be corrupt*. Your sting works on *altruists*. You've broken new ground!"

For some reason her praise made him flinch. Okay, he thought, you've had your minimum daily requirement of stroking. Back to business!

"So have you, love," he said.

She frowned, shifting gears at once. "Oh yeah. What's this about a message?"

"You better listen to it yourself."

"I guess so." She got up.

He pushed away from the door, and just in time remembered to say, and just in time had the wit not to preface it with *By the way*, "How's Laura?"

She winced, and came to him, and they hugged. "Later, okay?" she murmured into his neck.

Sure. Maybe in their golden years. "Yeah."

They held each other for a long moment, each relishing the physical comfort, each wishing it could be prolonged. Then they went to the kitchen, and he started a pot of coffee while the tape played back.

She played the whole message twice, and after she shut the machine off, for several minutes the only sound in the room was the merry bubbling of water. Just as he was about to set out cups and spoons, she shook her head as if coming out of a trance.

"You said there's a priest's hole in this dump," she stated, fiddling with the machine.

"Yeah. Down cellar." His blood began to pound: she was using command voice.

"*Now*. Bring Rosco!"

"I'll get a jacket—"

"Fuck the jacket. *Let's go*." She was already heading for the door to the basement.

He caught up with her at the foot of the stairs: she did not know which way to go from there. But she was right on his heels as he led them to the emergency exit, one hand in her purse, looking back over her shoulder. He had caught her urgency now, and didn't bother to conceal the code he punched into what looked like a broken calculator. A slab of paneling became a door, which opened to reveal the unlit tunnel. As he reached to turn the tunnel light on, they both heard the horrid sound of an alarm echoing through the house, and probably the neighborhood.

"Son of a *bitch*," he said. "Somebody just came through the front door." A different tocsin. "The fire alarm too! Damn—I *liked* this place." Suddenly his eyes widened. "Oh, shit—cover me! *The ninety-eight large*—" He began to turn back . . . and found that June was pointing her own gun at him.

"Did the brain fairy leave you a quarter last night?" she snarled. "Fuck the money."

She was right. He knew she was right. "But—"

She took the safety off. "Move move move move move—"

He moved.

✧   ✧   ✧

The best car in the underground garage was a '94 Honda Accord. June was better with cars, they'd settled that long ago, so Paul guarded her back while she got in and got it running, a matter of seconds. She had it on the street and accelerating before he could get his seat belt buckled. "Where are we going?" he asked.

"How the hell do I know? Downtown, for now: try and maximize witnesses, disappear in the crowd. After that, who knows?"

He nodded and watched out the window for cops. A few blocks later, he said, "You don't remember it at *all*?"

She took her eyes off the rearview mirror long enough to throw him an agonized look. "No! Not any part of it. If it wasn't my voice, I wouldn't believe it. Except for one other thing."

He nodded. "Our visitors."

"No, they only confirmed it. I believed it before we ran—that's *why* we ran."

"Okay: what's the one thing that convinced you?"

"The part about Angel Gerhardt having an orgasm."

"I don't get you. That part almost convinced me you were hallucinating."

"When I left Dad's house this morning, I was wearing panties. I'm not, now."

Paul turned pale, and then ruddy. "Jesus."

Suddenly she started to laugh. "You want to hear something stupid?"

"Sure."

"I actually feel better now than I did when you called. And I'm scared shitless."

Chapter 4
Strike One

As they came through the door they knew they were too late.

They did what they could—hurled orgasms after both their targets, *hard*—but were unsurprised to miss. Too much distance, too much building and wiring in the way . . . and almost at once, the targets were enclosed in something that insulated them from the tasp.

Knowledge of the certainty of failure slowed them no more than the door had—that is, not at all: they burned the living room floor away beneath their pounding feet and hit the basement running. Walls received no more respect. But the door they finally came to was made of sterner stuff, fighting a heroic fifteen-second rear guard action before it too succumbed. So did the one at the far end of the tunnel. By the time they emerged into the underground parking garage its robot door had fully closed again.

They let it live. To go quickly through so public a door would court attention; to trick it into opening normally would take too long. Without hesitation they backed out of the garage and retraced their steps toward the single-family home they had just renovated.

Once they were back in the tunnel, and its door to the world was fused shut again behind them, she put away a weapon widget and took out a scanning widget. "Lead lining," she announced. "Not just this tunnel: half the basement. Positively Murphian."

"This whole set-up has to be a Cold War relic," he said. "Basement bomb shelter with a secret way in and out."

"Thanks," she said. "I didn't quite have enough irony to choke on. Somewhere, Joe Stalin is chuckling. I don't like this."

"We'll reacquire," he said as they reentered the house proper and sealed the tunnel behind them.

"Of course we will. But meanwhile we have *two* active leaks—and the second target we know nothing about."

"We know everything June knows about him," he said soothingly.

"Yes, and she thinks he's an endearingly helpless boob. Do you think a boob outfitted this house?"

The house's security measures *had* been impressive, for this ficton. Impressive enough to keep their preliminary site surveillance shallow, for fear of being spotted. For that reason, the priest's hole had come as a rude surprise. And the speed—no, the quickness—with which it had been used was certainly unsettling. "No," he admitted.

"This is ungood," she said. "Two competent paranoids, in a fairly sophisticated ficton, on the loose with a Time bomb in their heads."

"So let's learn all we can about target number two," he said. He waved his hand like Peter Pan scattering fairy dust, and multicolored sparkles dispersed in all directions.

Upstairs in the den, Paul's hard drive powered up. Elsewhere in the building, photos of him were identified and scanned; samples of his DNA were collected and analyzed; his belongings were inventoried. In the basement, in the room where they stood, a barely visible trail of red sparkles began to form in midair, denoting where a heat-source of human temperature had recently passed. The brighter the sparkles, the more recent the passage. The *redder* the sparkles, the longer the human had tarried there. She traced it down a hallway to a place faint but carmine, and used her scanning widget. "There's something good here," she said, deactivating an excellent booby-trap.

"Be careful," he said, approaching.

"Don't b—" she said, and the second booby-trap blew her through a wall. He was barely able to cancel most of the sound. A lot of upstairs came downstairs onto both of them. He fought through smoking rubble to reach her side.

She lay on her back, blinking up at him. "I am finding it very hard not to dislike Paul Throtmanian," she said, her voice gentle in the sudden silence.

"Are you all right?"

She scanned herself—and winced. "I came through fine—but love . . . I'm afraid that was the Last Straw."

He turned to stone, and it did not help enough. "You're sure."

"My whole defensive system overloaded. For good. I'm an ordinary mortal."

He flinched, but said nothing. He owned no words equal to the occasion. He dropped to his knees beside her and took her in his arms.

This was a body blow, for her and for him and

for their marriage and for their mission. They had both known this day might come, for either or both of them—had spent centuries preparing themselves for it, knowing that preparation would be no help. Sure enough, it was not. Suddenly it was a very sad day . . . and nowhere near over, with utter disaster on the horizon.

They shared their heartbreak in silence for several seconds.

"I dislike Paul Throtmanian," she said then, her voice even gentler than before. "Let's go see what he was protecting."

He helped her up. Her clothing was already starting to repair itself—as if to underline the point that she no longer could. Her temper was not improved when she found that Paul's hiding place had concealed money. "Oh for God's sake," she snapped. "I thought it was something *important*."

He was almost as annoyed that the cash had been destroyed—it certainly could have come in handy for *them*, particularly just now—but he could not say so without implying criticism of her judgment. Worse, accurate criticism. Fortunately the stream of incoming data still being assimilated and analyzed throughout the house picked then to yield up a useful distraction. "Ah," he said gratefully, "there's a lead."

She held the flagged datum before her mind's eye, studied it, and nodded just as gratefully. "Good. It's a place to start, at least."

"Do we want to involve the law?" he asked.

She started to answer . . . caught herself. "You decide. My judgment is a little off tonight."

It was one of the bravest things he had ever heard her say. He saluted it by ignoring it. "I'm on the fence," he said at once. "My inclination is obviously to go for a full-court press; I'd call out an air strike on them if I could think of a cover story. But the way they bugged out of here, on a second's notice, without even stopping for the cash . . . maybe our only chance is for them to think they've gotten clear, and relax just a hair. I think the cops might simply keep those two alert."

"Tough call," she agreed. "Make it."

He juggled the universe, backstopped but all alone. As he thought, he heard a clock ticking, louder than one had ever ticked for him before. Sweat sprang out on his forehead for the first time in decades.

"More data," he said. "We *know* one of them; we know *about* the other—the one with the testosterone. We need to integrate everything we just got here with everything June knows about him."

Ignoring the ticking, they closed their eyes, joined hands, joined minds, and did as he had proposed.

Chapter 5
Cute Meat

June tried to walk as if the right shoe still had a high heel, and scanned both sides of the deserted street, searching the shadowed places for danger and the arc-lit places for a door out of the world.

At age twenty-eight, she had just made what she intended to be her last professional mistake, overestimating not the character but the intelligence of her partner. The Slider was so innately lazy, she had assumed he realized what a valuable asset she was to him. She had trusted him completely to handle the blow-off; it was well within his talents. Instead he had simply skipped, left her standing there to take the gaff when the mark tipped. Caught flatfooted, she had been lucky to get clear with nothing worse than a couple of slaps, one good punch, and a broken high heel. In the Slider's stupid estimation, the extra half of the take was compensation enough for the inconvenience of having to find and train another skirt at his next address; never mind that the new girl would have *half* June's brains, skills or talent at best. As a result June herself was on the street at 4 AM in Toronto with no money, no safe address or identity, no local friends, and a dull nauseating ache on the left side of her face where the fist had caught her.

She understood her error, and looked forward to explaining his to the Slider one day. Some equations, she would tell him, contain certain terms so valuable that they *cannot* safely be subtracted or replaced. Or perhaps she could match his own laziness and say it even more succinctly: a good place to carve an "equals" sign occurred to her . . .

But first she had to make sure she *was* clear, get off the street. The mark might have yelled copper—or he might be in his Porsche now, casting through the night streets for a redhead with a hitch in her walk. Her hair and makeup would probably pass under streetlights—if she kept the unmarked side of her face to the street—but even the option of playing hooker and flagging down one of the rare motorists was closed to her: she looked like after the rape rather than before. It was so late, other pedestrians were rare, and none she saw looked like a serviceable champion. The cabs had all melted or corralled up or whatever it was they did when you really needed one.

That left a rabbit hole. Scarce, at 4 AM in downtown Toronto.

Up ahead on this side of the street. A bar with a faint light on inside . . .

Horse Shoes & Hand Grenades, it was called. The owner had hubris—June was absolutely certain every male who had ever spoken of it had referred to it as "Horseshit and Handjobs." She squinted through the partially frosted window, saw a shadowy figure behind the bar. Thank God— someone as lazy as the Slider, still cleaning up at this hour.

Her knock startled him; he spun and stared from side to side of the vast window that fronted the street, trying to locate her. He looked young and dumb and just cute enough to believe himself irresistible.

Perfect.

She knocked again, more weakly than before, and allowed herself to slump.

This time he located her, and at once began shaking his head and waving his hands in a reasonably impressive catalog of all the myriad ways there are to pantomime *Go away; we are closed*, a statement so self-evident as to be insulting. Marceau himself could not have returned the serve more powerfully: she managed—long distance, in bad light—to convey *need, desperation, apology, tremulous hope* and *earnest entreaty*, without so much as raising her hands or ever drawing undue attention from her sexual desirability.

It might not have worked in America, say, but in this blessed country even the bartenders were candy. Knowing he was defeated, but unwilling to acknowledge it yet, he stayed behind the bar and gave her *harassed* and *frustrated*. She riposted with *abject surrender*, and saw him fold. She was already digging tissues and another item from her purse as he put down whatever he was fooling with and came around the bar, and by the time he got the door open the tears she was wiping away looked genuine.

He was still doing *harassed*, but now that he could

see her left cheek and general state of disrepair, felt obliged to add *concerned* and just a touch of *generically gallant*. Nonetheless he began by wasting his breath. "I'm sorry, miss, but we're closed."

"I know," she said, wasting some of her own. "But I just . . . I . . . look, I just had a really bad experience, okay? I'm a little shaken up; I thought he was going to . . . look, can I just duck inside for a second and clean up? Maybe after that I can figure out what to . . ." She let her voice trail off.

"Look, lady, I'd really like to help, okay? but the boss is gonna be back any minute, and honest to God, if he finds out I let anybody in here after closing he's gonna—"

He certainly had a lot of breath to waste. "I'll only be a minute, I swear." She paused a moment to let him begin his response, then overrode him with, "Look, I got female troubles, give me a break, okay?" and took a deep breath of her own to set the hook.

He emptied his lungs in a sigh (breath smelled okay, a good omen) and, in the Slider's memorable phrase, folded like a full wallet: slowly but thoroughly. "Jesus Christ, you're breaking my stones, lady. All right, look, come on in, the ladies' can is, uh, over there, just make it *quick*, all right?"

"You're very kind," she lied, and brushed past him, leaving him to close the door.

Once in the toilet, she relaxed and took her time. The cheek wasn't as bad as she had feared (thank God the son of a bitch wore the diamond on his other hand). She decided it would pass with a little work, and did it carefully. Then she addressed the shoes; by wedging the remaining heel under the sink tap, she was able to snap it off—lowering her apparent height by an inch or two. The tear at the collar she managed to repair with a safety pin, although it required taking off the blouse. Since it was off, she took off her bra too and treated herself to a full field bath, swabbing the sweat and fear-stink from her armpits with paper towels and rolling on fresh deodorant. The bra went into her purse, and several buttons were not rebuttoned when she put the blouse back on. She brushed out her hair and restyled it to present an altered silhouette. She removed and reversed her skirt, changing its color, and rolled its waistband under to shorten it by a couple of inches. She redid her lipstick with care. As an afterthought she slid a finger down her panties, moistened it, and rubbed it off on each earlobe. She assessed the results in the mirror, and felt some of her self-confidence flowing back.

Time to boat this sucker, she thought. She made sure her purse held condoms, and left the toilet.

He was exactly as she had imagined him: pacing behind the bar, muttering to his feet, drumming his fingers on every flat surface he passed, miming *impatience* to an empty house. He spun at the sound of her approach and stumbled slightly. When his eyes locked on her, there was an audible click. He had clearly been preparing to resume their Dueling Mimes with a strong combination of *put upon* and *endangered by your thoughtlessness* and *in no mood*, but the impression collapsed as his targeting computer claimed all available processing power.

She waited, let him speak first, and as soon as he did she overrode him with a husky "Thank you, kind sir. I really . . . owe you a lot."

"You're welcome," he had to say. "But look—"

"I really hope you mean that," she said. "Because right now I'd do just about anything for a stiff bourbon."

He wanted to say no firmly and at once, but was distracted by the half-grasped changes in her appearance; by the time he refocused, too much time had passed and it came out ineffective. "Jesus, lady, my boss—"

"I'm sure he wouldn't begrudge a lady a single drink," she said. "Not if he knew what I've been through tonight."

"Look, a cop glances in and sees you here this time of night and we got license trouble—really, they already gave us a couple of warnings: this time they're gonna—"

"I'll sit over here out of sight, then," she said, and at once took a seat at a table which was both well outside the cone of light from the single lamp above the register, and shielded from the window by a cigarette machine.

He glared down at his shoes and relaxed to the inevitable. "One *short* one," he said, and turned to hunt for a bourbon bottle.

She studied him as he built her drink. He was younger than her; call it three calendar and about a century subjective. He was of pleasing height, shape and aspect, in shape but not obsessive about it. He was clean shaven, wearing a black turtle-neck and dark slacks. He moved with easy grace, light on his feet, but appeared very tired, fumbling for things he needed and pouring with only a sketch of professional elegance. As he went by the register, she noticed the key sticking out of its lock, giving it the absurd air of a windup toy. Something indefinable about his upper lip gave her a mild but distinct urge to bite it. When he brought her the drink, she noticed the bulge in his pants, without being caught at it.

She thought about all these things, and then she made him sit down and told him a long and gaudy and quite fictitious tale about how she had come to need succor at this hour, sipping her bourbon slowly as she created. The story might well have produced an erection on a statue of John Diefenbaker, and when she was sure he had one, she slid a hand into her purse. "I've taken up enough of your time," she said. "Let me just pay for my drink and I'll let you finish up and go home." She stirred the trash in her purse. "Do you have change for a twenty?"

He blinked at her, turned to look at the locked register, turned back to her. "You don't have anything smaller?"

"Afraid not," she said, smiling sweetly.

"Forget it, it's on the house."

"No, really, it's the least I can do. You want your accounts to balance."

"I already closed out the register. Thanks for offering, but it isn't necessary."

"Well, let me give you something for your trouble, then. Really, you've been a life-saver: just give me back a ten and a five." She began to take out the imaginary twenty. This was *fun*.

"I wouldn't dream of it," he said quickly. "Look, have you got some place you can go for the night? That creep could still be back at your apartment—"

"I . . . I'll think of something," she said.

"Why don't I go back there with you, right now, make sure the coast is clear?"

"But didn't you say you have to wait for your boss?" she said sadistically.

He blinked twice. "Uh, well, if he's not here by—" He glanced at his watch. "—now, it usually means he's not coming. Really, I'd be glad to lock up here and—"

"I don't think I want to go back to my place, just yet. I don't think I'm ready. You wouldn't know of anyplace else . . ."

He went for it like a starving trout. "Uh . . . look, what's your name?"

"Angela," she said.

"Angela, I know how this might sound, but . . . there's a fold-out couch at my place." He met her eyes squarely. "And I swear you can trust me."

She looked him over carefully. "I almost believe you," she said softly.

"You can," he said. "I've got my share of faults, but I won't ever lie to you."

"I hope you mean that," she said.

"I do," he assured her, quiet sincerity in his voice.

She took her time deciding, for the pleasure of watching him mime *steadfast*, and finally said, "I don't even know your name—no, don't tell me yet—but I'll go home with you, if you'll give me a truthful answer to one question."

"I'm not," he said. "Never even been engaged."

"Good, but that wasn't the question."

"What, then?"

"How much did you clear?"

He shook his head slightly a few times. "Beg pardon?"

"How much did you take off the guy tied up and gagged on the floor behind the bar?"

His eyes went to her right hand, still deep in her purse. They were the only part of him that moved. His own hand must have yearned to go

to the bulge in his pants she had seen earlier—
the one a few inches from his erection—but it
didn't even twitch. She was impressed. "You heat?"

"No," she said. "And *I'll* never lie to *you*, either.
Not anymore. Sound like a plan?"

It was his turn to take his time making up his
mind. "Yeah," he said finally. "I guess it does.
When did you tip?"

"You were too graceful to be such a lousy
bartender. And you left the key in the register."

He was impressed. "You're good."

"Yes," she said.

"I figure I'll probably net somewhere around
two large."

"Chump," she said fondly. "It's time you went
professional. Let's book."

"I'm sick of the place," he agreed. He rose, got
a briefcase from behind the bar, said, "Sorry 'bout
that, cap," toward the floor, and came back to take
her arm.

As they walked out the door they nearly collided with a cop. He glanced at them with idle
curiosity, looked away politely, then registered the
briefcase and began a double take. Before he
could complete it his jaw collided with a male fist,
distracting him so much that he failed to notice
June's foot rising like a Shuttle launch toward his
groin. Its impact folded him like an *empty* wallet,
presenting the nape of his neck to her companion's
elbow, and he ceased to be a significant part of
their lives.

"*Now* you can tell me your name," she said,
when she had made sure the cop was out.

"I'm Paul Throtmanian." He was breathing
audibly but under control.

"I'm Susan Hughes."

"Want a gun or a badge?" Paul said cheerily.

"What would I need with a gun?"

"Good point." He flexed the fingers of his right hand, winced, and started to walk away.

"Chump," Susan said—but softly, to herself—and got the cop's wallet and pocket change.

She told him her right name after the third orgasm. His third; she had long since lost count.

ABSTRACT, ACQUIRED DATA:
PAUL THROTMANIAN, 31 OCTOBER 1995:

BIRTH NAME:
Paul Donald Throtmanian
BIRTHPLACE:
Riker's Island (holding cell, Women's Corrective Facility)
BIRTHDATE:
1 April 1970
MOTHER:
Lada Loven (apparently legal name; birth name: Ilse Throtmanian; deceased)
FATHER:
not known
CURRENT LEGAL NAME (THIS ADDRESS):
Ralph Metkiewicz
KNOWN ALIASES:
Peter David Talbot; Philip Dwight Tanager; Sebastian Tombs; Richard Stark; Dick Starkey; John Archibald Dortmunder; Samuel Holt; Ernest Gibbons, Sr.; James Tiptree, Jr.; Dr. Lafe Hubert, M.D.; Neil O'Heret Brain; B.D. Wyatt; Edward Hunter Waldo; Preston Danforth Tomlinson; Parker Meyer Spenser; Travis T.

Magee; Tak Hallus; Penforth Naim; Susan Donim; Dr. Winston O. Bourgee; Paul Nurk; John Nurk; Edison Ripsborn; Marcus Van Heller; Paul Teale

CURRENTLY ACTIVE ID:

Metkiewicz; Gibbons; Hallus; Naim; Donim; Smith; Teale (various)

REGISTERED VEHICLES:

- 1994 Toyota Camry to Metkiewicz (this address; disabled)
- 1995 Porsche to Naim (location of record: 10659 Point Grey Rd.)

KNOWN RESIDENCES, LOCAL:

- this address; expired
- 10659 Point Grey Rd., Vancouver, BC V8U 4R6 (legal residence of June Bellamy as "Carla Bernardo")

KNOWN RESIDENCES, NONLOCAL:

- 9787 Flagler St., Key West, FL [zip unknown] (summer home of "Ernie and Dora Gibbons"; currently sublet)

CITIZENSHIP:

Canadian (2); American (3); Cuban; Japanese; all valid and current

EDUCATIONAL HISTORY:

entered Chaminade HS, Mineola, NY, 5 September 1982; withdrew two months short of graduation; no further formal study indicated

CREDIT HISTORY:

labyrinthine; no credit history as Paul Donald Throtmanian after 1982

MILITARY HISTORY:

none recorded; inventory suggests advanced weapons training

WORK HISTORY:

various; all apparently virtual except for a

summer job as shipping clerk, K&K Chemicals, Syosset, NY, as Paul D. Throtmanian, 1985

TAX HISTORY:

none, any jurisdiction

ARRESTS:

- 1 April 1986, Old Bethpage, NY: Suspicion of Arson (NYS orphanage), as Paul David Throtmanian; dismissed LOE; file open

COMPLAINTS FILED:

none, any jurisdiction

CONVICTIONS:

none, any jurisdiction

WARRANTS OUTSTANDING:

none, any jurisdiction

Chapter 6
Grok and Roll

"There is no point in mobilizing the authorities," he said. Upstairs, the Throtmanian/Metkiewicz computer reformatted its hard drive three times and then boiled its own ROM; flames began whispering in two nearby floppy disk caddies, two filing cabinets, a lockbox under the bed in the master bedroom, and at three points in the basement.

"There isn't even any point in chasing that pair ourselves," she said. "We need to phone home."

His shoulders tensed, then slumped as he realized he agreed. Centuries of success, ended. Only the third full-scale Red Alert in their entire tenure, and the first time they had *ever* needed to yell for help.

The day had begun so *well*. . . .

Their own vehicle, a generic grey Honda Accord, was parked immediately across from Chez Metkiewicz, and their clothes had finished regrowing themselves by now. Nonetheless they left the building by the discreet route, and circled a total of seven blocks to approach the car. They would have abandoned it, but it was registered to his current identity. Several local residents and pedestrians passed them as they reached it, and they were alert and ready with the tasp . . . but it proved unnecessary, as everyone's attention was focused on the smoke and flames emerging from the shattered door of the house across the street.

They left that block with care, scanning the sidewalks to make sure no disaster fans would need notice them to cross the street safely. Even after turning the corner he drove just enough above the speed limit to avoid being conspicuous, and maneuvered conservatively, until he found a spot on West 10th where an Accord could remain parked indefinitely without attracting interest. The distant sounds of the fire engines leaving the substation were audible as they got out of the car; for once that fine brigade would be too late. They rounded the corner and walked south at a speed appropriate to their personas, and for another twenty meters into the dark mews between West 10th and West 11th. They stopped abruptly there, and stood in perfect silence and stillness for five seconds, making quite sure they were unobserved.

Then they became invisible and rose into the air and flew southwest at barely subsonic speed.

Like circling seven blocks to get the car, stashing it *felt* like a waste of time and energy. But the roundabout method got them home nearly two full minutes sooner, without compromising security.

There they found no good news.

Chapter 7
Woolgathering On The Lam

Paul said, "I think it's time to stop underestimating these people."

June, involved with a "footlong" sub (nineteen centimeters, counting projecting silage), did not respond. They were in the safest place they could think of to dine at 10 P.M.: on a bench by the harbor at Jericho Beach. An overhanging tree shielded them fairly well from the intermittent rain. People approaching on foot could be observed for hundreds of meters in silhouette before they reached small-arms range; there were a hundred and eighty directions in which to flee at need; innumerable cloutable cars were parked nearby; there were even cloutable boats moored at hand, and three different places of concealment to which one might swim underwater if need arose. The twinkling panorama of Vancouver's downtown—the Emerald City indeed—was arrayed on their right, with Stanley Park jutting out into the water to the left of it like Nature's Last Stand. Distant lights twinkled and shimmered at the tops of the ski runs across the water in North Vancouver. A tiny Asian man waded with rolled trousers at the water's edge well to the west, ignoring the drizzle, stalking tomorrow's breakfast. Dark water lapped at the shore, too gently to obscure approaching footsteps.

"I think it's time to change tactics, too," he went on. "I've been on the defensive for over an hour, now, and that raises my lifetime cumulative exposure to damn near a whole waking day. I think it's time we scared the shit out of *them*."

"Paf 'ime," she said, then swallowed and repeated, "Past time."

"So we need a plan," he said, and took a bite of his own sub. He hoped that she would take up the conversational ball while he chewed, but she took another big bite of her own food. When he had cleared his mouth again, he tried, "So what are our assets?" and took another mouthful.

"I come up with bugger-all," she said.

"Zheevuf, Zhu'," he said, and then, "Jesus, June!"

"Am I missing something? As an asset, a hot car has the shelf life of a donut. We have to consider both of our addresses blown. All three cars gone or useless. Every ID we have is hot, including passports. Chump change. No weapons. No good way to get out of town without new ID. Three real friends in the world, each of whom would regard us as radioactive typhoid HIV-positive lepers with Ebola fever if they knew what's after us. And I wouldn't blame them."

"Hell, *I* don't know what's after us. Maybe we're all of those things. All I know is, I'm a dog who just got chased out of his own damn house, and if I don't do something about it I gotta lie down and die."

"I agree," she said. "I simply said we have no assets. Except fear, terror, and a fanatical devotion to the Pope. So how would you like to start?"

He looked down at his sandwich, and gave thought to pitching it into the sea . . . following it, perhaps, with the portion already consumed. Then he sighed, and took a deep breath, and bit off another hunk.

"Okay, no asshetsh," he said, chewing vigorously. "Exshep Key Wesh, maybe, if we cang 'et there . . ."

"I think we have to consider that blown, too," she said.

"Not for awhile, maybe," he said. "There's no paper on it back there at home."

"It's in the computer."

"Jesus, June, the fucking *NSA* couldn't hack into my private partition in less than a week: even *you* might have some—" His voice trailed off. "Oh."

She nodded. "We've already *seen* them do things the NSA couldn't do."

"I said I was going to stop underestimating them. Right." He resumed eating, frowning.

She corrected him. "What you said was, 'It's time to stop underestimating these people. . . .' Maybe that's doing it again."

"Huh?"

"I've stopped assuming they're people."

He spat out a mouthful of sandwich and stared. After a moment, he wiped his mouth and said, "What, then? Martians? Sauron of Mordor? Cthulhu? Christ, Scientist?"

She shook her head impatiently. "I don't *have* any labels for what's after us. And I'm not looking for any. If I think of them as humans, I'll be subconsciously expecting them to have human limitations. If I let myself think of them as Martians, I'm liable to hunt them with a water pistol. If they're Sauron, I'll start looking for the Ring—you see? I can't afford preconceptions: this is more than our lives on the line."

"There *is* nothing more than our lives."

"Yes, there is!"

"Not so loud—"

She lowered her volume to a passionate whisper. "I'd rather the bastards rape me and torture me to death and crap on my corpse than monkey with my mind. They're welcome to anything else they're smart enough and strong enough to take from me, including my life—but they *can't have my memories*. Those are all I've *got* out of all this."

He kept silent, from surprise at her passion and confusion at her words and a general instinct to lower their average sound production. He had known that what had happened to June was very bad; awful, sure. He had not realized until now it was skin-crawling. . . .

Well, which *was* more important to him? Staying alive? Or preserving the integrity of his mind? *You can live, Mr. Throtmanian, but you'll never be able to trust your own memories again as long as you live . . . never know for sure what has been or will be taken from you—or, if you prefer, we can put you out of your misery right now. . . .*

What finally brought him out of his thoughts was the classic Sub Eater's Dilemma. (You've finished the sandwich; your hands are greasy; the paper napkin you were using is a sodden, useless mess; you have another napkin, but can't get it without soiling your shirt by reaching into your pocket for it with greasy hands.) He solved it as he did most problems, impatiently, running his fingers through his hair until it lay flatter and his hands were clean. June regarded him with fond distaste. "Can't take you anywhere," she said softly.

"Do we even know it's a 'they'? Do we know for a fact that there's more than one . . . Jesus, we have to call it *something*—more than one monkey demon?" He knew she would get the reference, having lent her the book. In Richard Fariña's novel BEEN DOWN SO LONG, IT LOOKS LIKE UP TO ME, the monkey demon was the symbol of all ancient evil; it *had* no limitations.

"Good point. Let's think it through using one, and see if we stumble. Okay: I trip over the demon in the woods, and I —" She hesitated. "— I have an orgasm, and it takes over my mind. It interrogates me until it's happy, disposes of my damp underwear, and lets me go. It doesn't need to follow me any more, any more than it needed to follow Angel Gerhardt. But now it knows I phoned you. It knows everything I said. It wants me to erase the message, but I have no way to do that because your machine is so primitive. So it goes to your place, but you're not there, you're out cleaning the sci-fi people. So the monkey demon stakes you out."

He held up a hand. "Interesting point. Why? Why not just enter the house, find out everything it can about me, and wait *inside* for me to come home? Or just erase the phone machine and tiptoe away?"

"I don't know," she said, "and it's the first thing like a limitation we've spotted on it. Maybe it could smell your alarms, and decided to let *you* turn them off. Mark for later analysis; onward. Then you come home—but it doesn't know you have, right away, because it doesn't know about your back way in, because *I* didn't—you'd hinted you had a bolt-hole, but you never showed it to me. For all we can prove, there was a second demon *behind* the house, with no idea you were strolling by under his feet."

"There was a back door alarm too," Paul said, "and I never heard it go off."

"To notice you were home only after a while suggests the demon or demons were monitoring the house with something like thermal gear, from outside: it took time for you to set it off. They thought I was in there alone, waiting for you."

"Okay, I buy that. I still see only one set of tracks."

"You're right," she said. "There's no reason to assume there's more than one monkey demon. On the other hand, there's no reason to assume there aren't fifty. And my mother is dying." At the non sequitur, she flung the heel of her sandwich from her, so heedlessly that it fell short of the water, providing not even the satisfaction of a splash. "So what I say is, screw the bastard or bastards. You want vengeance; I can relate. Let's deal with it in our next lifetime. Let's abandon our luggage, figuratively and literally. Forget Key West. Forget any plans we ever had that got as far as being spoken aloud. Forget anybody we ever knew. Let's just hit the restart button on our lives, right now. Make it didn't happen. Go someplace we've never been and create new personas and go back to what we were doing: educating the gullible. Yellow alert: I think the distant silhouette approaching from the west is a cop." Her voice did not change in pitch or tone in the slightest, on the last sentence.

Paul scratched his neck and peeked. "Still a ways off."

"Alone. Fat. Moving slow. I think he's just strolling his beat."

"Back to business, then: can we do that, you think? Just walk away?"

"There's only one weakness I've noticed about the monkey demon. I don't understand it, but I'm sure of it: somehow, despite all his power, he's as afraid of The Man as we are. He could have taken either of us out at any time, with anything from an axe to a nuke—but he doesn't want to attract attention to himself for some reason. I won't be terribly surprised if he sends a fucking curse after us . . . but he can't put out an APB. I don't think that cop is looking for us. About forty meters away now."

Converting that laboriously in his head to a hundred and thirty one and a quarter feet, a hair under forty-three and a quarter yards, Paul decided the metric system could stand to be damned one more time. "And maybe if the monkey demon notices we've disappeared, and after awhile nothing he doesn't like has happened, he'll decide we're not a threat and let us live. It plays. So let's see if it's safe." He stood and walked like a numbskull directly toward the cop.

June sat still, and discreetly put a hand into her purse.

"Excuse me, Constable," Paul said, pitching his voice just a little too loud for the time and place, the way a real numbskull would do. "My name is Ralph Metkiewicz, and that's my fiancée June Cleaver, and we've been talking about our relationship for hours, you know how it is, and we were just starting to wonder, sitting here trying to remember, whether we turned the gas off before we left my house, or . . . what I'm getting at, I'm sorry to bother you, I know this must sound stupid, but have you heard anything about a house fire or some kind of commotion up on West Thirteenth tonight?"

June held her breath. *That's my warrior*, she thought. *A hair trigger—everywhere except in the rack, thank God! Hope it doesn't get us killed . . . or even pinched. This is a lousy time to be trapped in a known location and have our faces on the news.*

The cop sized him up. After an endless few seconds, the registers of his eyes displayed: *Numbskull.* "Friend, if it doesn't concern this particular stretch of shoreline, I tend to get most of my local news from the TV, just like you. I was in your shoes, though, I think I'd conclude it was something worth going home to check on."

"You know, you're probably right," Paul told him. "Joan—Miss Cleveland there—excuse me, honey, *Ms.* Clevelyn—was just saying something like that. Risk versus game, or something like that. Weren't you, honey?"

"The term 'honey' is a demeaning sexist put-down, you *know* that, Ralph," she said. "It is not flattering to be compared to something wild bears paw and slaver over. And I think the constable is quite right—aren't you, Constable?"

For her the cop took no time at all: *Numbskull.* "Well, ma'am, all's I'm saying is, it wouldn't hurt to go check. I hope everything turns out alright for you both. Goodnight, Ms. Clevemumble—good night, Mr., uh, Metka . . ."

"Meskavitz," Paul said. "Thank you, Constable. Have a nice night."

"Anybody ever tell you you look like that starship guy on TV?"

"What guy?"

"Never mind. Good night."

Paul and June left their bench and headed west, listening carefully to the tired footsteps behind them. When Paul calculated that the fat cop was once again a shade under forty-three and a quarter yards distant, he murmured, "See? Good news: we were right about something."

"I *said* I didn't *think* he had us on his hot list," June said, a wonderful sentence to hiss through one's teeth.

"And that was good enough for me . . . 'honey.' What would have been better: wait a few hours for the morning paper to come out? Now we know we're not law-type hot, and we can plan our getaway."

"Fine. Go ahead."

"Jesus, do I have to do *everything* around here? You start. We want to go far far away. Tell me where."

"Not there."

"Huh?"

"Far far away is where the monkey demon will expect us to go. We want to get clear, sure—but some place so close to the known Danger Zone that only a numbskull would run that far and then stop. The monkey demon thinks he knows we're not numbskulls: that's our secret weapon."

He snorted. "By that logic, the smartest thing for us to do is pick up some marshmallows and wieners and go back to my place to toast 'em. We can join the crowd and ask in a loud voice if anybody's seen a monkey who can suck your brain and make you forget you saw him."

"Maybe that would be the smartest thing we can do," she said dryly. "I have a feeling the least threatening place we could be right now, in his estimation, is in a nice snug VGH mental ward with heads full of thorazine. It's something we *know* that makes us dangerous to him, and mental patients don't have any information anyone else cares about." She stopped, confused; instead of being squelched, he looked almost cheerful.

"You think he considers us 'dangerous'?" he said.

She suppressed an urge to smack him. "Amend that to 'annoying,' all right, Tarzan? 'Worth hunting and mindraping.' You want to pick up those marshmallows and franks? We'll have to pull a short con on a Seven-Eleven guy. . . ."

He sobered. "As Oberlin Bill used to say, it never pays to be *too* smart. Maybe a shade less audacity wouldn't hurt anything. Okay, nearby, but not too near—someplace we can get to without leaving a record or passing a security camera, with no ID and chump change. Well, I know one last good border crossing I think I can afford to use up—but I'm afraid we're going to arrive in the Land of the Fee smelling just like everything else that comes out of that pipe. Let's try and clout something with two changes of clothes in it—"

"The border's too far and too intelligent," she said. "Everybody tries to disappear to a crowded place where you can blend in easy. Let's go to someplace we'll stand out—to the *locals*, who we don't care about—and where we can hang out a lot of tripwires, where we'll hear early about any *other* odd strangers in town. We're both city kids, so we'll hide in the boonies."

"The Gulf Islands," he said. "A ferry."

"That'd work," she said. "But I've got something better in mind. Cast your mind back about a million years, to when we were free human beings, loose on the earth. What was I working on, when I had to go visit my mother?"

Paul stopped short, and stared in admiration. "Jesus. Of course. Whatsisname! Bonehead Island!"

June's recent trip south to visit her mother had

forced a working con onto the back burner: the mark had been ripe but June was too busy to pluck him, so she had been forced to reschedule. He was a yuppy software baron named O'Leary, presently away with his beloved on a long-planned trip around the world which would take him three months even in the absurd event that everything went as planned. Postponed opportunity had proven to be a blessing in disguise: O'Leary's luxury A-frame home stood unoccupied until his return.

"*Bowen* Island," June said. "Henry O'Leary."

"Where is that one?"

"It's one of the Horseshoe Bay jobs."

"Better and better," he said. "A little one. This likes me well. Have you noticed that things always start to look better after you eat a sub?"

"First we have to get there," she said. She was cheering up too, but was not yet ready to admit it. "Let's go find a doss. Tomorrow we scrounge a little, and then catch a ferry."

"Scrounge what?"

She thought. "We need a backpack, maybe an overnight bag, some binoculars, sunglasses . . . an ice chest wouldn't hurt. And cash, of course, at least enough for two pedestrian ferry tickets. And as much L.L. Bean as we can lay our hands on." She looked him over critically, and suddenly started to laugh. "And you'll need to shave." The laugh built as he stared in incomprehension. He had forgotten. "Nothing looks less respectable than five o'clock shadow all over your fucking head," she managed, and then lost it.

So did he, of course, and the shared laugh grew until they had to stop walking and hold each other up, and in no time at all they were kissing, still laughing but really kissing.

"Are we having fun yet?" he asked when they broke for air.

"Who stopped?" she said. But there was something indefinable in the placement of her eyebrows, or possibly her lower lip, that cued him it was time to stop kissing and get back to business.

Besides, the rain was starting to really come down, now.

The Lower Mainland of the province of British Columbia is more than generously supplied with islands; if you're missing one, it's probably there, somewhere. There ought to be a Lower Mainland salad dressing.

In 1995 one could drive thirty minutes south from Vancouver, almost to the U.S. border, and take a large ferry from the immense ways at Tsawwassen (providing one resisted the urge to attempt to pronounce it) southwest to any of the medium-size, generally well-populated Gulf Islands; these gathered like hungry pilotfish around the anus of the leviathan Vancouver Island, whose immense torso enclosed the Strait of Georgia between it and the mainland. Alternatively, one could drive twenty minutes north and then west to the feverishly picturesque Horseshoe Bay, and take a small or medium-size ferry from more modest docks than Tsawwassen's to an assortment of smaller and less populous (thus more interesting) islands in Howe Sound. These varied widely in state of development—from rustic Gambier Island, accessible only to foot traffic, to Bowen Island, relatively built up and well built. People were starting to call it Commuter Cay: it perfectly met the needs of the yuppie commuter, being as far from Vancouver (in every sense of the term) as one could get and still be within reasonable travel time. There was more than one Porsche on Bowen Island, and you could rent Buñuel movies or buy fresh Jamaica Blue Mountain coffee beans at the general store—but you could also get Cheese Whiz, frozen waffles and King Red Man chewing tobacco.

The Horseshoe Bay terminal was ideal for a fugitive, big enough for one to hide in the crowd but not big enough or important enough to be watched. Paul and June, carefully dressed and outfitted to suggest fairly rich people who had dressed down for the trip so as not to appear pretentious, would have been effectively invisible even without the drizzle.

Paul could not *believe* the security.

"There *isn't* any!" he exclaimed almost angrily. "Look at this place! No ID check, no cameras— I swear to God I don't smell a single cop, uniform or plain. There must be some, but they're all cooping." They were strolling along the edge of an immense parking lot which had filled in the last half hour and would empty in fifteen minutes, on the opposite side from the long row of washrooms, "restaurant" and other dollar-traps that were currently milking most of the cars' passengers while they waited for the ferry.

"They're probably helping a trucker with his engine," she said. "Usually they try to stay visible. In case someone needs to ask them a question."

Paul stared at her. "I will never in my life get used to this country. It isn't fucking natural."

"Thank God!"

"Christ, we could clout a car right here in broad daylight, if we had any use for one. I've seen three with keys in them."

"Where the hell are they going to go? Every one is boxed in."

They reached the front of the lineup, found a spot from which they could admire Horseshoe Bay. It was easy work. The stage-prop binoculars proved useful. The ferry was in sight in the distance, looking rather like Roseanne Barr—a white tub and proud of it, with great bumpers—and a cinch to beat the napping Hare in the swimming race, approaching Horseshoe Bay with the speed of the bell at the end of Geometry class.

"June?"

"Mm?"

"About your mother . . ."

She kept staring out across the gunmetal water. "She's still here. I can feel it. Still hanging on."

He nodded uselessly. He began to speak three times, producing nothing at first, and then, "We could," and "If."

She nodded, and put the binoculars on a bird. "Pop has enough on his plate just now," she said, tracking it. "He can't believe they moved to a country without socialized medicine."

"Yeah. I just . . ."

"I know." She put down the glasses. "And what I'm supposed to do is come into your arms and let you comfort me. You deserve that. You really do. I'm sorry."

He said nothing.

"I don't know if this is going to make sense," June said. "I want to try and say it just right." There was a long pause, and then the words came out quickly. "You and me. When we're together I want you inside of me, and me inside of you. You know that. When we're together and it's good I want to be naked for you, naked to you. I want you to come inside of my skull and *know* me, know me better than anybody else, know me better than I've ever been able to make myself known to anybody else, know all my secrets and all my sorrows." She stopped speaking, bent her head. The ferry was 25 percent nearer when she continued. "Well, it happened to me, the real deal, and it sucks. I feel like I've been raped by a column of ants. Like a burglar left turds on the carpet of my brain on the way out. I don't know, it—" She broke off again. When she resumed, her voice was thicker, her words clumsier. "So what I mean, us, it's for a while it'll be a little hard, okay? I'm trying to say hard the way it was, like before, feeling that way again for a little while, with *anybody*, I just—I've only *got* the two speeds, flat out and neutral, and I'm scared to touch the pedal. . . . I hope you can deal with that."

He had trouble enough dealing with the simple urge to reach out to her with his hands, then and there: the lunatic certainty that if he only touched her he could draw out some of her pain even if she said otherwise. And he did have the fleeting, guilty thought that running for your life is much more fun if you can get laid during the lulls. But he was a strong man, and loved her enough to give her anything she asked that would not kill him outright or spoil his opinion of himself. He took several deep breaths without being caught at it, and when he had himself under control, he said, as if agreeing on a restaurant, "Space. Sure."

The ferry was near, now. She checked his backpack, then picked up her overnight bag. "Thanks."

"Yowsah."

Then neither of them said anything until he

said, "Say when," and she said, "You'll know." By then the ferry was beginning its approach, snorting foam, and he picked up the cooler and they joined the rest of the foot passengers lining up at the gate.

They were much more plausible as rich people, walking a couple of feet apart.

Snug Cove, the ferry terminus at Bowen Island, was a lovely, sleepy little place, quaint but not yet aware of it, its "downtown" small enough that there was nowhere you could stand in it and not see forest, but just large enough to offer a choice of "restaurants." They dined in silence (as was expected of people dressed like that) at the least worst. The deck view of a rustic duck pond guarded by a magnificent old grandfather tree was splendid, but Paul was still moved to swipe tips on the way out. As they stepped back out onto a sidewalk which, between ferries, was empty as a politician's word, he spoke to his lady for the first time since they had left the mainland. "So how far is this place?"

"About a fifteen-minute drive, I think. I've never actually been there."

He groaned. "Naturally. We can't go around clouting cars, either; we have to *live* here. Is there any point in my even asking whether they have cabs on this overgrown speed bump?"

"Nope." She headed off uphill through the drizzle, toward the beckoning wilderness. He followed with as much good cheer as he could muster. Within what he thought of as a city block, the terrain leveled off—but the buildings and sidewalks went away. He was too much of a city kid to be comfortable walking anywhere that didn't have sidewalks, but his guru had once drummed into him that he must never complain (because she was sick and tired of listening to it), and so he soldiered on, scheming ways to humiliate an irresistible force. *Any place that has fifteen-minute drives should have cabs,* he thought from time to time, as the blisters began to form.

Suddenly June stopped, for no reason he could see. Distantly he heard the sound of a motorist, and envied him or her fiercely. "What's up?"

As though it were an answer, she moved a few steps to the edge of the roadbed, held out her hand, and stuck up her thumb.

He blinked, puzzled. "What are you doing?"

She sighed. "Just wait. And pray."

The vehicle, a truck that had emphysema too bad to be singing that loud, was almost upon them now. All at once it dropped its pitch, like Tom Waits nodding off in the middle of a song, and slowed to a complete stop beside them.

The driver, a senior citizen, stared at them. At a loss, Paul stared back. Both the old man's hands were visible on the steering wheel.

"Where you folks headed?" he asked.

Paul was too flustered to remember his cover; June supplied the name of the man whose house they were supposed to be sitting, and described its location. At once, as if some sort of agreement had been negotiated, the old man leaned to his right and opened the passenger door of his pickup, clearly offering them a ride. Up front, with him.

When June began walking around the front of the truck, Paul decided people must just do things like this in the country, in Canada anyway, and followed her.

Sure enough, without so much as displaying a

weapon, the old man put the truck very neatly in gear and took them where they wanted to go. He did talk nearly as much as a New York cabbie, in a voice clearly audible above the roar of the truck's renewed Waits imitation, but was willing to listen to June bullshit back—he even gave her something like fifty percent of the airtime. In the course of his own rambling he disclosed at least three pieces of information of use to anyone who wanted to come clean him out some night. He even waited to offer his name until June gave their current names.

"And it's all right to laugh when I tell you," he prefaced it.

"I wouldn't laugh," June assured him.

"Aw, go ahead, I wouldn't want to see you folks hurt yourself. My daddy's name was spelled L-Y-C-O-T-T, and he always pronounced it 'like it'— 'like it is,' he'd say, 'and you can Lycott or lump it!' And then my ma decided she just had to name me after her dead little brother Maurice. . . ." He waited until their faces showed they'd got it, thumped the dashboard and cackled. "That's right: I'm Moe Lycott!"

After a polite pause, they used the dispensation they'd been given and began to giggle. "You don't seem mad about it," June said.

"Hell, no," he said. "All my life, whenever I walk by, people point and say, 'Now, *that's*—'"

June obligingly supplied the punchline, and giggled some more.

Paul did not really think the bald husband of a chirpy yuppie woman who kept silent himself would be out of character, but eventually he felt he should produce at least a token attempt at polite discourse, to make clear that he was not the world's only wealthy skinhead. He cast through his mind for movies he'd seen involving country life, and at the next gap in the conversation, he said, "So Moe, do you have any cows?"

The truck was allowed to take a solo for the next forty-three and a quarter yards or so.

"I been a widower twenty year," Moe finally said, and immediately asked June something about her imaginary job back in the city.

Although June's directions had been general, Moe spotted the right mailbox with his cataracted eyes and let them off exactly where they wanted to be. He drove off before Paul could even begin to embarrass himself by offering to pay for the ride, leaving them the single word, "Goodnight," as though he no longer had a right to talk their ear off now that they were no longer locked into being with him. June turned at once and started down the weeded driveway, but Paul stood where he was for a moment, frowning.

"What?" she said, turning back.

"Nothing," he said. "I just feel like a tiger trying to hide in a slaughterhouse. This island is *candy*. Hell, Hopeless *Harry* could get healthy, here." He blinked. "I can't believe I just said that sentence." Hopeless Harry was the worst grifter either of them knew, a man with a face so quintessentially dishonest that he had once been stopped and frisked while dressed as a priest in a wheelchair; you had to admire his doggedness, but then you were done admiring him.

"Down, boy."

"I know, I know," he said. "I feel like the Invisible Man in the girls' dormitory, though."

As he had prayed, that got a faint grin. "Up, boy. Come on, let's check out our lovely new home."

The keys, as expected, were where people hide keys.

Much money had been both thoughtfully and tastefully spent on that home. The location itself was a postcard. The A-frame was a sketch drawn on the back of the postcard by a master. It had *two* decks out back, both cantilevered out over a dizzying slope that dropped what Paul thought of as about fifteen stories in about one block to Howe Sound; lush forest on either side framed the view perfectly, making it endurable. Next stop, Japan. Hi, birds.

"I can't believe this clown *didn't* actually get someone to watch a house this nice for him while he was away."

"Why? To make sure nobody moves in and trashes the place, or something? What do you think this is, civilization?"

There was a hot tub built into the lower deck, big enough for seven people or four programmers. The barbie on the upper deck enabled a reasonably bright child to cook half a beeve at a time to perfection, and the deck itself had a built-in cable-and-power hookup in its railing so you could take the portable TV/CD/tapedeck/tuner/VCR out there without stringing unsightly wires from the bedroom. There was an Aptiva in the den, with Pentium 133 chip and 32 megs of RAM, a ten-gig hard drive, a 25-inch monitor and an 800-dpi printer. There was a similarly equipped Power Mac in a corner of the living room; apparently O'Leary had taken all of his Powerbooks with him on his world tour. The brand-new state-of-the-art high-end entertainment console beside the Mac produced sound you could taste and video you could

smell in any room of the house including both
bathrooms, and could be remotely programmed
from most of them. The fridge and freezer could
have supported a midsize restaurant; the micro-
wave could have accomodated the other half of
the barbecued cow, with the gas stove for the
potatoes and vegetables; there was no room in the
house without at least one ceiling-high shelf of
books (most either old friends or intriguing); the
construction and carpentry were ostentatiously
breathtaking throughout; the interior decor said
you deserve this quietly but very persuasively, and
it came as something of a relief to Paul when he
managed to find (in the garage) a single, inexplicably uncomfortable chair.

"I don't want to con this guy," he said to June,
when he found her sorting through excellent drugs
in the drawers of the guest bedroom. "I want to
be this guy." He smelled a bag of marijuana, and
sighed. "I love this part of the world."

"You haven't seen what he's sleeping with," she
said.

"True. What *is* Mrs. O'Leary like? You never
told me."

"What's that got to do with what he's sleeping
with?"

"Ah," he said. "You were working a Diabolique."

"A modified Diabolique," she agreed. "What he's
sleeping with has a Y chromosome. Likes girls just
as much as Henry does, thank goodness, or I'd
have had to be big sister fag hag."

Paul nodded. "I wondered how old Henry was
dealing with the problem of bringing his mistress
along on a world cruise."

"By the time they all get back from being
locked in a hotel together for three months, all

the way 'round the planet, the boyfriend will be happier than ever to have me help him set up a burglary-gone-wrong on the happy couple, and run away with me. I just hope he stays greedy and half-smart, doesn't decide to ad-lib and lever them both over the rail somewhere along the way. I won't blame him if he does, but I want this place for the whole three months if I can get it."

The turn of this conversation was giving Paul a powerful warm furry urge to tear off all that L.L. Bean, peel his lady like a grape and throw her on the guest bed, so he put down the bag of marijuana and said, "I've got the water and heat back on, and the hot tub is warming. Is it time to go next door—wherever the hell *that* is—and start establishing our cover, so nobody has the cops swing by?"

She shook her head, and dropped a large chunk of hashish on top of the cocaine in the drawer. Coke was just money one shouldn't flash, to both of them. "That's covered."

"What, you mean Mo' Like It? We don't even know how far away he lives; he could be a hermit at the other end of the island."

"Doesn't matter. On an island this size, the jungle telegraph is like the Internet: all users are equidistant. Twenty bucks says at this moment, one of the neighbors is asking what the world is coming to, when even decent people are shaving their heads."

"Twenty Canadian? Or American?"

June shut the drawer. "Whatever. And I have a much better idea than borrowing a cup of credibility."

"Go."

"Why don't you tear this goddam L.L. Bean off

me, peel me like a grape, and carry me upstairs to the master bedroom?"

Don't ever let anybody tell you enough money can't heal, sometimes, Paul thought. "That bed there's a lot closer," he pointed out.

"Yeah, but I want to be carried further than that."

He shrugged. "Works for me."

Even for a strong man in love and his prime, yuppie clothing is oddly hard to tear; Paul had to settle for merely rumpling everything but the panties. June didn't seem to mind.

He was very careful, very alert, until she signaled clearly that he did not need to be; then he burst open and died and was annihilated and, timeless time later, painstakingly reassembled from a kind description. Perhaps it should have been disappointing to both of them that she didn't come, too. But she did not always, when they made love, and often didn't care, and could be relied on to cue him if she did. He offered anyway, licking her throat in a way that was one of their signals, but she declined with a warm hug and an uncounterfeitable kiss, and reached for the remote.

"*That's* why you wanted to come up here," he said sleepily. "Better TV."

"You know me so well," she said, and gave him a friendly tweak.

He fell asleep watching a genuinely astonishing commercial, in which an immensely fat hairy jolly man (immensely all those things) wearing only a jockstrap and a skipper's cap did—for a Pacific Rim audience—a *sumo* shtick that must have been to a Japanese what Step'n'Fetchit is to a brother.

It turned out he sold junk. *What a country!* was Paul's last coherent thought.

Then he slept, and dreamed that he was Gnossos Pappadapolous, and the monkey demon was chasing him and his buddy Heffalump through New Mexico desert. When it turned into Batista's Cuba and guns started going off, Paul tried what Gnossos had done in the book—run in circles; scream and shout—and it worked: he became Exempt. But not Heffalump, the only human being Gnossos ever genuinely loved: Heffalump was down, and Gnossos was hip too late. He tried to change the dream channel, and found himself in Heinlein's JOB: A COMEDY OF JUSTICE, he and Margrethe on an ocean liner, suffering from *mal de merde*. This was insufficient improvement: Margrethe was stacked but so was the deck, which promptly sank out from under them. So he went deep, and found darkness and quiet for awhile.

June switched to headphones when she saw he was asleep, found the satellite channels and watched a Japanese porn movie dubbed into Chinese for an hour, marveling at the endless variety of ways different cultures have evolved to make idiots out of themselves while doing something necessary, all in the name of a little quiet in the pants. *Hasn't there* ever *been a sexually sane culture?* she wondered for the thousandth time in her life. *Will there ever be one?*

Just before she drifted off, she thought, *I almost came. Next time I will. I won't let the bastard take that away from me, too.*

Her sleep was dreamless when it came, and she woke hungry.

Chapter 8
The Fans Hit the Shit *Back*

Pacing in his bedroom, the evening after the con, Wally said, "Let's total up everything we know for sure about the son of a bitch."

He's uncircumsized was Moira's first thought, but she probably would not have said that even if her husband had not been armed. "He's very smart; he probably has five o'clock shadow all over his body right now; he has our lives, AKA ninety-eight thousand dollars, in a big brown bag; and with his head shaved he looks a little like Captain Picard. And he was raised in America. That's all I'm sure of." She rearranged the pillows behind her.

Wally stopped pacing. "You think he's American?"

"I didn't say that. Maybe he's a Canadian citizen, maybe he's a Landed Immigrant, maybe he's just a visitor come north to shear the fat stupid sheep of Niceland for a few weeks. But he was raised in the Untied Snakes." The pillows were giving her trouble.

"What makes you say that?"

She burrowed her shoulder blades into the pillow mass, and finally achieved comfort. "He used the word 'table' to mean 'temporarily remove from consideration,' rather than the correct, rational, AngloCanadian meaning, 'put forward for immediate consideration.' He was raised in America, all right."

Wally smiled. "By God, I think you're right. He *did* say that, I remember. It didn't take at the time. Very good, love." He frowned. "Wait, now. What about that G.S.T. line?"

"Misdirection," she suggested. "He's subtle."

"Which one?" he argued. "'Table' or 'G.S.T.'?" She echoed his frown.

"Let's mark that one 'tentative,' for now," he said. "I'm considerably more confident that he's a fan, possibly even a Truphan. Inactive, maybe—about as gafiated as you can get, now, thanks to us—but at some time in his life he smelled corflu, I'd bet my collection on it."

"Not necessarily," she insisted. "Ten or fifteen years ago, I'd have said anybody who could sting us like that would *have* to be a fan. Who else would try? But fandom's had a lot of media exposure, the last decade or so. A lot of mundanes have noticed us going through hotel lobbies in costume and asked the desk clerk what was going on. Anybody on the Internet could have stumbled over all that PR we tried so hard to make eye-catching, and found out about VanCon. From the membership data he could infer the size of the nut in the bank, and even the bank . . . and the names of the only two chumps with signing authority."

"Sure, maybe," he said. "But constructing the scam itself . . ."

"—doesn't even require that the bastard ever read a book in his life," she said. "The movies are full of time travel these days."

"He used the word 'ficton,' I'm sure of that," Wally said.

"True," she said. "Okay, so he's read Heinlein. That just makes him literate and lucky. It doesn't mean he reads sf for pleasure, let alone make him a fan. Much less a Truphan. No fan could be capable of this. Not even Splatt."

Wally resumed pacing. "Dammit, you may be right. But even so, I think we have to put out the Word."

"To *fandom*? Come clean? *Why*? Didn't we just get through begging Steve and Sybil in Toronto to keep the story to themselves? And apologizing to a dozen friends for terrifying them with hallucinatory warnings about an earthquake? They already all think we've started taking drugs." Suddenly Moira's stomach hurt.

"Moira, our fannish reputations are dead, forever, the moment the first major VanCon bill comes due. *We have no other explanation for where the money went*. We can't even say *we* stole it, unless we can explain why we haven't got it any more. There's only one way we can prevent our names becoming *the* fannish byword for Stupidity for the next century, now. The only hope we have in the world of ever being allowed in a Con Suite again, the rest of our lives, is to catch that hairless ape, ourselves, personally, and get back every cent we handed him—in time for the con to go on. That gives us two weeks, absolute max. And I think fandom is our only lead."

"Beatles," she said. "Internet Beatles forums—chat groups—"

He shook his head. "You don't have to leave traces *anywhere* to know all about the Beatles. The information's in the water supply. I mean, there are probably starving hermits in Pakistan who know what the original title of 'Get Back' was, for—"

Moira's choices were, get up and get the Pepto Bismol, or come up with an idea. "I got it!"

Wally misunderstood. "Okay, I was just trying to—"

"No, no, I mean I got an idea. Another lead, besides fandom!"

Wally stopped in his tracks. If he had been the protagonist of Jack London's "To Build A Fire," suddenly confronted with a Zippo, he could not have become more alert, more hopeful, more frightened. " . . . tell me," he whispered.

Moira began to—and from nowhere came the thought that it would be kinder to let him guess it himself, and that her husband could use some kindness now. " 'Fool, fool—back to the beginning is the rule,' " she quoted softly from their favorite bedtime story.

For a moment she could *hear* his neurons firing . . . and then his eyes began to glow, as if in illustration of the memory behind them. "Yes!" he cried. "*Magnesium . . .*"

"How many places could there be in the greater Vancouver area where a man could buy that much?"

The question hung in the air for a moment. And then they chorused together: "I don't know, but I know somebody who'll know somebody who will!" and raced for their computers.

Wally, having been both standing and nearest the door at the starting gun, won the race handily; Moira arrived (looking not unlike the Bowen Island ferry) just in his wake, to find that he had already booted both their machines. She slapped her modem to life and waited for her Finder to load.

"I'm tryin'a think, but nothin' *happens*," it reported truthfully, in the voice of Curly (the real one), and began rebuilding her virtual desktop.

As always, it took too much time. By the time the desktop appeared on-screen, she had begun to leak helium. "This may not work out as well as we hope," she said slowly.

Wally's system had loaded faster; it just took much longer to *do* anything. "Why do you say that?" He moused like Monk taking a solo, off-rhythm but strong.

"Think about Jude. Or whatever his name is. That's my point: can you see a con-man that good buying a kilo of magnesium *in this town*? Under his own name? And leaving a valid address?"

Monk let the bass player have it. "Oh shit." Wally pushed his chair back from the desk, and rubbed his eyes. "Any two, possibly, but not all three." He looked like he was going to cry.

"We should still try, though," she said hastily, and opened her Net browser. She wished she had gotten the Pepto Bismol on the way there.

"Yeah, we will," Wally agreed, his voice tired and defeated. "And we'll check the Beatles forums, and we'll search the Net for 'con-man' and 'grifter' and strings like that, and maybe we can even get Vicki's brother Jack to hack us into the cops' network and look for Jude's footprint, and none of it is—"

"Genius," she said. "I married an intuitive genius."

Wally blinked. "Certainly. What I say?"

"What does Vicki's brother *do* for the cops?"

Wally was hesitant to let hope return, but this was good. For the second time, he chorused along with her: "He draws pictures of people you didn't think you remembered!"

Jack was a police sketch artist—one of the first to realize that the WYSIWYG revolution had transformed *his* profession as much as any other, for no other image-medium can be as quickly and easily changed, fine-tuned, as a computer paint document. He was by training as good a psychologist as he was an artist: he had once, as a parlor trick, drawn Wally and Moira a sketch on his Powerbook of a waiter who had served them the night before, using only the memories he drew out of them with his questions and his trackball. An hour later, a friend who'd had the same waiter a week earlier had ID'd him from the sketch.

"That's really good, love," Wally went on, excited again. "He can even add hair and stuff, or show ways the guy could disguise himself, beard and glasses and like that. We could show them to the clerks at all the chemical supply houses, and—" He broke off.

"And?" She didn't want to ask, but it was the only question she had.

He took his time answering. "And let's face it: unless and until some clerk says, 'Sure, I know that guy; I got his address and his Visa number, and come to think of it, his fingerprints are on the slip,' we still have *shit*."

For the first time in decades, Moira searched for words.

Wally switched his computer off cold, swiveled his chair to face her, and when he spoke his voice was awful to hear. "Let's admit it. We're screwed. The Yankee son of a bitch is just too smart for us."

CHIRRRRRRUP, said the phone.

Oh Finagle, NOW? Moira thought. *Five seconds earlier and whoever it is would have gotten a busy signal on that line. When the luck goes bad, boy—* But almost instantaneously she flip-flopped. Nuisances have their place. When your husband has just made the most terrible, humiliating admission he has ever made or could make, perhaps a good distraction is not unwelcome. Even a poor one. "I'll get it," she said, and started to rise.

"I've got it," he said bitterly, and picked up the phone. "Yeah, who is it?"

The caller ignored the perfectly reasonable question, but identified himself nonetheless. "Enough I had," came a voice with what Moira had always called a pronounced Martian accent. "No more, you are hearing? Any more shenaginans like the last night, police I call, yes? My wife is upset, I am upset, you should be disgrace. You are hearing me, flying saucer boy?"

"Gorsky!" Wally groaned.

Well, I asked for a nuisance, Moira thought. *I hit the Lotto.*

"Dem right Gorsky. Too much, too long I put up. This is decent neighborhood, Kemp, till you come with science fiction condom people. No more! I tell you: you tell wife who has different last name: police come next time. You tell naked Metkiewicz too: police come *his* house too—and one more thing: my dog puke one more time, I come punch you face. You got no right poison lawn where dogs live around, you—"

Moira had turned to stone. It was Wally who found his voice first: an eerily calm, peaceful voice. "Naked who?"

"Naked Metkiewicz—how many naked men play big joke with you last night? You tell him I know where he lives: they got special prison for naked men, what is call? fleshers. He will—"

"You know where Medgawhatsis lives."

"*Metkiewicz*, Jesus, M-E-T—" Gorsky spelled it, contempt plain in his voice for anyone who needed to be told how to spell Metkiewicz. "You bet I know where he lives. Ha ha. He is not so smart he thinks, yes?"

"How do you know where he lives?" Moira heard herself say, and cursed herself because it was the wrong question.

He answered it anyway. "Ha ha. Big surprise, yes? He buys chemical for big boom from my warehouse in Surrey. His Visa I have . . . address I have, God damn, from sign for chemical . . . his fingerprint on paper. Police find easy. No more naked Peeping Dick nonsense, you tell him, are you hearing?"

Wally asked the right question. "What address did Mr. Metkiewicz give you, Mr. Gorsky?"

"What?"

His voice had been too dreamy; Moira repeated the question.

"How do I know what address? Is in warehouse. Why you don't know where your friend lives?"

For a fraction of a second Moira debated telling Gorsky that "Metkiewicz" was a thief, who had stolen their money. The scent of a burglar in the neighborhood would elevate even her and Wally to the status of provisional human beings in Gorsky's eyes. But he would insist on handing over his evidence to the police at once. "He's not a friend, Mr. Gorsky. He's an acquaintance. Someone we know from science fiction. He's having trouble with his mind, you understand?"

"I understand good, you bet it. Big trouble, sure."

"He was acting so crazy last night, after he left

we thought maybe we should make sure he got home all right, but we don't know where he lives."

"He go home naked, I know where he lives now. In hose goo."

He couldn't say "hoosegow" when I had time to laugh, Moira thought. "No, he wasn't that crazy. But I really think we ought to check on him. Is there someone at your warehouse at night?"

"Is watchman. But he can not get paper. Is lock."

Moira briefly explored her decision tree. Branch A: try to persuade Gorsky to give them the key to his Restricted Substances records and phone the watchman to expect them; rotsa ruck. Branch B: try to draw the address out of Gorsky's murky memory; forget it. Branch C: give up and hand the whole thing over to the police, like a civilian; make herself and Wally—and by extension, God help them, VanCon and the entire Lower Mainland Science Fiction Association—international laughingstocks within and without fandom.

Without fandom . . .

"But crazy naked man is bad thing. Hokay. You come over, I give you key, phone watchman to wake up."

Absurdly, Moira found herself thinking of the silly joke Wally had once made after they'd seen a video of Stallone as a mountain-climber, endlessly going up and down ropes to display his biceps. Wally had held up the video box, moved it up and down a few times, pointed to Sly's picture, and said, "Yo. Yo. Yo. Yo—" *Up, down; up, down—* "That's very kind of you, Mr. Gorsky. Thank you very much. We'll be right over."

"No crazy nakeds in this neighborhood I want."

Wally ended the conversation the way he

religiously ended conversations with that man. "Good luck, Mr. Gorsky." He disconnected.

They swiveled to face each other, and simultaneously reached to take each other's hands, and as their fingers touched they allowed themselves to smile.

"Hose goo," she said. "Oh, that is precious."

"The man next door has just walked on the Moon," Wally said, smiling bigger.

"Every once in a while, maybe a good deed goes unpunished," Moira said.

"We are going to explain to Jude that it's a fool who plays it cool, by making his world a little colder."

"Let's go get under his skin," she agreed. They put their silicon servants to sleep, and left the office. Like any Vancouverite about to leave home unexpectedly at night, Moira zapped the TV on to access the cable weather channel to find out whether rain-gear was required. It came on with a shriek of sound, tuned to the local news channel; the last time the set had been used, they'd been listening for earthquake warnings while running around the house packing. The screen filled with a long shot of a smoking ruin, and an earsplitting voice bellowed, "*OINT GREY COMPUTER PRO-GRAMMER RALPH METKAVITCH'S HOME WAS DESTROYED BY FIRE FOLLOWING AN UNEX-PLAINED EXPLOSION LAST NIGHT, AND THE PRELIMINARY INVESTIGATION REPORT SAYS THAT ARSON QUOTE CANNOT BE RULED OUT UNQUOTE. SO FAR POLICE HAVE BEEN UNABLE TO CONTACT MESKOWITZ, WHOM NEIGHBORS SAID HAD RECENTLY SHAVED HIS HEAD—*"

Moira tried for either the volume down or mute

buttons, and missed both; the set went off. She thought about turning it back on, and could not think of a point. She turned to her husband, and at the sight of his face she blanched. "Oh, Wally."

"It's not the despair," he said, his voice placid, conversational. "I can deal with the despair."

She nodded. "It's the hope."

"Yeah. It's killing me."

Sigh. "Me too, Wally."

CHIRRRRRRUP, said the phone.

"Do we answer it?" she asked.

Wally sighed. "Why not? We haven't got anything better to do. Maybe it's a Psychic Friend, calling to tell us where to find Jude. Maybe it's Dr. Kevorkian letting us know he's going to be in the neighborhood, *that*'d be useful—"

"I'll go."

"No, I'll get it."

She compromised, waiting until he caught up and then putting on the speakerphone. "Is this someone with good news or money?"

"*Both*," said the phone.

"Steve?"

"*I got a lead on your guy.*"

Silence.

"*Hello?*"

It was Moira who reinvented breathing first. "Say again, Steve."

"*I got your guy. Got an address and an accomplice, anyway—from the Net.*"

Moira would not have believed, if informed beforehand, that a heart could so simultaneously rise and fall. This might just possibly be good news—but it was probably worthless, and its cost could be dear. Had Steve started a fannish clock ticking on their amateur manhunt? Had he told anyone *why* he needed the data? "Steve, just *how* did you get this—"

Wally overrode her, slapping the *record* button on the phone machine. "What's the address you have?"

The vibrations of his voice had to be translated by the phone into a pattern of electrical signals; these had to cross half a continent, starting at the speed of light but arriving much slower due to switching delays; converting them back into sound waves took more time, then Steve needed at least three times as long to hear, grasp, and respond to them—whereupon the whole weary process began in reverse. All this time, Moira waited, absolutely certain that if she were just patient enough Steve would give them the late address of the former Ralph Metkiewicz, and they could hang up and get back to contemplating suicide. She and hope were quits for the night; maybe for good.

"*Pencils ready? One, zero, six, fi-yuv, niner, Point Grey that's ee why Road, Vancouver; postal code Varley eight Unicorn, four Rotsler six. Owner of record is a Carla with a sea Bernardo. He got mail there through an account registered to 'Penforth Naim,' that's en-nuh, eh, eye, em-muh, but obviously that's not gonna do you much good. Still, it's a start. You want me to repeat any of that?*"

Moira's operating system was hung, her cursor and her curser both frozen; Wally had to take it. "No, that's okay, Steve-o, it's on tape. I'm genuinely impressed. Tell me, though, how *exactly* did you dig all that up?"

"*Relax: I know what you're thinking. It's cool— really. I understand this is . . . uh . . . a sensitive matter. What I did, I logged onto the Net and tapped the fannish grapevine—*"

Moira moaned.

"No, really, wait a minute and listen. I didn't say anything about . . . about what happened to you guys, okay? Not a word."

When it was clear that Steve would wait until someone reassured him or hell froze over, whichever came first, Wally said. "You have our complete confidence, Steve. What did you say then?"

"I said I was putting together a Next Generation parody for VanCon, called 'Data Takes A Dump,' and I wanted to know if anybody had seen anyone around a con lately that looked like Picard and either was bald or wouldn't mind shaving his head."

The metaphorical lightbulb that appeared in the air over Moira's and Wally's heads baked their shadows onto the wall.

"Bless my soul!" Wally exclaimed. Moira backed up involuntarily until she hit the fridge, and gave thought to sliding down it to a sitting position. But she couldn't face getting back up again. "Steven," she said weakly, "would you and Sybil like a couple of sex-slaves for a year or so?"

"You'll have to take a number—damn city building-code won't let me expand the dungeon without a permit. Now, naturally I got about two dozen hits—hell, I got people who were willing to have plastic surgery to play Picard at a Worldcon, and have you noticed? there's no shortage of bald guys in fandom. But I'm pretty sure if any of 'em is your guy, it's the one I gave you. Yin the Stomach-Settling talked to him at the Registration Table at Vikingcon, down in Bellingham. You know her thing for Captain Picard: she remembers the dude good, even though he had hair then. She says he came on like a mundane, asked all kinds *of general questions about fandom . . . but then at one point she started a Lazarus Long quote and he finished it. He gave her his e-mail address so she could send some stuff about how to go about starting your own con, how to finance it and stuff. And some promo for VanCon."*

"As far as I know," Wally said, "that may be the second sign of sloppy workmanship he's shown."

"Well, actually it wasn't all that sloppy. He must have thought it was safe: the address he gave her went through anon.data.ru." This was a Moscow-based free Internet service, created and run by a volunteer and funded entirely by donations, which relayed e-mail after stripping off its identifying header—conferring effective anonymity on its users. *"Yin said on the strength of that she included some of her private porn in the stuff she sent him, but she never heard back."*

"Then how did you get a meat address?" Moira heard herself ask.

Steve made the vocal equivalent of a suicide's hesitation marks.

"Steve?" Wally said.

"Look, this is completely DNQ, all right? I mean, really. I keep your secret, you keep mine, okay? The guy that runs anon.data.ru. *is a friend of mine."*

The metaphorical flashbulb attempted to flare again, but it was shot.

"You told him the truth," Wally said.

"I had to. He wouldn't have breached security to help me find an amateur actor. He's only EVER opened his files twice, and nobody knows about either one or he'd be out of business. Both times were to stop criminals in progress—and I mean, he's got a comfortingly narrow definition of

'criminal.' But 'thief' fits. He says this guy is too
clever to be walking around."

"Roger that," Moira muttered.

"Did he let you browse 'Mr. Pen Naim''s traffic?" Wally asked.

"*Negatory. He says catching crooks is one thing,
reading their mail's another. I have to agree.*"

"Yes, I suppose so," Wally agreed, rubbing his
forehead. "I'll settle for reading his entrails."

"*Well, I'll tell you what my friend in Moscow
said.*"

"Please do."

"*He said 'bolshoyeh luck.'*"

"Thank him for us. Discreetly but profusely. No
one will ever know where we got the information,
I promise him that. As for yourself, I would begin
to outline a summary of just the highlights of all
the many ways we thank you, but this is your
dime. We owe you big-time."

"*I'll relay your offer to Sybil. She happens to
have an opening . . . and a position available, too.
Good hunting, you guys. Remember, if you lose
him, you're no worse off than you are now—you
can't be—but if you get him, you'll live forever.
Later.*"

The speaker clicked off. There was silence.
Wally reached up and shut off the phone machine,
hit rewind.

Moira said quick "OhWallyifthefuckingtape-
didn't—"

Wally cut her off. "One, zero, six, fi-yuv, niner,
Point Grey that's ee why Road, Vancouver; postal
code Varley eight Unicorn, four Rotsler six. Carla
with a sea Bernardo: cute. Penforth Naim: too
cute. Let's go see Ms. Bernardo."

Moira saw his hand twitch toward his pants

pocket, toward the little .22 he had bought from a helplessly giggling Rastafarian on Bathurst Street. She kick-started her brain. "Let's walk around her and kick the tires, first. And let's let our fingers do the walking." She pointed toward the office.

He hesitated, and his hand twitched again. And then he relaxed. "Never make decisions in haste that don't call for haste. If she's there now, she'll be there in an hour. You take municipal and provincial, I'll take federal."

"The other way round," she said, already on her way, physically and mentally.

An hour later, they parked their Toyota across the street from Carla Bernardo's house, which lay on the water side of Point Grey Road. It was, even more than its companions along this stretch, shamelessly opulent. It did not even have the decency to wear hedges, and its floral display was positively obscene even by streetlight.

"What's 'cute' about the name Carla Bernardo?" Moira asked.

"You don't want to know. Dammit, I don't see any lights on in there."

"Well, it's late."

"Not to a thief. Maybe they're out working; we can wait here and ram them in their own driveway."

"We could look through the garage window and see if there's a car in there."

"Screw it; let's just go knock on the door and see what happens." He started to get out of the car, but Moira could be a very effective anchor. "What?"

She looked him in the eye. She kept her voice

very low and calm. "Wally? Do you want to out-think this guy, for once?"

"More than I want to win a Hugo."

"Give *me* the gun."

He opened his mouth . . . and in spite of himself, he began to smile. "Oh, that is good. That is smart. I smell like fear and testosterone: if he's there he'll watch my hands and you can put one through his knee."

She was mildly surprised to realize that she was actually prepared to do that. "You remember how good I was with a paint-gun that time in Biloxi." They had once and only once attended a con that was eighty percent War Gamers, drawn by a special GoH; to her own surprise, Moira had ended up *winning* the only paint-gun stalk she'd ever been on, nailing the enemy commander square in the groin. (He had earlier made a remark she found offensive.)

"You hit what you aim at," he agreed. "Here." With some difficulty, he extricated the gun from his pants, checked the safety, and passed it across. As he did so, his smile turned wry. "It's technically a lady's gun anyway, the Rasta said."

She moved her hand from his shoulder to his cheek. "Wally . . . I promise you I won't shoot him until you hit him at least once, okay? Unless he runs."

He turned his face and kissed her hand. "Thank you. The safety's on the right."

"I saw how it works." She placed it carefully in her purse, and hung the purse from her right shoulder, unzipped.

They left and locked the car and, since it was late at night, crossed Point Grey Road on foot without the customary side effect of dying. There was a light drizzle in the air, but both ignored it. "There's one in the chamber and four more," he said. "I insisted on firing it before I bought it. He just laughed and turned his boom box all the way up. It put a hole in a dumpster."

She stopped on the minuscule sidewalk and looked at him. "In a dumpster?"

"Well, it didn't come out the other side. But I think I heard it hit the back."

"Did it shoot straight?"

"I don't know. Uh . . . I was aiming at the dumpster."

She nodded. "Good enough. Five rounds, got it. Let's check the garage before we knock."

They walked through a florid floral quotation from Butchart Gardens and circled around to where they could squint in the window set into the center door of the three-car garage. "Jesus," Wally said. "A Porsche. And something else generic on the right, maybe only a lowly Thunder-bird or something."

"Looks like a Camry to me." She took her hand from the gun and rummaged in the purse until she found her Swiss Army knife; went over to the edge of the door and examined its track. She found a place to wedge the knife, and opened some of its exten-sions to tighten it in place, trapping the Porsche in its bay. "There. Now if they get past us and make it to the garage, we only have to catch another Camry. *Now* we ring the bell."

Wally examined her in admiration for a moment—she felt it—before he followed.

She let him ring the bell. Its melody was like a commercial for a laxative—lovely on first hearing, cloying at the fifth repetition . . . binding by the tenth.

She was afraid he might get angry then—his
face was dark as he turned away from the door—
but his voice was calm. "Okay, we gather information. Let's try neighbors. Wake 'em up if we
have to."

"What do we tell them?"

"Whatever they want to hear."

To their surprise, they hit pay dirt on the first
try. The neighbor immediately to the west of Casa
Bernardo was a find from the point of view of
just about any collector.

Her face alone was worth driving a long way
to see: it had started out pretty once, many years
ago, and then she had dieted until the bones
showed clearly, and then she had had it repeatedly
lifted until, on first viewing, one felt the cruel
impulse to bounce a quarter off her cheek. Even
in the doorway light, the line where the nasal
region of her skull gave way to cartilage was clear;
in better light, Moira was confident she could have
traced the way that cartilage had been rebuilt. The
woman looked overall like a concentration-camp
survivor onto whom absurd balloon breasts had
been grafted by Dr. Mengele, dressed in the Bitch
of Buchenwald's housecoat and given Szell's
cigarette holder. For their purposes she was the
ideal menagerie: mean as a snake, nosy as a cat,
territorial as a pit bull, shameless as a ferret, loud
as a gull, smart as an ox, and drunk as a skunk.
They had won the Blotto.

She opened the door talking; it was a full
minute before they were able to fold and insert
their names. The moment she grasped that they
were interested in any gossip she might have
about That Pardon My French But Cunt Next
Door and/or Her Stud Gigolo, it ceased being

necessary for Wally or Moira to do anything but murmur and nod from time to time, with an occasional cluck or tsk as seemed indicated. She even reeled away into the house—waving them sternly to wait where they were—and returned with several photographs of an astonishing zoo-parade of zombies at a recent Do in her back-yard: three shots had Carla Bernardo in frame in the background, and one of those included a clear shot of Jude/Metkiewicz/Naim with a full head of hair. They were in their own yard, at a raised poolside, visibly sneering at the party. Mrs. Never Mind What My Name Is, I Live Here was unwilling to give Wally and Moira any of the photographs—but *was* willing to sell them the shot with both targets in it for the approximate cost of an exclusive McKinnon, since it also depicted guests she particularly despised (for reasons they were obliged to hear). She even took one of Wally's cards—Moira's she ignored—and swore to call him the *instant* That What I Said or Her Love Slave came home. She assured them she would know, day or night; they did not doubt this. Then she gave Wally a quick but nonetheless sloppy bour-bon kiss he was too shocked to dodge, and closed the door in their faces, but Moira did not shoot her through it.

"You know," she said as they walked back to their car, "I hate to say it, but I'm almost starting to enjoy this. Stephen Cannell couldn't have written her dialogue better."

"Monologue," Wally corrected, wiping his mouth and spitting.

"We were getting *stale*, Wally: we gotta start hanging out with mundanes again. You know, if a pygmy shrunk her, she wouldn't get any smaller."

Wally began to giggle. "If you unscrewed the top of her head, her whole skeleton would come squirting out from the pressure—" He chortled. "—and there'd be this little glove left, shaped like Linda Hunt—" He whooped. "Unzip the *back* of her head, and her face would be in your face—"

"Keep it down. A sincere laugh in this neighborhood is unusual enough somebody might call the cops—and I'm holding a firearm."

He reduced his mirth by increments to a silly grin, and they got in the car. "Okay, now we're getting somewhere. We know there's two of them, we have their pictures, we know a lot about their habits, and we have their house staked out for us by a force of nature. All we have to do now is—"

"Honey, I, uh, I have a bad feeling about that part."

His grin flickered.

"Maybe you'll think this is hard to buy, with that Porsche sitting there in that garage and all that money blooming all over the place . . . but I think maybe why I *buy* it is that Porsche, just sitting there. . . . Wally, honey, I don't think they're coming back here. I think something happened, something spooked them, some other con blew up in their faces, probably. Jude's house got torched last night, and according to Roboneighbor they left here on foot a few hours later. I think they're on the run."

"We have competition," Wally said, in his testosterone voice.

"But maybe we're a jump ahead of them," she said quickly. "That . . . life-form back there would have mentioned anybody else asking about Carla, so we have information nobody else does."

"Sure—about why Motormouth doesn't like her other neighbor Mrs. Wong."

"Think, Wally. She said they left in the middle of the night dressed for a day of hiking. . . . I remember distinctly the way she made five syllables out of 'L.L. *Be-ean-uh*' . . . and she said they were carrying an ice chest and a backpack and an overnight bag. Carla's a Canadian, from Vancouver, she knows you can't get cabs on the street here. They're running for the country somewhere, on foot."

"Terrific," he said. "That narrows it down to three hundred and sixty possible degrees. Maybe they dug themselves a bunker over in the Endowment Lands—excuse me, Pacific Spirit Park."

"It means wherever they run to, it won't be far. And not where anybody else would expect a conman to run to, not downtown or the 'burbs or another city altogether."

He nodded. "Yeah. That's good."

"Everybody else will be watching the airport and the bus station and the highways and the Tsawwassen Terminal . . . and meanwhile they'll take the bus or Skytrain or the Seabus or . . . I don't know, the Horseshoe Bay Ferry."

"But we still don't know which, or how far."

"No, but look on the bright side. Country grapevine works even better than city grapevine—if you're listening to it."

His fickle grin returned. "Wherever there's a Nowheresville . . . there's a fan with a modem. Those two will stick out *more* there—to us. Oh, I like it, darling. Let's go get their pictures scanned in and cropped, and put them—no, get Steve to put them out on the Net. You're right. Maybe our luck is finally starting to turn."

He should really have known better than to make a U-turn on Point Grey Road at night. On that long straight pipeline they were visible for a kilometer in either direction, and the cops' end-of-shift was approaching, leaving them with tickets to unload.

Fortunately, Canadian cops do not search stopped vehicles—or their passengers' purses—without a good reason. The pair got back home with nothing worse than a ticket that would put points on Wally's license . . . and one set of slightly damp underwear. His, if you must know.

Chapter 9
Peeking Ahead

Rain was just beginning to fall as they arrived. Ignoring it, and being ignored in return, they landed in front of their home in Pacific Spirit Park, entered the house, and became visible again.

She found that she was both exhilarated and exhausted. (These terms relative to her normal emotional state: any human observer would have thought her serene.) The simple intellectual knowledge that one has become mortal, can die, changes a thing like flying. The sensation was oddly invigorating, as if in pathetic compensation for its cost.

He did not notice, nor did she hold it against him. He was too worried for her to empathize with her fully right now; she would have to do something about that when she had time. And they were both too busy.

"I'll make coffee," she said. Human domestic customs, adopted for cover and practiced for drill, had worked their insidious comfort over the centuries. The ritual would help her ground herself, and him as well, even if the caffeine itself was superfluous.

He nodded, understanding. "I'll build a fire." He used his hands.

Both had long practice in achieving and sustaining calm; it was a large part of what they did. By the time the hearth was crackling and the coffee was steaming, they were ready to see the humor in the situation, and nearly ready to appreciate it.

"E.T.," she said. She blew across the surface of her cup, grateful for the professionalism which had caused her to develop that habit, now that her lips could be burned. "Only it's Extra Temporal, rather than Terrestrial."

He smiled, understanding the reference. "Yes. Time for us to Phone Home. Talk about call forwarding!"

She sighed. "Never expected to do it."

"I know. I haven't tried to peek ahead to the end of a book since . . . well, a long time ago."

"And we made it necessary."

Another would have accepted her tone as flat, neutral—but he did not need ears to hear his mate's pain. He spoke sharply, for him. "We cannot afford to be ashamed of our failure just now. The stakes are too high. The least important thing about this disaster is whose watch it happened on. The most important thing is to report it fully and try to get it dealt with. I love you."

She steadied. "Agreed. I love you."

He gestured, and a small piece of polished quartz left the rock collection on display in a corner of the room and came to them. It hovered directly between them, picking up flickering highlights from the fire, so that to each it appeared a sparkling third eye of the other.

They began to fill it with thought together.

❖   ❖   ❖

Even as the first datum was entered, the message began containing information. Its very formatting structure said that it was composed of purely human thoughts, thus largely in words, these words being late 20th Century Canadian English. This declared the identity of its senders, strongly hinted at the nature of the problem itself, and implied the mode of thought that would have to be adopted in order to consider it effectively.

Having created a self-explaining "blank sheet of paper," they began to "write" on it.

First, in the largest type, the addressee:

Everyone.

Next, the desired delivery time; i.e., the specific (sidereally expressed) date on which the quartz beacon was to begin announcing itself, and continue until acknowledged:

The instant we left.

Then, priority:

Ultimate.

Next, summary of text. This was the first part they hesitated over long enough for a contemporary timepiece to measure the interval. Finally:

A Class One Paradox threatens. We urgently request Anachrognosis to resolve it; delivery soonest.

They *had* to pause, there. One simply cannot make a truthful statement on the order of *it will now be necessary to rape God* and then go on to explain why and just how, without stopping for a moment and waiting for the unprecedented thrill of awe and horror to fade. They had just asked that one of the most fundamental principles of their society of origin be massively violated, in order to preserve it. Since the whole point of their present existence was to make such a request unnecessary, they felt the antinomy perhaps more strongly than would anyone who heard it.

Thunder sounded outside, somewhere to the north.

Statement of problem:

Here they dumped everything either had experienced since the Tar Baby had shrieked. Literally everything. The context from each of their points of view. Every single vagrant thought or sensation the mook had ever had, up to the instant when his shovel had said *clack* and he had said "Aw, fuck." (He'd had no thoughts after that which were relevant.) Every single random thought or sensation June Bellamy had ever had, up to the instant when she touched the shovel. Everything they had done in response to this catastrophe, and every thought they'd formed while doing it. All the data they had gleaned from Paul Throtmanian's house and ancillary sources.

Summary of conclusions:

The targets Throtmanian and Bellamy are much too intelligent and educated to be permitted to know what they know. Given time, they will draw obvious conclusions. They are top professionals at escaping capture by any reasonable contemporary means, and have proved themselves resourceful in evading the most sophisticated methods available to us. One of us has already been rendered mortal while tracking them.

Prognosis broke down into two sections. First:

(Without Anachrognosis—) Exposure. Paradox. Catastrophe.

(With Anachrognosis—) A very good chance of salvage and safety.

And at last, they came to the part they metaphorically sweated most over: their specific request.

The heavens outside wept inconsolably onto their roof as they thought it over. There were several ways to approach it. After agonizing for nearly a full minute together, they selected the one which seemed to them to require the absolute minimum of anachrognostic disturbance, and the smallest possible outrage of human free will.

We request that Paul Throtmanian and June Bellamy advise us on how to catch them.

It was done, now. All that was left was a final trivial detail: specification of the delivery date for the requested information. They had already asked for "soonest"—but now they must tell the addressee specifically when "soonest" would be.

He glanced over at the TV by learned reflex, snorted, glanced upward through the ceiling to a satellite with considerably better raw data, and made his own analysis.

She saw his face change, checked his figures—and reached the same conclusion.

It had long been established—indeed, since the very first attempt—that it was a Very Bad Idea to hurl a parcel back through time to a ficton where it was raining . . . or snowing, though that was rarely a problem in the Pacific Northwest. In that historic instance, in Nova Scotia in 1972, the energy liberated by the simultaneous annihilation of several hundred snowflakes had been sufficient to offset the Egg's terminus by a crucial few meters, into a tree—nearly killing its occupant, the first-ever time traveler.

For as long as there was rain, or even mist, in the air, they could hope for no package from home. They could not even submit their request for one until they could confidently specify dry target ficton coordinates.

"Why am I not surprised?" she asked quietly. And then for the first time in more than a hundred and fifty years, she began to cry.

He swept the coruscating bit of quartz out of the way and took her in his arms. "It will be okay," he said, the way you say something when you hope saying it will make it true.

"After all this," she sobbed against his neck, "are we going to be ruined by the damned *weather*?"

"We've always had that hazard here," he said. "We can shorten it a little. Three days. Maybe two; let me work up a first approximation."

She struggled against his embrace. "If those two get *one* whole day to sit and think about what they already know, it's all over."

"Not instantly," he insisted, the muscles of his upper arms and shoulders bulging like kinked hoses. "Even if they figure it out, we could have *days* to get to them before they *do* anything about it."

She gave up the physical expression of her struggle. "Sure. And right now they could be gaping up at the clouds and drowning, like turkeys."

He did not slacken the physical expression of his caring. "Things are bad. We will do our best. And then we will wait to see what happens. Shall I refine that approximation now, or would you like to do it?"

She squeezed her eyes shut until the mandalas came. "I'll do it. I was always better with weather."

Chapter 10
The Biter Bit

In paradise, Paul was in a funk.

He didn't do it often, for a man. June's inclination was to let him indulge himself. But he seemed to *want* to be busted for it.

He had thrown himself savagely into his period of enforced play, as if determined to have fun or die in the attempt. He had hot-tubbed until he pruned; eaten till he creaked; drunk till he puked, and screwed till he couldn't any more for awhile. Then he had filled the house with Wagner at terrifying volume while filling the huge satellite TV screen with German porn—some of the really astonishing stuff; the kind that would in a few months embarrass the Munich police into harassing CompuServe for letting foreigners export disgusting hard-core erotica to their God-fearing nation. Then, of course, he had screwed some more. (She'd been forced to admit, howling along with the Valkyries, that the Master Race had its points. As she'd hoped, the ability to climax had returned to her— Hoyoto! But it hadn't been especially *friendly* sex.) Afterwards he'd switched the music to the Beatles, and dived into O'Leary's books for several taciturn hours. When he emerged it was only to boot up the big Mac in the living room and sample his host's games. He found an alpha version of a WWII submarine simulator with superb graphics called War Patrol, designed by Gordon Walton, and became impervious to human contact for half a day, happily stalking defenseless convoys and torpedoing hospital ships.

June joined him for half an hour, out of loneliness, and the game was diabolically interesting. But it was a prerelease version, even more prone to crashes than Wagner, and she could not see the point of a game that would kill her sooner or later no matter how smart she was. She drifted off and watched the rain fall on the lower sundeck. The next time she wandered by he had stopped playing and was typing some sort of text document, but she knew from the set of his face that it would not be a good idea to read it over his shoulder. A little while later, reading in the bedroom, she heard the keyboard-tapping downstairs cease abruptly, and the door to the lower deck slide open and closed again. When he did not return within five minutes, she left the TV and went to make sure he hadn't fallen over the side.

She saw him at an angle through the glass of her own sliding door, wearing a mackinaw, standing down on the lower deck by O'Leary's big Zeiss telescope, a hand resting on it. It was aimed not at the drizzling sky, but at the bay laid out below. His other hand held a pair of binoculars, through which he seemed to be examining the horizon. As she watched, he took a look through the scope, visibly sighed, and went back to the binoculars.

For the first time it began to dawn on her that he was in some kind of trouble. Paul was a city kid to his bones; he enjoyed looking at nature as much as she enjoyed looking at blood.

But what the hell could his problem be? They had been on the run before. They had even been on the run from superior forces before, and taken shelter in much meaner quarters than these. Okay: so Something Bad was out there, and for all they knew might be vectoring closer even now—was that any reason not to enjoy life in the meantime? Why was he acting like a citizen?

She slid her door open and stepped out onto her own smaller deck, and was shocked. He was smoking marijuana! The light rain and the roof overhang that shielded her from it combined to enclose the smell. It was not the first time he'd ever gotten high—but it was definitely the first time she could recall him doing so while danger was known to threaten. They were both firm believers in alertness during working hours: God knew nothing else had saved their bacon only two days earlier. "Jesus, Paul," she said, leaning over the rail and waving at the thick fruity scent.

Red eyes blinked up at her. "Hey, baby. Wanna toke?"

He looked so miserable her heart softened. "One of us better stay on duty," she said gently. "You have fun."

He snorted and looked away. "Yah. Fun."

She let that line sit there for a little bit. When he raised the binoculars again, she asked, "Whatcha looking at?"

"The only straight line God ever made," he said, resting his elbow on the Zeiss to steady himself.

She found herself thinking about that. Were there any straight lines in nature besides the horizon? Come to think, even raindrops didn't fall straight, did they? "Curved," she said thickly. God, was the stuff *that* good, that two breaths of his exhaust were zonking her? Or was it just empathic contact high with her lover?

"Technically, yeah, but you can't see that from here. Looks straight as a citizen, doesn't it? Has to be where humans got the idea for straight lines . . . and without them, what would people like you and me color outside of?"

"Go easy on that stuff, okay? It smells powerful."

"The year I was born," he said, "New York State did a study comparing the effects of alcohol and marijuana on drivers. I ever tell you about that?"

"No."

"They assigned five levels of stonedness for each drug, and learned how to reliably bring experienced volunteers to each level—from barely buzzed to shitfaced. Then they had 'em all drive an obstacle course, sober and at each of the five levels of intoxication for both drugs, and compared results. At levels one and two, grass made you a *better* driver. Faster reflexes, wider peripheral vision, expanded depth of field, more caution. After careful thought and due determination, the state decided the study was too good to publish or release. They prefer the ones where you count how many fatality-accident victims had smoked pot in the previous forty-eight hours: the more people get high, the more 'proof' they have that it 'causes' all those accidents. My mom happened to type most of the raw data while she was in the joint, and she told me about it."

"I wouldn't dream of arguing with your mother," she said, "but remember: that's B.C. boo you're smoking. They didn't have that shit in the '70s."

He put down the binoculars and looked up at her. "True. Maybe I better check the old reflexes, huh?" He slipped off his mackinaw, faced her and crouched.

"Paul—"

Nothing wrong with her own reflexes; she managed to get out of his way, and still had a whole half second to appreciate the beauty of his tumbling flight and the catlike grace of his landing. Dizzily, she reconstructed what she must have seen: he had sprung high, used the floor of the deck on which she stood to continue his ascent, and grabbed the rainslick upper railing just long and hard enough to let his legs come up and over and fling his body forward, finishing up in a half crouch before her. "So," he said, not even breathing hard, "you sure you don't want a hit?"

"Christ," she said, annoyed at her momentary fear and at him for causing it. "I hope you don't develop a taste for coke, next."

"Right. I'm just trying to relax and have a little fun, alright?"

"I noticed," she said. "You getting anywhere?"

His cockiness drained from him. "As the fella said after a *ménage à trois* with a porcupine and a skunk, 'I reckon I've enjoyed about as much of this as I can stand.' I feel like a guy who's had his leg cut off—I itch, but I can't find the place to scratch."

Good. Keep him talking now. Anything at all. "So what's all this about straight lines?"

Paul made that sound which can be either an aborted chuckle or suppressed nausea; context offered no clue which. "Well, it just seemed like there had to be one, right?"

"In nature, you mean? I guess so. Why?"

"Hey, think about it. The greatest joker Who ever lived—" He waved upward at the weeping sky. "—I mean, the truly *funniest* sonofabitch of all time . . . the guy Who filled the universe with punchlines—" He mimed boxing. "—pow, pow, pow, punchlines . . . shit, there'd just *have* to be a straight-line around *somewhere*, now wouldn't there?" He pointed at the horizon, where grey day was becoming rainy night. "There it is. The set-up for the cosmic joke. The sweet salty place we came from, that tries to kill us every time we try to go back." He began to laugh, the helpless belly laugh of a driver who wakes after the crash to see his toddler wearing the dashboard for a hat.

She took him in her arms and tried her best to stop the ghastly laughter with compression of the thorax. "*Good* straight-line—" he choked out between spasms. "—stare at it—long as you want—*still* won't see that old punchline comin'—oh God, baby—"

She held on, searched her memory for soothing things her mother had said to her when she was a heartbroken child. "Better soon . . . better soon, honey . . . I'm here . . . we're okay so far . . . it'll be all right . . . we'll figure out what's the matter, we're too smart not to . . . and once we do, we'll know how to fix it, you wait and—" She broke off. He had stopped sobbing, was looking at her with astonished eyes from a distance of three inches.

"You don't get it yet," he said. "You really don't get it." He worked a hand between them and wiped at his nose. "Jesus, I'm really surprised."

"Get what?" She wasn't going to like this. She let go of him.

"You haven't worked out the punchline yet." He

grimaced, covered it by rubbing at his eyes. "Hey, why should you? I'm the one it was aimed at. 'You just happened to be comin' along at the right time, sucker.' You want me to spoil it for you? Or you just want a hint?"

She took a deep breath. "Spit it out."

"How did I get Wally Kemp and Moira Rogers to give me ninety-eight large?"

There having been no part for her in the Jude sting, Wally and Moira had never become real to her. She fell back on first principles: "By selling them something they wanted that much."

"No, I mean, who was I? Who did they think I was?"

"A time traveler. It really was brilliant, you know."

He waited for her to get it, so she tried. Finally she lifted her eyebrows: I'm stumped, get on with it.

"Who," he said, "are we running from?"

At first she thought he was crazy. The more she thought about it, the more terrified she became that he was not.

"Tell me something else it could be," he said, "that fits the facts we have so far."

She flailed. "Mad scientists," she tried. "I don't know, aliens, maybe." She was horrified to hear herself suggesting something even more X-Files than his notion, but could find no better.

"If you find star travelers who have some reason to be afraid of us monkeys more plausible than time travelers, hey, go for it," he said. "I figure like this: you tell people you came across an alien artifact, either you end up in a shirt with real long sleeves and buckles, or you end up in the same room with Maury Povich: either way there's no reason for anybody to burn your house down. But you tell people you stumbled across a *human* artifact that can't be made yet, an anachronism of some kind . . . and maybe you end up making a paradox, and the universe goes away."

June had endured just enough sci fi in her life to understand the argument. Time travel had to be stealthy if it was to be done at all. Change history, and all hell broke loose. Whoever wanted them dead was trying to move like a virus: with *discreet* deadliness. Oh God, it made sense . . . more than anything else she could think of.

The word "denial" was in her vocabulary—but only as a legal strategy. She had spent her life training herself to face facts. She couldn't stop, just because the facts had turned weird . . . could she?

"My brilliant idea," Paul said sourly. "I'll tell you something I wasn't ever gonna tell anybody: it wasn't even original. I got it from a fifty-year-old story by a writer named Cyril Kornbluth—the guy that wrote 'The Marching Morons.' I figured it was okay to lift the gimmick in this other story because what he did with it just wasn't practical. His grifter pretends to be a time traveler, and pulls off a sting—a lot crummier sting than the beauty I put together, by the way: it never woulda worked in real life—and then the punchline is, the real time travelers hear he's blowing their cover, and they come boil his brain. Naturally I didn't waste any time worrying about *that* little hazard—hell, no! I'm a rational man. Only in a science fiction story would time travel turn out to be real—and unlike Wally and Moira, I don't wish my life were a science fiction story. Guess what, honey: it is anyway. Whether we like it or not."

The true horror of their situation washed over her, and she began to laugh herself.

Unlike Paul, however, she had no trouble at all stopping. She sat down on the deck with her arms wrapped around her knees and thought, *hard*. He sat beside her and let her think, silently watching the dull grey glow go out of the world to the west.

"I don't get it," June said finally, breaking the silence. "I believe you, I guess, but I still don't understand it. How the hell does this time traveler think we threaten him? By knowing he exists? How does that make us any different from Kemp and Rogers? What are we supposed to do with the information? Sell it to Geraldo?"

"We know where he has something buried. We don't know what, but it must constitute proof he's a time traveler."

"So what? Everybody who sees it forgets."

"You didn't—for long enough to phone me."

"So why doesn't he just move whatever it is fifty meters east? We'd never find it again."

Paul shook his head. "I don't know. He must like it right where it is, for some reason. Maybe it's his time gate, and once you set it up you can't move it." He frowned at the rain. "I wish I could call up Wally and Moira and ask them. They've had experience thinking seriously about this shit."

She shook her own head, impatiently. "Horseshit. They don't know any more about time travel than we do. And they probably don't even realize *that*."

"Maybe not, but they can think about this kind of stuff logically without boggling," he said. "They actually know some real science. I haven't got a good enough sense of what's really ridiculous, and what's only weird."

"So we do that: stick to what we know, and

apply logic. How about this one—this is the one that keeps sticking in my craw: how come we know as much as we do? How come we know anything at all?"

"Huh?"

June went into lecture mode. "You're a time traveler. You have powers beyond those of mortal men. You bury something you want to stay buried. So you booby-trap it: if a guy hits it with a shovel, he gets hit with a mind-ray or whatever, he forgets what he was doing and wanders off. Now: won't you give the damn mind-ray a large enough radius to *also* get his buddy who wandered off a few meters to take a pee?"

He nodded. "That bothers me some, too. You shouldn't have had time to make that long a phone call before you got bagged."

"Maybe it was just a robot security system that mook triggered—"

"Even so. It obviously read his mind; it should have noticed a better mind nearby. It would have if *I* designed it, and I'm probably not as smart as a time traveler."

June winced at the last clause, and spoke quickly to distract him, lest he hear what he had just said. "So we want to figure out why it didn't notice me at first. Let's just riff and see what happens. How am I different from Angel Gerhardt? I'm smarter . . . right, and the mind-ray only notices stupid people. It'd be getting a great reading off of me, now. Uh . . . let's see: I'm female, I weigh less, less upper-arm strength, I probably have nicer tits—"

"Try it this way," Paul said. "How were you different from him *that afternoon?*"

"Okay, let's think about that. I probably had less

cocaine in my system . . . I wasn't planning to commit a crime, not that day, anyway . . . I was depressed from thinking about my mother . . . I didn't have a backpack or a shovel—"

"The depressed thing might be something," he said. "I admit I can't imagine what—but it's something mental, and this is a mind-reader we're talking about. I think so, anyway. Maybe depression is something he blocks out as long as possible."

"Great. In that case, I could walk straight up to him, right now, and he'd never even notice me." Thoughts of her mother were trying to steal her attention, but June pushed them back under the covers. She knew—somehow—that Laura Bellamy was still alive, down there in California, and she had made up her mind not to start grieving until it was grieving time. But the mental association did give her an idea of what to do next. "Look," she said, getting to her feet, "I'm coming up empty. It's time for me to do my thinking thing."

"Not a bad idea," he agreed, remaining where he was. "It's what you were doing when this whole clem started. And this is a good place for it, as long as you stick to the path. Take an umbrella and a flashlight." June's "thinking thing" was a ritual he was familiar with, and respected, even if it didn't work for him. Faced with an intractable problem, she liked to surround herself with the physical, visual, olfactory and aural stimuli she found most conducive to thought—by walking in woods (for preference; a park or picnic area would do in a pinch) or along the shore while listening to good music on headphones. "I think I saw a Walkman in the bedroom," he added.

"Yeah," she snorted. She took hold of the railing and did some stretches to work the kinks out. "I noticed it, too. What the hell is the point of _owning_ a Walkman if you're going to leave it behind when you go on trips? I swear, the ones with the money are always the least— WOW!"

He rolled away from her, came to his feet in a half crouch and spun twice like a ballet dancer, snapping his head around for each turn. "_Where?_"

"No, no, relax—I just had a rush of brains to the head. I was wishing I had my own FM headphones with me, so I wouldn't have to go put on something with a pocket to put that heavy Walkman in, and deal with the cord, and so on . . . and that made me miss my headphones, sitting back home in Vancouver . . . and that reminded me that as I was leaving the house for the last time, right after you called, I looked for those 'phones and couldn't find them. They weren't where I always hang them by the door."

Paul straightened, shivered slightly, and shook adrenaline-energy from his fingertips, but kept his temper. "Okay. And from this you infer . . . ?"

"I know I had those 'phones on my head when I walked into Pacific Spirit Park. The jockey had put on a whole side of Coltrane ballads." Her voice was becoming dreamy as she forced the memories to the surface. "I remember 'Nancy With The Laughing Face,' and 'Little Brown Book,' and something I didn't know, and then another Strayhorn . . . 'Lush Life,' that was it . . . I remember 'Lush Life' starting . . . and then the next sound-memory I have is walking out of the Park . . . and thinking for the thousandth time in my life that Philip Glass must have stolen half his lick from listening to birds! Paul, I was hearing birds—"

Paul's eyes glowed. "You didn't have the radio on anymore. Oh, I *like* this. You're absolutely right: this is a 'WOW.' " He began to pace the deck. "Check me out on this. This Gerhardt mook starts to bury his stash. In doing so he triggers . . . I know it's a feeble pun, but let's call it a mental detector. It reads his mind, erases the parts it doesn't like, and sends him on his way, clueless. It ought to pick *you* up, too, what did you say, fifty meters away, call it fifty yards, right? Only *you have an FM radio right next to your skull*, and that screws up the mental detector for some reason. So you get to watch the whole show. The mook buries his stash somewhere else, and goes home, and you put a message on my machine. Alright: for the Hawaiian vacation and ten thousand dollars cash, what does June Bellamy do next?"

"I dig up his stash," she said at once, and then, more slowly, "and maybe I take my radiophones off to wipe away the sweat—"

"Or maybe a *second* mental detector has been put on the stash, now, to keep tabs on the mook if he should ever shake off the whammy and come back—and the FM radio gag only works at fifty meters."

"I like the first one," she said. "It explains why they take the risk of not giving me my headphones back after they're done."

"Okay," he agreed. "I like it, too. You realize what this means? For the first time, we have a *clue* how we can possibly defend ourselves, if the bastard catches up with us."

"We're doing it again," she said.

"Doing what?"

"Thinking of him as 'him.' I said I wasn't going to do that."

"Hard not to."

She nodded. "Well, now that we're agreed he's not a monkey demon or a spaceman, 'it' doesn't work anymore . . . and who knows better than I how few women warriors there are in North America? But we still ought to keep reminding ourselves that 'he' could just as easily be 'they,' at least."

"Point taken. Tell you the truth, I kind of hope there *are* two of them."

"Really? Why?"

"Well, we seem to have found a counter for the mental detector slash obedience ray slash brainwasher."

"Maybe."

"Without that, the best these guys can possibly be is supernaturally good . . . so if there's two of them, that makes it a fair fight." Even in the growing dark she could see his grin. "I *like* a fair fight."

"God, testosterone is an amazing thing. I'll settle for there's only one of him and we kick his ass without working up a sweat."

He shook his head, still grinning happily. "One way or another, I'm working up a sweat. I disapprove of people who do B&Es on my sweetie's skull."

It came to her that testosterone had its uses. "Not to mention people who spoil your greatest triumph and burn your house down."

He shrugged. "Those things too. For them I'd hurt him. For you, I'm going to kill him."

A primitive thrill made her tingle, and a few more uses for testosterone occurred to her. "You say the sweetest things," she murmured, and moved nearer.

But he was not quite ready to segue from blood lust to the other kind. "I'm glad it pleases you," he said, "but I have to be honest: I think my motives are more selfish than anything else. *Nobody* is going to know you better than I do."

She pressed her attack, ignoring his body language. "Darling, our relationship is based on enlightened mutual selfishness, you know that." Her tongue made a demand of his neck. "Our interests coincide." She could smell him shifting gears. "You kill him, and I'll make you a lovely loincloth from the hide." Her fingers asked a question of his penis. "Now drag me into the cave and exploit me, you brute."

As she was being carried in from the deck, she remembered that he always lasted forever when he was stoned, and she shivered with anticipation. Her lover's funk was definitely over. They had a plan . . . and just possibly the beginnings of an edge.

"The first thing we do tomorrow morning," he said sleepily, "we find out where's the nearest place to score a couple of sets of FM headsets. Shit, one of us may have to go back to Vancouver; I'll be surprised if they stock 'em out here on Gilligan's Island. Maybe I could work up some kind of headband rig to hold a Walkman against our skulls—did you notice whether O'Leary's has FM? Or is it just the tape kind? June? Are you listening to me? Hey—are you *crying*? God, was I that good, or are you—"

"Mom is down."

He stared.

"I just know, okay? She's gone."

"Aw jeeze—"

"Shit, I can't even call Pop and console him." And *her* funk began.

❖   ❖   ❖

By the middle of the next day, it had so thoroughly thickened the atmosphere in that lavish little A-frame that Paul volunteered to walk to "town" in a low-probability search for headphones with FM radios built in, despite the ever present rain. Better to soak than choke.

Although he kept his ears open for the sound of Tom Waits along the way, he was not fortunate enough to encounter Moe Lycott, and he could not quite suppress the instincts of a lifetime enough to stick his thumb out for the occasional stranger who did drive past. Consequently it was midafternoon, and he was footsore and sweaty under his mackinaw, by the time he reached the cluster of shops by the ferry terminus. He looked with longing upon the first tavern he came to . . . then remembered his marijuana binge of the night before, reminded himself sharply that he was on combat-alert, and began to walk on by. But the first step hurt so much, after the momentary respite, that he converted the second into a pivot and trod heavily into the welcoming shade where ice-cold beer lived.

He emerged with a much lighter step half an hour later, scoped the street without seeming to, and made his way to the general store the bartender had suggested, humming softly.

Two beers was not enough, however, to make him follow the bartender's suggestion that he ask for "Space Case," despite assurances that this was the name of the clerk most likely to be able to help him. Instead he simply looked over the two clerks available in the little shop, figured out which a yokel would be most likely to call Space Case, and approached that one. "Uh, excuse me—I wonder if you could help me out."

"I can try. Define the problem."

Ah, a technical mind. "My wife and I have decided we prefer radio to tape. It's more unpredictable, eh? And we do a lot of walking, and gosh, to get the same amount of choice from a Walkman that a radio offers, you need an extra pack just for cassettes. Plus I always get the cord caught. You wouldn't by any chance happen to have a couple of sets of dedicated FM headphones around the shop, would you?"

Space Case grinned, brushed stringy hair from his face, and pointed to the wall behind him. "Ask me a hard one. Panasonic okay?"

Paul squinted. "Are they powerful?"

The grin widened. "Well, that's your basic good news/bad news situation. The good news is yes and yes, and the bad news is yes."

Paul reminded himself that he was supposed to be a Canadian, too polite to mind having his chain yanked. "Beg pardon?"

"You ask me if it's powerful, you're asking three things. First, does it play loud? Answer: yes, it'll play just as loud as anything else in the world with earphones—as loud as the law allows, and no louder. Second, does it pull in all the signals, even the weak ones? Answer: maybe better than the tuner you have back home; your whole skull kind of acts as an antenna, fillings and all. Those are the good news. Part three: does it put out a strong field? Answer: well, yeah, kind of, relatively speaking."

Paul's ears grew points. "I don't think I follow you. A radio receiver puts out a signal of its own?"

"Well, a weak one. So does a Walkman, or a CD player, or a computer. It's why they don't want you to use one in a plane during takeoff and landing. Which by the way is a total crock: the field strength falls off so fast with distance, you're as likely to interfere with the pilot's electronics as you are with his menstrual cycle. Airlines are just lawsuit-happy."

"So why is this bad news?"

Space Case took two sets of FM headphones from the wall and set them on the counter, then recaptured his hair and tucked it behind his ear again. "Well, a lot of experts say it isn't, actually. But I notice that your personal skull gets a lot closer to one of these than the cockpit does. Even a Walkman at the end of one of those little cords gives you more distance. And there's this cube-square thing happening."

"So if the experts are wrong, and there *is* any danger in low-level electromagnetic fields . . ."

"This is about as good a test as you can get," Space Case agreed. "Short of building a cabin under a power line."

Paul frowned. He wanted the things more than ever, now . . . but staying in character required him to appear dubious. "Are you saying they're dangerous, then?"

Space Case shrugged. "I'm saying, anybody who claims to know that *for sure* either way at this point in history is lying or kidding himself. Put it like this: Panasonic is willing to undertake the risk of selling them to you . . . and I'm willing to accept the karma of taking your money. I'm just into full disclosure. Like I say, a lot of experts say they're perfectly harmless. But the way I see it, an expert is an ordinary person, a long way from home."

Paul considered, wrestling with a tiny, absurd dilemma. In New York, he would simply have bought the headphones now—long since, in fact.

But as a putative Canadian, he needed a polite reason to ignore the salesman's clear reluctance to sell them, to override the other's judgment. He took refuge in quotation. "Well, as a great man once said, 'You can go as far wrong by being too skeptical as by being too trusting.' I guess I'll give Panasonic the benefit of the doubt: let me have two sets, please."

Space Case grinned even wider. "A fan!"

Paul blinked. "Beg pardon?"

"That was a Lazarus Long quote. You're a fan, right?"

Very faintly—in fact, almost below the conscious level entirely—an alarm went off in the back of Paul's mind. Those who lie for a living must pay close attention to any mental notes they leave themselves . . . and one part of the prophylactic debriefing procedure he'd automatically put himself through as he had walked out Wally and Moira's door with ninety-eight thousand of their dollars in his hand had been to instruct himself: *For the next little while, if anyone asks you if you know anything about science fiction, say no.* "Sorry," he lied fluently. "I don't know this Nazareth fellow. I was quoting an English teacher I had once, Mr. Leamer."

"Ah. Well, never mind; it's a long story. Pun intended. Several books long, actually. Will that be cash or charge?"

"Cash, please."

"How are you fixed for goo?"

Paul stopped sorting bills by color, and stared. "Could you run that by me again?"

"You said you and the wife walk a lot. I got some great blister goo."

Paul had made up his mind over an hour ago:

he was going to walk back to Casa O'Leary with his new radio headphones, and then he was never ever going to walk anywhere again as long as he lived. Painkiller he already had. So the only operative consideration was, what would a *real* walker say to an offer like this? "No, thanks," he said. "We've got some prescription stuff her sports medicine doctor gives her."

"Oh yeah? What's it called?"

He took refuge in incompetence. "I know it as 'foot gunk.' It's white, if that helps any."

Space Case kept his face straight. "Yeah, that narrows it down some."

Out of professional admiration, Paul kept his own face straight, and kept playing dumb. "Really?"

"Yeah, all them white ones are only manufactured on days that end in y."

He did his double-take so beautifully he drew a shout of laughter from Space Case. "I suppose they *are* just about all white, eh?" he said with a great show of rue. "I wonder why that is."

"I'd imagine," Space Case said, still chuckling, "for the same reason every brand of creme rinse you can buy for your hair looks exactly like ejaculate. You want powerful magic, invoke semen."

Paul obliged by looking mildly scandalized but too ashamed to admit it, and left, well pleased. Even the nosiest clerk tended to forget the dull ones quickly.

All the way back to O'Leary's A-frame he strained his ears for Moe Lycott's truck, without success. Halfway there the rain suddenly went from drizzle to downpour. He went through a kind of epiphany, and by an act of the will forced himself to stick his thumb out, the way he'd seen people do in old movies. This turned out to be sound strategy: the savage satisfaction he achieved when fourteen successive cars blew by him without slowing was more comfort than a ride would have been. Even here, there were traces of civilization. . . .

He arrived home lamed but in a fine sour spirit that tasted like unsweetened chocolate, and hung up his mackinaw prepared to resume the burden of not being permitted to comfort his lover—

—only to find something out of a nightmare.

Sitting, safe and sound, in the chaise longue on the lower deck, under the overhang of the deck above. Serene and tranquil, internal thunderclouds past, funk miraculously over, days ahead of schedule. Heartbreakingly lovely in the grey light of rainy afternoon: his lover, his partner, his best friend June. Who at his approach looked him square in the eye, and said, quietly and without a trace of humor, words which frightened and shocked him more than being stalked by a brain-raping house-burning time traveler had:

"Paul, I'm getting out of the business."

Paralysis. There were so many possible responses— so many sheafs of different *kinds* of possible responses—that his quick wit and quick body alike were mazed, and he made no response at all. He stood there expressionless and motionless and almost thoughtless, for the first time in years simply waiting to find out what would happen next.

"However this thing with the time traveler works out, I'm through," she said. "I'd like to keep half title to the Key West place, if we're alive when this is over, and the stash in Chicago. The rest is yours. The store, all the other cushions, the software, everything. I'm cashing out."

His eyelids closed of their own accord. He could

think of no reason to raise them, but then he heard a voice rather like his own, miles away, croak, "You're leaving me?" and opened his eyes to see who had said that and what she would answer.

It must have been one of those two tiny copies of him swimming in her eyes who'd spoken. "Not unless you ask me to," she said carefully. "We can keep separate finances, and you won't talk about work at home. I'll go where you go, and lie for you, and cover you when you have to run, and catch up when I can. I'll bind your wounds and tolerate your bullshit and I'll bury you if it comes to that. But I won't so much as rope for you: I won't even consult. I'm through."

Idly he wondered what new—legit!—profession she would dream up for herself, flexible and portable enough to be compatible with a mate in The Life: he knew it was certain to be interesting. But that was a consideration for the distant future—whole minutes from now. At the moment the important thing was to get his heart restarted. *Unh*. There . . .

"You want to hear something amazing?" his voice said. Yeah, it was coming from one of those little reflections in her eyes: the distance and volume sounded about right. "My feet don't hurt a bit. Not at all. You feel like going for a hike in the rain, I'll be glad to come along."

"Paul—"

"It's like the old joke," the reflection interrupted; he lip-synched along. "You're supposed to lead up to a thing like that. First you say, 'I've found Krishna; please call me Moonbeam now.' Then you say, 'Your test came back: it's cancer of the penis.' *Then*, you say you're retiring."

She returned his gaze steadily, and said something so absurd he and the reflections all had to smile: "I'm sorry."

For the first time Paul understood why the commander of the Light Brigade had followed those blundering orders and mounted an impossible charge. Because there is no despair so vast or cold or stony that some drifting idiot seed of hope cannot take root, wither, and decay there, all in an instant. "June," he said, in the freedom of futility, "your mom—"

"She didn't like what I do, Paul. She never said so. Not once, or we could have argued it, and maybe I could have persuaded her. But we both knew."

"Of *course* she didn't like it: she's your mother, she was scared for you—"

"She was ashamed of me. I think she was wrong, most of the time, but she was ashamed of me. Not because she had to lie whenever her friends asked what I was up to; she didn't mind lying at all. Because the truth hurt her. She wanted to be proud of me. And she was—but not all the way."

"If she'd understood—"

"I'll tell you the worst. I've been sitting here reviewing the last year or so, and *I'm* ashamed of me, too."

He had been stunned for some time, now he was shocked: different things. He raised his arms as if to summon divine witness. "*Why?*"

His reflections, thrashing around in their tubs like that, made them spill over and run down her cheeks. "Our standards have been slipping."

"Bullshit."

She shook her head hard enough to displace the tears, but they were replaced almost at once.

"What did we say, back at the beginning? *Only jerks*, right? Only people that deserved it."

"That's right," he agreed. "You're the one who taught me that. I was feeding on anything with blood when you found me. And feeling shitty about it."

"Think about my last two games. How about Frazier?"

"He hired us to kill his wife!"

"And you said yourself it was a shame not to go through with it."

"But—but then it wouldn't have been a sting. It would have been . . . *work*."

"The point remains. Being driven beyond his endurance doesn't make a guy a jerk. Remember, he even asked us to make it quick and painless."

"Sure—till I told him that'd be extra."

"Being on a budget doesn't make you a jerk either. She had no money, there was no real insurance on her to speak of: all he wanted was his sanity back. We didn't even leave him enough to try again."

Change tack. "Well, what was wrong with Wo Fat? *He* had it coming."

"Sure, he deserved to get stung. I *ruined* him. Not because he ripped off immigrants. Because he offended me. Because he treated me exactly the way his culture had raised and trained him to treat women. The way I encouraged him to treat me, to set up the gaff. What I was trying to do was sting his whole sexist society."

"So?"

"So I forgot it's half women."

Paul was lost. "Okay, so maybe you've slipped into a couple of grey areas, lately—"

Water had continued to leak, silently and slowly,

from her clear eyes. Now she began to cry: different thing. "I've even got you doing it lately."

"*Huh?*"

"It really was brilliant, honey. I never wrote a better scam in my life. But tell me: just what did your Wally and Moira do to deserve to lose ninety-eight large that wasn't even theirs?"

For the second time he waved his arms. "Are you nuts? They're true believers. Sci fi fans, for God's sake."

"Those are lapses of taste, not lapses of morality. And you didn't just take their money. You also took their friends' money, entrusted to them. Right now their universe is forever fucked because they wanted John Lennon alive and the Beatles back. Accept that criterion and we can sting anybody over thirty, and anybody younger than that with taste."

He got a grip, and patiently began to explain to her why she was wrong. Assembling his arguments, he discovered she was right.

The only trouble with owning an unusually acute and flexible mind (aside from the loneliness) is that you can't make it blind or stupid when you need to. Paul Throtmanian shifted gears instantly for a living. Against his will, his universe now precessed about two degrees, and clicked into a new alignment, for the second time in as many minutes. He tried desperately to put it back the way it had been, but it wouldn't go. He had been stunned and shocked, now he was horrified: different thing.

"My God," he breathed. "We *have* been slipping. You're right. We've been acting like . . . like executives, or muggers or something. Robbing anybody who comes along." He shook his head, in awe as much as horror. "Haven't we?"

Her crying escalated to sobbing. "I never got to work it out with her. She died ashamed of me. It has to stop."

He had *never* seen her sob, not even when that mark in Calgary had broken her finger. After stunned, shocked and horrified comes terrified. "Okay," he cried, and threw himself on his knees to embrace her. "Okay," he kept saying, over and over. "Okay, it stops now."

He didn't mean it yet. But he already knew he would, eventually.

After they had been silent and still for awhile, he suddenly began to giggle. She pulled away and searched his face, more than glad for something to laugh about. "What?"

"J-just one thing b-bothers me—"

All of a sudden she got it, and began to giggle herself. "The time traveler—"

He nodded. "If he gets us—"

"—we'll forget we ever made this decision!"

They howled.

Later, as he helped her to her feet, she gripped his shoulder. "So we won't let him get us. Right?"

"Well, now that we've finally got a good reason . . ." He stopped smiling, then, and put his hand over hers. "We won't let him get us."

"I love you," she said.

He squeezed her hand tightly. "And so well."

As they cleared the doorway, his feet began to hurt again.

Chapter 11
The Immortal Storm

"Excuse me, ma'am," Wally said. "I'm sorry to bother you a second time, but I intend to break and enter Ms. Bernardo's home shortly, and I was wondering if you could help me."

He held his breath, poised like a cat to spring to safety, while she blinked blearily at him.

In America it might not have worked. But Canadians could still afford a romantic view of crime. "Why, yesh," she said finally. "I believe I could be of shome asshistance."

He had to wonder why she had failed to slur the last two sibilants. For that matter, why hadn't she shooshed last night, when she'd been just as drunk? "Thank you, Mrs. Live Here. That's very kind of you."

He still did not relax. He was not poised to escape an adverse reaction, but to dodge any more attempted bourbon kisses. Moira had agreed with him that this audacious approach, long shot though it might be, was the only possible way to burgle a home on Point Grey Road, but she had been extremely emphatic on precisely how far he was and was not authorized to go in securing assistance. If her sensitive nose detected a single

171

molecule of bourbon—or worse, soap—anywhere above his collar or below his belt when he got home tonight . . . well, he wouldn't be able to *go* home, no matter what he found out at the Bernardo house.

"Why do you call me that?"

He slapped his forehead. Clumsy start. "I'm sorry. I have this . . . well, odd sense of humor. When I asked your name last night, you said, 'Never mind, I live here,' so I'm afraid ever since, I've been thinking of you as 'Mrs. Live Here' in my head."

She pursed her lips and blinked some more. "All thingsh considered, that'll do. But it's *Ms.* Live Here. Call me Liv for short."

"Ah." Oh God, don't let that mean she's single. "Well, Liv, is there any particular method of entry you would recommend? I'd prefer to keep this as discreet as possible. Actually, I'd like it if no one ever finds out I was in there; frankly, we're sort of hoping to come up on Ms. Bernardo's blind side. If you should know anything about the nature of her alarm system, for instance—"

"I only know one thing about it," she said, blinking, "but it's a pip. There ishn't one."

Wally blinked back at her. "Bless my soul. Really?"

"She told me once it was ludicroush to spend a penny on shecurity on Point Grey Road. She said she had no alarm, never locked her windowsh, and, for icing on the cake, as she put it, she always left the back door shlightly ajar."

"You know," Wally said slowly, "that makes a kind of sense. You see an open door, unlocked windows, you assume someone's inside."

She nodded so savagely she nearly unbalanced.

"Damn right it make shense! Spesh'ly here. There hashn't been an *attempted* break-in on thish shtreet in . . . well, shince I've been here. Early this century. And do you think my fucking inshurance comp'ny'll let *me* do the same goddam thing? Bugger, they will! That'sh why I'm gon' help you: I wanna see *her* 'shurance comp'ny get what they desherve for being so shenshible and decent."

His brain kept trying to find the pattern in her intermittent slur; it was giving him a headache. She seemed most successful with sibilants spelled with a c. Could her tongue *spell?* "Of course. So you think it would be safe for me to just . . . pop next door, go round back, and try the door?"

"Long ash you don't look furtive," she said. "That'll get you shot anywheres around here."

"Oh, I won't," he assured her.

"You're poor," she said suddenly, as if challenging him to disagree.

"That's right," he said.

She snorted, fruitily, like a small horse. "You poor guys alwaysh got more intreshsting minds than the kind o' jerksh I gotta hang out with. Why'sh that, you think?"

"We need to," Wally explained.

She nodded as thoughtfully as if provisionally accepting his solution to Fermat's Last Theorem. "That soundsh right. Anybody on thish block wanted a break an' enner done, they'd hire it done. Too damn rich to be intereshsting."

He wanted, badly, to ask her how she had conceived the notion of both slurring and not slurring the sibilant in "interesting," and whether it required practice or had come easily to her—but he knew it would constitute a digression, and in any case, artists are seldom able to explain their methods satisfactorily to the layman. "It hardly seems like break and enter if I don't have to break anything, does it?"

She smiled her feral smile, tightening her face so much that for a moment he feared her eyeballs would pop out. "Far'sh I'm consherned, you can exshplore that ashpect of your artishtic vision once you're inshide. I promish not to hear a thing. And the old Chink on the other shide's deaf as a boot. Wing Wang Wong, or whatever her name ish."

Now she was slurring c's—and even an x! "I really appreciate your help," he said. He was already backing away as he began the second syllable, out of the sheltered doorway and into the rain. This proved to be nice timing: her aborted lunge was unmistakable. "Goodbye, Liv, and thank you."

"Good luck, Handsome."

Wally had last been called handsome by a woman not Moira while auditioning for a part in a fannish play that was to have been performed at a small regional relaxacon, some eighteen years before—and he had not gotten the part. "Cuddly" he could aspire to; "handsome" exceeded even his fantasies. Nevertheless he was within ten steps of Carla Bernardo's back door before he next remembered to be terrified again. There was something to be said for drunken myopia—and nymphomania, too, if it came to that.

His pulse quickened when he saw that the door was not, as advertised, actually ajar. Liv Here might—in fact, almost certainly did—suffer from that condition Moira called rectofossal ambiguity. ("Fossa" being Latin for "a hole in the ground.") If he tried that door . . . was he going to trigger the alarm system Liv had assured him didn't exist, and end up with his own rectum in a torsa ("sling")?

Did he have any choice?

The door opened at his touch like a nymphomaniac's legs, easily, thoroughly, and silently.

Wally stood there before the open door, absolutely motionless, in drizzling rain, for a full five minutes. He told himself he was listening, but the rain and his pulse would have drowned out anything short of a pistol being cocked next to his head. It took him nearly the whole first minute to realize that there was a radio playing in the house, a talkjock whose topic tonight seemed to be the old Canadian standby, "America: Threat or Menace?" If Wally had merely been a junkie with his whole body screaming for a fix, he'd have left. Only one thing finally had the power to drive him inside: the vision of Moira's face when he reported back. He found that he wanted, very badly, to hear her say, "My hero!" so that he could say, "Aw, shucks."

Once in the house, however, he simply doffed his rain gear and got to work. He lost some time and some shin skin to his reluctance to turn on any lights—successfully establishing by way of consolation, however, that anyone else in the building was dead or deaf, and that a human heart can't actually explode. He also managed to silence the talkjock, at least locally. But once he penetrated to rooms with no exterior windows, where he felt safe turning lights on, things picked up quickly. Not only did he locate the computer in the second room he tried, and not only was it a make and model and operating system he was reasonably comfortable with, its security encryption program yielded to him even more sluttishly than the door had.

As he had guessed, "Carla Bernardo" had characteristically been a hair too cute for her own good: the password that cracked her shields was "Tammy Lynn." It was an obvious choice, if you had some experience at what hackers and crackers called "social engineering"—and if you realized "Carla" had made up her name by reverse-combining those of the notorious, recently sentenced Canadian monsters Paul Bernardo and Karla Homolka. The first of the young girls they had raped and murdered together— a few weeks before their wedding—was Karla's fifteen-year-old sister Tammy.

Wally didn't even bother to read a thing: just fired up the modem and uploaded everything he could decrypt to one of his own hard drives back home. It came to something over fifty megabytes. Then he scanned the stuff which had not been encrypted, and uploaded some of those files to a separate folder at home. He could see Moira smiling, in his mind's eye, and grinned back at the screen.

When he was satisfied he had every byte he could locate and wanted, he reformatted Carla's whole hard drive three times—wiping it irrecoverably—and entertained himself as it churned by thumbing through the Japanese pornographic comic book collection he found in a drawer. She had some better ones than he and Moira did.

Finally the computer chirped for the third time and drew him back from a particularly absorbing *manga*. He nearly left, then, but things had gone so well thus far, he was in the mood for a little adventure. So he searched Carla's office, finding nothing of lasting interest, and then her bathroom, learning only that she was not a natural blonde, and then her bedroom, where he found behind the false back of a bottom dresser drawer a lockbox whose combination was the same as her computer password. Its contents caused Wally to leap to his feet and dance the Monkey, for the first time in twenty years. A little work before a full-length mirror distributed these things about his person so well that even a sharper observer than Liv might not have noticed Wally was a bit more cuddly than usual.

On his way out, he stopped by Carla's office again, stole three of the *manga*, and added them to the swag, tucking them inside his belt in the back, under his shirt.

He recovered his rain poncho and left by the back door again—leaving it ajar—and returned to the street around the opposite side of the building from the one by which he'd entered. By the time Liv saw him and began cawing, he was within twenty steps of his car. Even walking carefully so as not to spill his pornography, he was able to make a clean getaway.

Halfway home, stopped at a traffic light on Broadway, he found himself unable to suppress an impulse to beat his fists on the steering wheel and howl with animal glee. He glanced to his left and saw a pedestrian staring at him from the sidewalk. "Vancouver," he cried happily through his rain-streaked window.

The pedestrian smiled, nodded, and waved.

The light changed and the mighty hunter went home to his mate.

Who literally greeted him with open arms. And open nostrils.

"My hero!" she cried.

"Aw, shucks, ma'am." Wally knew he was grinning the uncontrolled grin, the one that made him look goofy, but he couldn't help it. He had successfully carried out his first burglary, and he had passed his sniff test, and he had just heard and spoken two of his very favorite clichés—and the best was yet to come.

Moira hugged him tightly, putting english on it. "Really, Wally, you did great. I've been going through some of what you sent, making a start, anyway, and there's—what?"

He had disengaged from the hug just far enough to silence her with an upraised finger. "Go to the meditation room," he said, "and wait for me there."

She frowned, studied him carefully, and one eyebrow lifted slightly in alarm. "Wally, that's the goofy grin. Am I gonna like this?"

"Want to see another grin just like it? Bring a hand mirror to the meditation room and wait for me there."

"Hey, where's your coat?"

"Read on," he suggested.

She sighed. "Should I put on music?"

He shook his head. "There'll be plenty. Trust me."

She looked exasperated. "That's the trouble. I do."

He went back to the car, recovered his coat, and carried it inside in his arms. He locked the door behind him and made sure the phone machine was armed before joining Moira in the meditation room. He found her there, sitting on her *zafu*, measuring her breath. She had not fetched a mirror. Again he made sure the door was sealed behind him, then dropped into tailor's seat opposite her, setting his bundle down between them. Declining to feed him any more straight-lines, she waited serenely.

He adopted his Panel Moderator voice. "Having stolen all the really *important* items—that is, the data—of which you were just about to deliver a preliminary summary that I am, I promise you, most eager to hear—I turned my attention briefly, before I took my leave, to mere material things."

She kept waiting, but her lips seemed to tighten ever so slightly.

He nodded as if she had said something. "I hear you. You're thinking: no matter how lavish or fine they may be, I don't want any of the possessions of those people in my house. I felt much the same way when I began my search. Doubtless you're wondering why I'm going around Robin Hood's barn like this, why I've got what I found bundled up in my coat. If I'd left it all where I had it stashed when I left the place, you'd have felt most of it as soon as you hugged me a minute ago, and then there might have been trouble. I thought it would be better all around if we did this here. Are you ready?"

She took one more deep breath and nodded.

He unwrapped his booty.

He let her have five seconds to absorb the basic gist of the contents, and then placed his fingers in his ears, and in a loud clear voice, provided inventory details. "The Canadian is forty-seven thousand five hundred in used nonserial fifties. The American is thirty-five thousand in new nonserial twenties. The handgun is a Glock nine millimeter, fully loaded; there was no extra ammo. The comics are great. The passports are all—" That was as far as he got.

One of several reasons Moira had been in more or less constant demand for fan theatricals over the past few decades was her scream. It might have made a Hammer Films alumnus weep with nostalgia, or won a nod from Coltrane—evoking all the stark despairing terror of a virgin accosted by the Ripper on her wedding night, yet delivered by a vocal instrument with the raw pneumatic power of a Sophie Tucker or a Mama Cass. At the previous year's Worldcon Hugo ceremonies, where she had performed for two thousand pros and fans in an immense hall, the tech crew had not found it necessary or even advisable to mike her. The effect in a small soundproof room was impressive. Even with his fingers deep in his ears and his palms cupped over them, Wally paid for his fun. He had expected to, and paid up like a man. But then he made a very bad mistake: he took his fingers out of his ears—just as she did it again.

Shortly he managed to pry his eyelids open again, but he kept on seeing paisley swirls and neon mandalas. Gradually, as in one of those tests for color-blindness, some of them resolved into Moira's face. The lips were moving. He waved and gestured to indicate the transmission was unsuccessful, but they kept moving. He closed his eyes to conserve processing power and concentrated. White noise slowly arrived from the far end of the universe, rose to the level of static—then, as with the visual data, some of it coalesced into a parody of Moira's voice.

"—*alize what this* means? *This is wonderful. This is horrible. It couldn't be better, and it couldn't be worse. Who's* writing *this mess, Wally?* What did we ever do to deserve this? Stop *grinning, dammit!*"

He hadn't realized he still was. He made it go away with a massive effort, and his hearing improved slightly. "You understand why I did this *here*?" he asked. His voice sounded to him flanged, distorted, like John Lennon in "I Am the Walrus," a comparison that irritated him.

She nodded impatiently. "Of course. Everyone on the block would be dialing 911 right now if we weren't in a soundproof room. But Jesus, Wally, the way you set it up I thought it was gonna be something *good*."

What in Finagle's name did he have to do to *please* this woman? "This isn't good? One: sitting right there on the floor is on the close order of ninety-five percent of what we got taken for; I did the math. As far as I can tell it's all real and it all spends. Two: it's enough—as of now, VanCon can happen after all, and we even got some of our own money back! Three: that means hereinafter, I can be assured that my motives in continuing to stalk these bastards are at least eighty percent pure personal vengeance; I don't know about you, but that gives me a lot of spiritual satisfaction." His hearing was improving; by now he sounded like Lennon in "Strawberry Fields." (The first half.) "And four: now we *each* have a gun, and neither can be traced to us. Tell me the downside, because I don't—oh wait, I get you. Here we are in the middle of a manhunt, and we have a convention to run again. Okay, so we give up sleeping on alternate days, instead of every third—"

She cut him off. "What would have happened if we'd gone on the Net this morning and announced exactly what had happened to us? That we got taken, and VanCon was vaporware?"

He frowned. If this was a sequitur, the connection escaped him. "Well . . . put it this way:

the only upside would have been that we'd never have heard another live filksong in our lives."

She nodded. "Total humiliation, and lifelong expulsion from the councils of fandom. Possibly even total excommunication from fandom itself. We'd have had to have plastic surgery and change all our ID to ever see another huckster room."

"And your point is . . . ?"

"Obviously that's unthinkable. But what would happen if we went on the Net right *now*, and truthfully reported events as of this minute? VanCon's still on, but here's why it almost didn't happen?"

He flinched slightly, and then made himself think about it dispassionately. If she wanted to be Socrates, he could bat around a theoretical proposition as well as Phaedrus. "Uh . . . let's see . . . still total humiliation, for sure . . . but probably no banishment. It'd be just too much fun to have us around to laugh at. Best guess, I'd say we'd be making significant progress toward living it down in—I don't know, ten years? Twelve? A couple of fannish generations, call it, before we'd ever be given anything but scutwork to do again. Long after we died, they'd still be telling neos about us. And the neos would be laughing. Except for the occasional sweet one who would pity us."

She reached out and took his hand. "Wally?" she said. His hearing was now nominal; nonetheless her voice sounded strained. "Those two jerks are still out there someplace, with new names and maybe new faces. We're looking for them, granted, but we don't even really know for certain they're still in *Canada*, much less in the Lower Mainland. They're experienced, professional vampires, and they've just learned how nice fans taste, and

perhaps you'll join me in flattering ourselves that
they are very fucking good." She had his complete
attention; Moira rarely used that word. "Answer
me this, honey: *how important is it that fandom
be warned?*"

Wally screamed. Not in the same league with
one of hers . . . but it was closer to his ears.

That postponed the first real quarrel they'd had
in months for another several minutes.

It escalated, when it finally came, to yet another
iteration of The Quarrel. Their version, that is,
of the one all couples lucky enough to have the
privilege will write together and perfect over the
years granted them: the basic chord structure over
which they would improvise The Dozens together,
every time fate lashed them into song. It was no
more interesting than any other couple's quarrel,
full of You're Always and You Never and If You'd
Just Once; its chief function was to allow them
each to say things of which they would later be
intellectually and/or emotionally ashamed—an
instinctive human response to crisis so primitive
it makes fight-or-flight look like an intelligent
advance. By now they knew where each other's
vulnerable places were, and were reasonably
confident they could take each other's best shot.
(Pity the singles and loners, who must make do
with bar fights or politics.)

As in postmodern music—indeed, postmodern art
of most kinds—communication was subordinated
to personal expression; the results were thus
unlistenable for anyone but the artists, and will
not be recorded here. When this set had had time
to seep into long-term memory storage, each
would forget most of what they had said, and

remember most of what the other had said, but they would process it differently. Wally would be deeply scarred by the very worst of her barbs—but would almost never consciously think of them again until the next jam session, and thus would take decades to deal with them. Moira, on the other hand, would replay his cruelest words over and over in her head daily for several weeks, until she had worn them smooth, then string them with the others on a secret necklace she could finger whenever it suited her to be depressed.

Fortunately for them, they both suffered from a chronic condition that might be called stupidity fatigue. Even driven by fear, frustration and shame, half an hour away from rationality was about the maximum either Wally or Moira were built to tolerate. This session followed their basic pattern: two extended solos, a spirited duet, a reprise of the theme, and then a smooth segue into their trademark ending. Wally always won the putative argument, whatever it happened to be, and then discovered his prize was a barren, blasted desert, and scrambled to apologize and surrender. This allowed her to apologize and accept his surrender, and at last they were free to return, tired but oddly refreshed, to whatever their actual problem was.

Which usually had neither changed in the slightest, nor suffered visibly from being used as an emotional dodgeball.

"Alright," he conceded finally, and swallowed a mouthful of the coffee cake she had fetched to seal the truce. "We have to warn fandom. It is our fannish duty. But do we have to do it *immediately*?"

"Let's use worst-case analysis," she suggested. "Say Jude and Carla walked from Point Grey Road down to the water, climbed into a float-plane and flew straight to—let's say, Edmonton. Okay, how long does Jude need to set up his next victims? How long did he need to set *us* up?"

He stopped a forkful short of his mouth. "Well," he said, "it must have taken him awhile to select us as targets, and research us both—"

"Worst-case scenario, I said. Assume he selected and researched multiple targets, and now he's going across the checker board: jump . . . jump . . . jump. Or maybe she does the research in advance for him. Like a celebrity surgeon: he holds out his palm, she slaps the next scalpel onto it. Whatever: once he knew he was coming after *us*, once he knew which window we'd be sitting beside, how much time did he need to take us?"

He took the bite, and chewed and swallowed it, before he was ready to say, "Half an hour to shave all over. Maybe an hour or two to buy and set up the magnesium. Then he could go as soon as it got dark enough. Oh, damn."

"We have no way to be sure we're the first fans he's hit, Wally."

"Butter me!" He spilled tea on his lap. "Ow. Oh, Moira, that's a horrid thought."

"And even if we are, he could have destroyed two more clubs already, by now. Every convention in North America with a Beatles fan on the concom is at risk, this minute."

He prodded futilely at his soggy slacks with a handful of kleenex she'd given him, and gazed morosely at the results. "Heaven help me, I think I'd actually rather be a monumental sucker, than *just another* monumental sucker." He shook his head. "Isn't that appalling?"

"Well," she said grimly, "if we are, we can at

least be the first ones who didn't fail the test of honor." She turned and looked pointedly toward the office, where the computers waited. "We can sound the alarm. Even if we have to pull our pants down to the world to do it."

For the first time he could recall, Wally didn't feel like finishing his coffee cake. He sighed, assessed the results, and sighed again. "I guess it's time to put my Asshole Principle to the test."

Some years before, he had suddenly stopped their car on a country road, gotten out and walked around it several times, shaking his head and mumbling, then slowly climbed back in and propounded to his wife the stunning new insight he had been vouchsafed: that every living human, and every one who had ever lived, was an asshole. He had challenged her to name a single exception. Jesus? Trashed a harmless currency exchange, which merely let foreigners give sacrifice to God in legal tender. Handpicked a round dozen custodians for the most important words ever spoken: every man jack of them both illiterate and too stupid to find a ghostwriter—staged the most important event in history and forgot to invite the media. What an asshole. Albert Einstein? Instigates Manhattan Project; says Oops: major asshole. John Lennon? Saw his future with utter clarity—began the last Beatles album with the whispered words, "Shoot me," wrote and recorded a prescient solo song called "I'm Scared"—then a few years later, forgot and stuck his head up again: poor asshole. Robert Heinlein had given Wally's theory the most trouble—but even the First Grandmaster of Science Fiction had disparaged marijuana, and once permitted one of his more authoritative characters to refer to homosexuals as "the poor in-betweeners."

To be sure, Heinlein had more class than any other three assholes put together, but . . .

Once Moira had accepted her husband's basic premise, that *everyone* is an asshole—and she could not dispute it; she had a fair amount of self-honesty—she'd seen the obvious corollary. The trademark of the true, dyed-in-the-wool, hopeless and irredeemable capital-A Asshole (Wally had explained) is the fixed belief that there exist some people, somewhere, who are Not Assholes. This immediately gives rise to the passionate desire to be mistaken for one of them. Wally himself—he now saw—had been wasting enormous amounts of energy, time and invention on *trying to keep anyone from suspecting that he was one of the Assholes*. "Dignity doesn't have to be a suit of armor," he had told her. "It can be as weightless and transparent as a force field." And from that day forth, both had tried to refocus their efforts—to settle for being perceived (by anyone whose opinion mattered to them) as a pair of competent and pleasant and capable assholes. Assholes with class.

And, damn it, with senses of personal honor.

Building on his anal metaphor, and punning on a joke they both knew, so ancient it was almost due to come around again, she gestured with her head toward their office and said, "Time to answer the question, 'How far is the old log-in?'"

He took one last look at his coffee cake and heaved up from his chair. "About thirteen steps away, I'd say." He helped her out of her own chair, and they each put an arm around the other as they walked those steps to the gallows.

"Let's compose it on your Mac," he said as they waited for their machines to boot. "Then we'll save it as text-only, and both upload it. Gee, there are still a few clubs that aren't online yet, too—we better fax them. Don't you have a database for them somewhere?"

"First let's just sniff the Web and make sure we aren't too late," she said. "Maybe we'll get lucky: somebody else will sing first, and we can go down as a subtitle instead of a headline." Her browser stabilized on-screen and she began a staccato composition for keyboard and mouse.

He knew she could netsurf better and faster; he left her to it, and began to triage their e-mail. First he identified the VanCon traffic, which had to be sorted into business (hotel and other subcontractors), pro (the Guests of Honor and honored guests), and fan (everybody else with a right to yank on their chain). All three folders bulged with unread posts which he was just beginning to realize he was going to have to deal with after all, now that the con was tentatively back on. But he left them all unread and pressed on. Next he culled out and filed several professional messages—related, that is, to the cottage industry by which he and Moira earned their bread: writing and distributing stable software patches for existing computer operating systems, which made them more useful for the handicapped. He was briefly tempted to stop and read one of these messages, a beta-tester's critique of a new program intended to assist one-handed typing and eliminate mousework altogether in Mac System, but restrained himself. Finally he was down to personal mail, and began to read it—for once leaving his Joke of the Day subscription for last. If there were going to be a report of a major fiscal fiasco anywhere in fandom, this was (after the Web) where it was most likely to be.

Two sentences into the third message, he turned to stone in his chair.

Even a statue can read good news, though, given enough time, and happily the text of this message was short enough to fit on Wally's over-sized screen without scrolling.

When his screen began to shimmer at the edges, he remembered to blink. He stopped when he realized he was making it strobe. "Darling?" he said faintly. "Anything?"

"Bugger all so far."

He reached out, groped, found her wrist and clamped down hard. "Have you committed us to anything yet?"

She stopped work, looked down at his hand on her wrist, then up at him. "Of course not—we said we're going to write it together, didn't we? Aren't we?"

"Maybe not."

Her eyes widened, and she gripped his hand with her other one. "Tell me."

"Take a look at this e-mail from Steve."

Sender: stevethesleeve@eworld.com
Received: from vanbc.eworld.com
(vanbc.eworld.com [204.191.160.2]) by dub-img-2.eworld.com (8.6.10/5.950515)
    id JAA08556; Tue, 2 November 1995
09:58:32 -0400
Received: by vanbc.eworld.com
    (Smail-3.1.29.1 #32) id m0uJKeR-0690WpC; Tue, 14 May 96 06:58 PDT
Message-Id: <m0uJKeR-0690WpC@vanbc.eworld.com>
From: stevethesleeve@eworld.com (Steve Tomas)

Subject: Forwarded message from Space
Case
To: moira@eworld.com (Wallace Kemp)
Date: Tue, 14 May 1996 06:58:30 -0700
(PDT)
X-Mailer: ELM [version 2.4 PL24 ME8b]
MIME-Version: 1.0
Content-Type: text/plain; charset=US-ASCII
Content-Transfer-Encoding: 7bit
Content-Length: 1291

Found this in my mailbox this morning.
Will be happy to forward any reply
you want to send.

--- Forwarded message from Space Case
(John Edw. MacDougal, III) ---

From spacecase@teleport.com Mon May 13
22:33:15 1995
Message-Id:
<999605140533.WAA05535@desiree.teleport.com>
From: spacecase@teleport.com (John Edw.
MacDougal, III)
To: stevethesleeve@eworld.com (Steve Tomas)
Subject: smooth fen
Date: Tue, 14 May 1995 05:29:51 GMT
X-Newsreader: Forte Free Agent 1.0.82

Dear Sleever:

On 31 October 1995 00:19:57, you wrote:
>If you happen to run across any new fans,
or even just
>fellow travelers, who look like they'd cast
well as

>Captain Picard, let me know ASAP. (Please route thru
>me as Wally and Moira are busy with VanCon coming up.)
>As you might imagine, close facial resemblance is not
>as important here as willingness to go bald for awhile
>--and if he's articulate, so much the better. Please
>pass the word.<

Don't know if helps, but am out here on Bowen Island, hard by your friends' meat address, and gent just walked into my store today with 3-4 days' beard -- all over head. Backs of hands, too. Not stilyagi: if had to guess, would say he bet Reform in last election. Late 20s, tall, in great shape, narrow face. IMHO, with right makeup could make wizard Picard -- and if wife he mentioned let him shave head once, might again if asked quickly enough.

Funny thing: specifically stated was NOT fan -- but quoted Lazarus Long . . . accurately. Perhaps one of those legendary poor bastards who got self de-fan-estrated for life, for some ripoff or cosmic concom blunder. Or perhaps, as he claimed, favorite English teacher once passed off Heinlein quote as own. Pleasant cobber, seemed a little dull to be fan. But note for whatever may be worth he also claimed to be hiker, and was full of shit about that. Still, get that lie all time out here . . .

Want me to ask grapevine for his 20?
Probably take <5 minutes and .5 droplet of
sweat. Please advise.

CU at VanCon; will have latest NSS updates
for our panel as promised.

-- Space Case
   Regional Rep, National Space Society

O *   *   *   *   *   *   *   ***>=======»   ∞

--- End of forwarded message from Space
Case (John Edw. MacDougal, III ---
--

--
stevethesleeve@eworld.com
stevethesleeve@eslvcr.whimsey.com (Steve
Tomas)
http://www.whimsey.com/~steve/
Key fingerprint = B9 4F BO 4U 2B +/ 2B 4Y
I8 69 4U 82 1C U8 12 6C

"He's on Bowen Island," Moira said, pounding
on a thigh (Wally's) with a fist (hers). "With his
girlfriend, enjoying the spoils of war. There's only
one or two ways on and off that island. And we
have a large war chest to hunt him down with."

"And two warm guns," Wally murmured dream-
ily, temporarily immune to physical pain. "Double
happiness." He began to sing. "Bang bang, shoot
shoot . . ."

She had to lean past him and use his keyboard
to reply to Space Case.

Chapter 12
The Lifehouse

Johnson would have found the successive days of almost relentless rain frustrating—even though waiting was his life, and his life was long—had it not freed him up to devote most of his time and attention to cheering up his dying wife Myrna. This had the side effect of cheering him considerably as well.

Their emotional state during this period is difficult to convey to a normal human; different postulates controlled. Most adults who mate know, and sometimes reflect, that they will one day see their loved one die, *if they are the lucky one of the pair*; it has been thus since before we invented language. Johnson, however, had lived several long centuries without ever truly believing in his heart that this fate could come to *him* some day. (And in that respect, at least, was like all other men— save that in his case it had not been denial, but only optimism.) The fact was emotionally wrenching—could have been devastating, if he had not regarded death as a correctable nuisance.

Myrna did, too . . . but understandably, she needed more cheering up than he did. She was the one who was probably going to have to do the dying.

And even that (maddeningly) was not certain. Her body was newly mortal, but not particularly fragile—especially for its age—and the Great Change was not impossibly far away. With luck and good management, she might very well survive, enfeebled, until the day when the long Masquerade could end, and she could have not just immortality and invulnerability and youth again, but literally anything she could conceive.

Unfortunately, luck and good management did not appear to be in inventory just at present, which was where/when they were needed. "Might not die" is admittedly better than "will certainly die"—but not a hell of a lot better, for one who has long been immortal.

So Myrna's husband did his best to cheer her.

Music was one of his favorite methods of sharing, a nonprescription mood-elevator almost as potent as sex and laughter themselves. The artistic challenge he faced was that he had been writing her love songs for some seven hundred years, during which he had been perpetually on duty but almost never busy. The subject had been picked pretty clean: believe it or not, there are a finite number of ways to say "I love you."

Happily, the dilemma itself suggested a line of attack, and by the evening of the third rainy night, he was able to take up his current guitar, borrow a sprightly tune no one was using at the moment, and sing to her:

I want to tell you how I feel, love
But it ain't exactly news
Got no secrets to reveal love
But I'm gonna say it anyway,

'cause I'm alone and you're away
I haven't got a blessed thing to lose . . .

(so here goes:)

Water ain't dry, the sky goes up high,
And a booger makes pretty poor glue
You can't herd cats, bacteria don't wear
hats
—and I love you

Sugar ain't sour, it's damp in the shower
And murder's a mean thing to do
Trees got wood, and fucking is pretty
good
—and I love you

I'm belaboring the obvious:
You will have noticed all the good times
This is as practical an exercise
As taping twenty cents to my
transmission
so that any time I want to
I can shift my pair o' dimes . . .

(but God knows:)

Goats don't vote, and iron don't float
And a hippie don't turn down boo
Dog bites man, the teacher don't
understand
—and I love you

Sickness sucks, it's nice to have bucks
And the player on first base is named
  Who

*Kids grow up, and fellows pee standing
  up
—and I love you*

*Guess I didn't need to say it
Just a message that my heart sent
And I kinda like the way it's
More redundant than is absolutely
necessary according to the Department
of Redundancy Department . . .*

(I must close:)

*Fun is nice, you can't fry ice,
And the money will always be due
Bullshit stinks, and no one outsits the
  Sphinx
—and I love you*

*Living ain't bad, and dying is sad
And little we know is true
But that's just karma—baby,
you can bet the farm on this:
I do love you.*

"I call it 'Belaboring The Obvious'—or is that redundant?" he said, after the last notes echoed away.

He had already gotten the smile he had hoped for. Once he had set down the guitar, he got the kiss, too.

Smile and kiss were both like oil of cloves on a toothache, like the warm bath of pharmaceutical morphine, melting pain for each spouse. Their telempathic connection caused this analgesic energy to oscillate back and forth between them like alternating current, reinforcing itself, and generating a third, resultant field that acted to stabilize both. Their vibrant love had been the sole constant in a millenium of slow tedious change; they knew well that it was stronger than death, and that they differed from all the other lovers alive only in that they could explain why. Johnson, a scholar of his wife's body language, decoded runes in their hug which indicated that while this was not yet the right time to proffer an erection, a fellow who was patient and played his cards right might not die of waiting. Every songwriter loves applause, however promissory.

As they disengaged, he caught himself reaching for a cigarette. He was not addicted to nicotine, of course—he and Myrna could self-generate any desired drug effect they wished—but his cover persona appeared to be, drawing smoke deep into his lungs in public without ever actually meta-bolizing a molecule of it. And he was meticulous enough about tradecraft that he had formed the policy of smoking even when in private, sometimes, so his home would smell right to the rare visitor. It was that (true) habit which had caused his hand to start toward his breast pocket.

What stopped it was the realization that his mate no longer had the power to decide which of the molecules she inhaled might have her leave to remain, and which must depart.

Well, irrational antitobacco hysteria was currently epidemic in this ficton anyway, part of the general paranoia inevitable in a large complex society of innumerates and scientific illiterates. It would actually be good for his cover to quit smoking, at this juncture in history, make his persona even less interesting. And their home less musty—not that either ever smelled anything they didn't choose to. He mentally accessed the housekeeping nanobots' controller, and added cigarettes and related materials to the list of objects defined as "trash," to be disassembled for parts the next time it was convenient.

—and was surprised to feel a pang, almost as sharp as an addict might have felt. The small change in habit was his first overt acceptance of the great change that had come into their lives, his first tacit admission that he was helpless to cure, and must endure, this thing.

Myrna caught all this, of course, and instantly took over as morale officer. "Honey," she said, referencing a book they had both enjoyed, "let's go and look at the kids."

He hesitated a fraction of a second. Was it appropriate to comfort a dying woman by taking her to visit one of the world's great mausolea? But he knew her intuition was superior to his own. "Sure."

The Lifehouse lay less than half a kilometer from their home. They walked the distance, as humans would (under an umbrella Myrna would actually have needed if she'd been alone), not just for the sake of their cover, but simply because they wanted to walk in the forest in the rain together. It was always best, they had found, to approach the Lifehouse slowly, and with humility.

The rain had dwindled for a time to a barely visible mist, that did not so much fall as roil. This should have been frustrating—for if it would only clear up that last little bit, even for a few minutes, they could inscribe their quartz beacon with a requested delivery date of *now*, stomp it into the mud, and receive an instant response from the future.

But one of the first principles of Waiting is that there is no such thing as *almost done*. The rain would stop when it stopped; very sensitive detectors would alert them the instant that occurred; meanwhile downpour or mist were the same.

The damp forest was full of trapped ozone; they allowed it to mildly exhilarate them. Everything had that strange muted vividness that comes of poor light passed through a billion tiny prisms. The rain-sound that had been blanketing the high frequencies like a treble filter was suspended now; viridescent trees still dripped their accumulated moisture, but those sounds arrived with crystal clarity. So did a rich stew of smells. The rain forest ecology could be *felt* going about its business all around them, industriously making hay while the sun didn't shine.

And so, hand in hand beneath their umbrella, mud sucking shamelessly at their boots, the scent of sweet rot in their nostrils, they came to the place where the mook Angel Gerhardt had recently tried to bury two ounces of something laced with cocaine.

They perceived that the repairs they had made to the site were holding up. The great elm was vertical once more, the bank on which it stood rebuilt to a convincing naturalness. They stepped up detector range and sensitivity to the maximum, satisfied themselves that the most intelligent life-form besides themselves within a kilometer was a bull raccoon—and, this time, that there were no electronic devices save their own functioning anywhere within the same range. Then Johnson gestured, and a yonic tunnel gaped in the side of the bank with a lewd wet sound, opening like a man-sized mud sphincter to reveal the stainless surface of—

—the Lifehouse.

Their Lifehouse.

Their child, in a sense. Many children and children's children, in another. In yet another— just as valid—merely a highly evolved descendant of a hard disk, packed with a great many zeros and ones.

It was a crystalline sphere two meters in diameter, externally identical to the Eggs used to travel back through time, but it had never carried a living passenger—in that direction. Now, after a millennium of creeping *forward* through time again in the only way possible—like everything else, at the rate of one second per second—it held millions of passengers . . . albeit only potentially living, at present.

This particular Egg, like all the other Lifehouses on earth, was packed absolutely full of the most dense and stable information storage medium permitted by the laws of physics. Its capacity was most meaningfully expressed not in giga-, tera-, peta-, exa-, or even zettabytes, but in yottabytes, or sextillions of bytes. It could hold a *lot* of yottabytes—so securely that the society which designed it had actually abandoned, presumably forever, the concept of data backup.

Paradoxically, this sphere of ultrastable memory visually resembled nothing so much as a translucent model of Jupiter: a slow, majestically churning globe of chaotic milky fluids, that appeared dimly lit from within, as if for the convenience of the student.

Suspended in those roiling fluids, as incorruptible patterns of data, were virtually all the

human beings who had died in the Pacific Northwest since the dawn of time.

There in the Lifehouse, if all went well, they
would wait safely, in something very like the
Christian concept of Limbo . . . until the day
came when their descendants were ready to grow
them new bodies and resurrect them to life
eternal.

And if, through Myrna's and Johnson's failures
as guardians, that day should never come . . .

Well, the dead would never know they had died
a second time, at least.

Was there any consolation in that? Or not?

Myrna had always loved to visit the Lifehouse,
always wished they dared do so more often. It did
not put out any trace of any field that any
instrument could detect . . . but it always seemed
to. Whenever she felt overwhelmed by that profound melancholy which sooner or later must come
to any immortal, who watches everything around
her dying in pain and needless terror, she would
come to the Lifehouse and put her hand on its
cool surface and feel better. This was part of the
antidote to Death. A monument to monkey defi-
ance of entropy, to the stubborn, eternal refusal
of the human spirit to surrender to fate.

She had wondered if it would feel any different,
any less comforting to be here, now that she knew
in her guts she might well end up in that glowing
milky swirl herself one day. She found that it did
not. Mentally she compared the Lifehouse to every
popular human conception of afterlife, including
utter nothingness, and found it a reasonably
congenial place to be dead for a few decades. No
hymns to memorize, no harp lessons. No hellfire.

No petulant paranoid demanding hosannas. No houris forcing figs and camel milk on you. No grinning Krishna with a rampant erection. No Great Wheel, no Eightfold Path. Absolutely no sensation of the passage of time at all, by all reports. Simple suspended awareness, like a paused CD.

She found herself picturing the way it would probably be.

One silly thing or another would kill her. Whatever the proximate cause, her heart would cease to beat, and decline to restart. Blood pressure would fall to zero, along with cranial oxygen supply. Brain temperature would begin to drop. At some point, an indetectably tiny but quite sophisticated nanocomputer in her medial forebrain bundle—precisely like the one to be found in the brain of every living human being older than minus eight months—would conclude that she was a goner.

And, as with everyone else who had ever died, her whole life would pass before her eyes . . . as a high-speed data dump.

Forewarned, and used to thinking at computer rates when necessary, she would probably be one of a bare handful who had ever been in a position to fully appreciate that particular show—and hers would last considerably longer than was customary. Even at the ferocious speeds that would be employed, and even though she had been in the habit of making regular deposits in the Lifehouse's memory bank every century or so, it would take nearly five whole seconds of realtime to squirt a perfect copy of her *self* from her played-out body— wherever it happened to die—to the indetectable satellite that was always in the sky, and another ten seconds for the satellite to perform integrity tests and relay-bounce her back down to . . . *here*, to this very Lifehouse.

Where she would remain in stasis, in the form of Read-Only Memory, along with all the other dead. Until the time—subjectively, only an instant after her death—when she would come to awareness again, to find herself floating down a long tunnel diode, toward a bright light . . . being greeted by departed relatives and loved ones . . . being welcomed (in her case, back) into The Mind, the telepathic family of nearly all the humans who had ever lived . . .

It didn't sound that bad, actually.

Oh, the dying part itself would doubtless be unpleasant. But she had known unpleasantness before, in her near-millenium of stewardship. And it would probably be the *last* unpleasantness she would ever know. In effect, she would be trading some moments or days or weeks of pain for the privilege of fast-forwarding through some history that was becoming increasingly oppressive: the final darkness before the dawn of the Great Change. It might almost be worth dying, to miss the rest of the Nineties—let alone the decades that would follow.

But poor Johnson would be so lonely in the meantime!

"I keep wishing we could just talk to them," she said aloud.

"To Paul and June, you mean?"

"Yes. If we could just *explain* to them . . . bring them here, show them this, explain the stakes . . . perhaps they'd submit voluntarily to editing. You never know."

In her mind she constructed the argument.

Elsewhere in this country, right now, a man is learning to decipher the information storage code of the human brain. Before long he will know how to erase memories . . . and shortly after that, how to read and write them. In time he will have technologically assisted telepathy. By great good fortune he will be an ethical man: he will exercise the resulting power to conquer the world undetected—but only long enough to successfully give away his secret to everyone, everywhere, at once. Soon thereafter, inevitably, nearly all men will be telepathic, and nontelepathic man will join Neanderthal. The Mind will form: several billion brains, all equal, all forever free, all able to transcend solitude and death and pain and the need to sleep, working together without friction or language barrier. Soon, inevitably, they will understand the universe well enough to travel backward through time. Soon, inevitably, they will realize that almost as many brains' worth of memories as the Mind began with were trashed unnecessarily before it formed—and they will decide to conquer death retroactively. They will come back and make pickup on all their fallen comrades who will consent to live again in a different way. They will tailor a nanovirus that makes backup copies of human beings, and stores them in Lifehouses until there is a Mind to restart them, and they will release it ten thousand years ago. And the very hardest and most necessary part of the whole project will be concealing that knowledge from terrified ancestors, who needlessly believe themselves doomed to extinction.

Johnson knew her thought. He did not even bother to disagree. They both knew it was wishful thinking. Though they had never physically met either Paul or June, they knew both of them very well: they knew June at least as well as she knew herself, and knew Paul a little better than she knew him. Each human had the kind of fiercely independent, paranoid temperament that would find The Mind—the author and point of all this—a thing of horror. Both believed deep down that identity was a thing made of borders and limits; both would flatly refuse to believe that an ego could blend with any other without losing its integrity. To them, a self-cherishing telepathic species-wide family would seem an ant-like hive mentality: inhuman rather than superhuman. If they were apprised of all the facts, and given a simple choice—forget this ever happened, and wake one day to life eternal in the company of everyone you ever loved, liked or respected . . . or sound the alarm, and vanish forever along with the whole universe—well, humans could never be perfectly predicted, but the strong probability was they would proudly choose the latter.

When and if they were tracked down, they would have to be mind-raped: both were incapable of surrender. The irony was biting.

As Myrna and Johnson stood there in silence, contemplating the Lifehouse together, souls of the recently deceased rained down invisibly from the sky at random intervals, striking the receiver at the peak of the elm and racing down the heart of its trunk to the Egg beneath. Each time this occurred, a short report was generated and squirted to a database in the attic of their caretaker's cottage, a process designed to come to their conscious attention only in the astronomically rare event that the report read "file could not be written and was skipped." Idly, now, perhaps feeling that it would bring her into a slightly more intimate contact with the whole ongoing process to which she'd dedicated her life, Myrna tuned a fragment of her mind to that "channel," and monitored the names and vital statistics of the incoming new dead.

Just as one byte in particular tried to claim her attention, an alarm went off. Think of the alarm clock you've hated worst in your life, surgically implanted in your skull. Even as she and Johnson flinched, their hearts leapt with joy and relief.

The humidity had finally fallen below the critical value.

Johnson whirled and gestured toward home. The chunk of coruscating quartz crystal arrived in less than a second, decelerating smoothly to a dead stop in midair at a point precisely equidistant from them both. Their eyes met around it. Together they mentally inscribed it with the tick that described this particular instant of sidereal time. Johnson gestured again, and the crystal slammed down into the earth and buried itself deep.

At once, both began to back away from the spot.

The air became electric. A prickly scent, like toasting basil and cinnamon, came from everywhere. A faint, high, vaguely metallic sound converged slowly from all directions at once. Local temperature rose. Tendrils of steam rose from the damp grass. The sound swelled and contracted, like an explosion played backwards—

At the last moment, Myrna remembered to avert her eyes.

CRACK!

"Oh, shit," Johnson said.

She opened her eyes again. An Egg sat on the earth, directly above the spot where the quartz beacon had buried itself.

"Oh, shit," she agreed.

They had *not*, in their wildest dreams, expected to see two actual, corporate passengers in that Egg. A person could exist only once in any given ficton. But they had hoped—hoped *hard*—to see a chunk of quartz very like the one they had used to summon the Egg here/now: a memory-crystal containing the best advice of the future June Bellamy and Paul Throtmanian on how to track and capture their past selves.

What had arrived instead both looked and was considerably less impressive.

"Well," Johnson said philosophically, "like they told us back in training, the operative syllable in 'Anachrognosis' is the next-to-last one. Can't fight a big paradox with a little one. We should have known The Mind would turn us down."

Myrna said nothing.

"Look on the bright side," he said. "The situation just improved: from 'hopeless' to 'outcome uncertain.'"

"Yes," she said softly. "That is good news."

"We're going to get to repair our own mistake after all."

She noticed, just at that moment, that her neck hurt, and automatically tried to fix it herself so she wouldn't have to ask Johnson for a rub. And failed. For the first time in her long life . . . and not the last. "It's purely a coincidence those things usually home on shit," she said, suppressing a wince.

"Well," he said, apparently deciding that sardonic humor was better than none at all, "at least nobody can say we don't give a fucking fly."

The humor was metaphorical, of course. The thing that hovered in the center of the new Egg—

its sole contents, save for air—was not in fact a housefly. It just looked and acted precisely like one.

Externally, at least. But not superficially. If, somehow, it had fallen into the hands of a drosophilist, he might have needed several days of study to notice there was something distinctly odd about that particular specimen. He would probably never have identified the weaponry, would certainly never have located either the detection gear or the onboard computer, and could not have comprehended the power source if it had been explained to him. His best guess at its top speed would have been short by at least an order of magnitude or two.

For a climate so kind that even in November a single passing fly would elicit only mildest surprise, it was the perfect tracking device. The ultimate snitch: in cop slang, a shoo-fly. Or perhaps "gumshoe-fly" was more accurate.

If time travelers had the luxury of being allowed to alter the historical date of anyone's death, it might also have made a perfect Terminator. It was quite capable of saying "No problemo" in a German accent if the need should arise . . . and could not be stopped or destroyed by anything currently living or manmade. But while it would fight like a wolverine to avoid capture, it could not kill any life-form as advanced as another fly, even to save itself.

Given enough time, however, it could *locate* any life-form whose DNA parameters it knew, anywhere on earth or in its atmosphere, clear out to Low Earth Orbit.

It already had DNA and gross physical descriptions of June and Paul in memory. It could identify their skeletal profiles under any conceivable disguise, their retinal patterns through even opaque contacts, their fingerprints on a car door handle from treetop height. It knew every pheromone or sebaceous volatile their bodies were capable of emitting, far more intimately than the lovers themselves did, and could positively identify them in concentrations of less than one part per octillion. Like a Bussard ramjet, its high speed made it an excellent molecule collector. If either grifter were presently in Vancouver, it would have them pinpointed in less than a day. If they were within the Lower Mainland area, two days, or three at the outside. Perhaps a week, if they were somewhere in China. Worst case—say, a nominally airtight enclosure buried deep on the other side of the planet, with sophisticated countermeasures— call it ten days.

The question was: did Myrna and Johnson have as much as a whole day left, before some form of all Hell broke loose?

" 'Said the flea, "let us fly!" Said the fly, "let us flee!" . . .' " Myrna recited.

" . . . 'So they flew through a flaw in the flue,' " Johnson said, giving the tagline of the ancient limerick. It so happened that he had written it. "This fly won't leave a flaw in the flue, Flo. Slim Gaillard would have called it a 'flatfoot floozie with the floy-floy.' "

She wasn't really in the mood for word games— her neck was quite stiff, now—but he was trying his best. "Reet," she agreed. "Let's turn it loose-a-rootie."

He heard the subtext in her voice, dropped the banter, gestured sharply at the Egg. It promptly ceased to exist, utterly and forever. The Superfly, without so much as pausing to dip its wings in salute, took off like a silent bullet, reappeared briefly above the nearby spot where Angel Gerhardt's coke-laced baby laxative lay buried for all time, and departed in a northerly direction at just under Mach One.

They stood there in silence together for a minute or two, looking deep into each other's eyes. She found the strength for one last effort. "Well," she said, "the fly is cast."

He winced obligingly. "Very dry."

And of course, just then it began to rain again, wringing genuine giggles from both of them.

"Come on," he said, taking up the umbrella and putting an arm around her. "Let's go home. You look like you could use a neck rub."

She put her head on his shoulder, her own arm around him, and squeezed *hard*.

In the distance a faint false thunder was heard, as the trackfly exceeded the speed of sound. . . .

Chapter 13
The Shithouse

It was such a brief and such a kindly note, to have generated so much adrenaline:

> *Dear Mr and Mrs Dortmunder*
> *somebodys askin around the island tryin to find you two without you knowin. I didnt say nothin but they will find you sure by tomorrow or the next day. You seem like a nice young couple. I thought youd want to know.*
> *Regards,*
> *Maurice Lycott*

June always took a secret special pleasure in blowing her lover's mind. So few people could manage it. Even she, who could blow just about anybody's mind, usually had to work at it with Paul. The look on his face now, the color in his forehead, the little squeak in his voice as he said, "You want to *what*?" were enough to calm her down, and almost enough to cheer her up.

"Call Wally and Moira," she repeated.

He made three successive sounds, two moist and one dry, none of which graduated to the status of a proper syllable.

"You said it yourself: they've got the kind of minds that can think about time travel without boggling. For sure they've been thinking about it longer than we have—and reading the thoughts of better minds than their own, too. The more I think about this, the more my head hurts. You need a getaway: you call in a wheelman. You need something moved: you hire muscle. Right now, we need a time travel specialist in the string, *fast*. Two would be even better."

He closed his eyes, sighed, and opened them again. He began quietly, but built to a crescendo by the end of his question. "And you don't suppose the fact that both those airheads are presently consumed by a *passionate* desire to examine my giblets with rusty fucking *tongs* might present a few *trivial fucking obstacles*?"

She ignored his anger: it was not really directed at her. "You tell me—you know them better. Which would a true-blue science fiction fan rather do, in his or her heart of hearts? Avenge a sting— or meet a no-shit time traveler?"

"No *way* they're going to believe me a second time—"

"Way," she said, knowing he hated that particular neologism. "They're not stupid, you said. You *steam-cleaned* them, Paul, down to the last peso. They're wigless, gigless and cigless now. You know it, and they know you know it. The only possible motive you could have for coming back on them again with the same tale is if it's the truth this time."

"That's not—"

"That Kornbluth guy—was he a big name in sci fi?"

"One of the very very best. So what?"

"How much do you want to bet Wally or Moira once read the same story you did?"

He frowned and squinted ferociously, as at a sudden blinding light.

"Think about it, Paul. Everything I know about time travel, and half of what you know, we got from the movies and TV. They're lousy sources of information about *real* science, for God's sake. You want to blow this, through some equivalent of expecting to hear sounds in vacuum, or thinking cars blow up in real life?"

He gestured, like a beggar seeking alms. Shylock, crying, "My daughter! My ducats!" could not have sounded more conflicted. "But June—*ask a mark for help*? It's . . . it's not *decent*."

She shared his pain, but pressed on. "You don't like that argument? Here's one you're gonna love: it goes right to the root of your favorite root. So far we *think* we've worked up a few field tactics useful for defending ourselves against this guy's mind-ray—maybe—for as long as a pair of AA batteries hold out—maybe long enough to slip in under his radar. All to the good. But wouldn't you like to have a way to *threaten* the bastard?"

His frown eased slightly. "With what?"

"Look, we know he's afraid of exposure. Maybe even more than we are: we could go to jail, he could go to Never-Never Land. That in itself doesn't give us a whole lot of leverage, though . . . because ninety-nine people out of a hundred, we could tell them everything we know, in detail, with a straight face and corroborating exhibits, and all they'd do is call the men with the thorazine. *But suppose we convinced a science fiction fan, who's wired into the Internet?*"

Paul's frown released altogether; so did all his

facial muscles. "Oh, my," he said softly. "Oh la." He pulled his jaw back up, and shaped it into a grin. "Oh angel, I *like* it. That might be just about the only thing we could possibly do that would scare the living shit out of the son of a bitch. Will you marry me?"

"No."

His grin faltered. "Huh? Why not?"

"Paul, don't ask me that now, okay?"

Back to a frown. "I think it constitutes what I'd call a valid point of order," he said. "I may have been smiling, but it wasn't a joke question."

"I know."

Hurt twisted his features. "So?"

"I gave up on marriage a long time before I met you: it just isn't in the cards for me, alright? Please, baby, can't we just go on living in sin and get this fucking zombie off our backs and then see what happens?"

He turned on his heel and walked away.

"Paul?"

He reached the telephone's base unit and thumbed the intercom; a loud repetitive whoop in the next room announced the location of the wandering handset.

"Aw, come on—Paul?"

He retrieved the phone, punched keys. "Yes, in Vancouver, operator, I'd like a residential listing for a Wallace Kemp, that's kay ee em pee, on West 12th, please?"

"Paul—"

He held up a hand. As the digits were read to him, he punched them into the phone. When he had them all, he hung up, poked redial and returned the thing to his ear. "Ringing," he said.

"Paul, damn it to hell—"

He held his hand higher and turned his face away slightly.

They waited, alone, together.

After what seemed like an eternity, he disconnected. "Answering machine. They stayed in Toronto. Oh *damn*."

"Paul—"

"They *gave* me their fucking number there— and of course I burned it the minute I got home. Oh—" He began his swearing litany. It was different every time, and she had once heard him continue it for three solid sulphurous minutes before he slipped, and repeated an obscenity. Another time, the victim—a grown man—had fainted dead away, midway into the second minute. It was going to be impossible to interrupt him now until he had finished wringing the English language dry of its power to express his frustration.

She gave up and left the room, to attack the same task from a feminine perspective. Somewhere she couldn't be interrupted either, with a door that locked, and lots and lots of kleenex.

But of course she was wrong. One simple knock at the front door, and she and Paul were both as interrupted as they could be.

"Look," Paul said wearily, when they had all seated themselves, "the sooner you put those silly things away, the less chance you'll end up using them as suppositories."

"You're probably right," Wally agreed. "But I'm feeling reckless." His gun-hand looked dismayingly steady.

"It's not necessary, you know," June said. "We were just trying to call you when you showed up, only we lost your Toronto number."

Wally looked at her for a long moment. "That is such a preposterous assertion, I think I almost believe it." He glanced to Moira.

She shrugged. "My experience is that the really ridiculous is usually true. But I'm not losing the gun."

Her husband nodded, and turned back to June. "Why were you going to call us? You don't look like gloaters. You *know* you tapped us out. Oh, wait, I get it—you must have found out somehow that we hit your other place on Point Grey Road. What, you were going to ask us to give you *your* money back?"

June groaned. Another perfectly good address and identity, blown for good. Not to mention another large cash-stash gone. "You know," she said to her own partner, "I've had better weeks. Lots of 'em."

"Tell me about it."

"Our own has been excessively eventful," Moira pointed out.

"Let me take this," June said.

"Of course," Paul agreed.

There was no more than that to the exchange: half a dozen banal words, absolutely no ironic vocal undertones or pained expressions. But June clearly saw Moira grasp that she and Paul were presently in the middle of a quarrel. From this she inferred that Moira was no fool, and reconsidered her opening.

"Wallace, Moira, my name is June Bellamy, and this is Paul Throtmanian. I can't think of any reason why you should believe those are our real names, because I'm as good a professional liar as he is. But you have to call us something. It's a place to start."

"Call me Wally, June," Wally said.

She felt relief. She did *not* want to address herself principally to Moira, to seem to be trying the lame *let's us girls work this out while the boys hold weapons on each other* ploy. "Thank you, Wally. As I said, Paul and I were discussing phoning you and Moira. Not because you have brains—we have brains—but because you both have a particular *kind* of brains. And I think you've proven that, by tracking us. Frankly, I don't know how you pulled it off—and please don't think I'm asking how you found us: I haven't earned the right. But we have a problem we need your kind of brains to solve, and I'd like to explain it to you."

"Pardon me," Wally said, "but I want to get this straight. We're holding guns on you, and you're trying to *hire* us?"

"Basically," she agreed.

He nodded. "I'm beginning to like you, June. Proceed."

She carefully did not smile. "Thank you, Wally. Since you say you got as far as the Bernardo house, I assume you must know what happened to Paul's Metkiewicz place." She glanced to Moira for confirmation, got back nothing, glanced away. "From that and our hasty departure for here, you must have deduced that someone else is after us. Someone we are very respectful of."

"And you want to hire us as consultant hackers," Wally said. "Oh, this is lovely."

"Would you like to hear our minimum fee?" Moira inquired.

June turned back to her. "Please, let me define the job correctly first. It may not involve any hacking as such, for instance. What we really need is your expertise as science fiction fans." She saw

Moira begin to frown. "Please," she said quickly, holding up a hand, "I *know* that sounds like exactly the same sort of grifter technique my partner used on you: tell the mark what she wants to hear. Unfortunately, it happens to be the truth. Paul and I need a fan, badly. All I have to overcome your reasonable suspicion is logic. If you're really who we need, you'll see that logic. Will you listen?"

She was quietly elated when Moira shared a glance with her husband before saying, "Yes."

"Again, thank you. I'm going to make another assumption. I'm guessing you've both figured out where Paul got the idea for the game he ran on you. A story by . . . what's his name, honey?"

"Cyril Kornbluth," Paul supplied.

"*Told* you," Wally blurted, and flinched at the glance it got him from Moira.

"Thanks," June pressed on. "Kornbluth." She began slowing the pace of her speech. ("June," her mother had once told her, "it is almost impossible to speak foolishness slowly.") "I haven't read it, but Paul's told me about it. You've read it. A grifter pretends to be a time traveler. He works a long con." Beat. "*What happens to him?*"

Moira's eyes began to glitter a whole second before Wally's did. She covered superbly, kept her face serene and body relaxed. Wally managed to keep silent, but allowed his eyes to widen and his knuckles to whiten on his Glock, which happened to be pointed at his own ankle. Neither said anything for several seconds. Then simultaneously they turned to each other, exchanged a silent high-speed transmission, and turned back to June together. Wally's gun was no longer pointing at his ankle.

"You allege that the Time Police are after you," Moira stated. Her own gun was smaller, but nearer; June felt she could almost see the .22 bullet in there in the chamber. Dammit, this *did* sound exactly like another con, improvised to fit their known weakness. They were right to be angry. It was time to go for broke.

"I have a . . . call it a skill," she said. "I call it the eye of power, or just the eye. I have not tried to use it on you so far—" She did so now, on Moira, gave her both barrels. "—but you can see that it is very powerful. I can sell a turd to a perfumier with the eye of power." Moira nodded involuntarily. "I am now going to look away from you both and talk to the bay out there for a few minutes. You can shoot me any time you become convinced I'm lying to you. If you can think of any other explanation for what's happened to us, I promise to believe it." She switched off the eye, continued to meet Moira's eyes long enough for her to grasp that, then slowly swiveled her chair until she could just see Moira's gun in her peripheral vision.

And then she told them, as concisely and accurately and dryly as she could, everything that had happened to her since she had first seen the mook in Pacific Spirit Park.

She was quite surprised not to be interrupted even once. Her opinion of science fiction fans rose somewhat, in consequence. She did not try to hide her own complicity in Paul's sting. When she came to the only part she had intended to gloss over, how she and Paul came to be in tenancy of this particular dwelling, she changed her mind and told that straight too, giving O'Leary's name and a rough sketch of the game she had been planning for him, blowing it thereby.

For her finale, she got up, went to the phone's base unit, and activated the speakerphone feature. "I just thought of one small piece of evidence that can corroborate at least one tiny thing we've told you," she said, over the sound of dial tone. "I wish I had more." Signifying for them like a mime, she pushed the redial button. After four rings, they all heard a click, and then Moira's recorded voice saying, "This is what it sounds like. Do the obvious at the standard cue." June disconnected before it could beep at them.

Wally and Moira exchanged a glance.

"You both must know the Sherlock Holmes quote about eliminating the impossible," June concluded. "Paul and I are down to the X-Files, ancient hairy gods, a mad scientist, or a time traveler. I don't know about you two, but time traveler is the only one of those I can live with. I would reject *that* as impossible . . . if I had anything at all to replace it with. Do either of you see any possibility I missed?"

There was a long silence.

"And you see why we need *you?*"

Outside, the rain stopped.

She was mildly surprised when it was Wally who broke the silence. "You've defined the job. I will stipulate the problem is interesting to us. Will you hear our consulting fee now?"

She swiveled back to face them, and took Paul's hand. "Please."

"Ninety-nine thousand Canadian dollars."

Paul's hand tightened on hers. She squeezed back. "You've already—" she tried.

"—recovered a large fraction of what you took us for, yes. That's a separate transaction. That's why we're probably not going to shoot you. This is different. Ninety-nine thousand dollars is the fee your partner set for giving us an education, in *his* area of expertise. We won't work for less."

June looked at Moira's eyes. They meant it.

Paul groaned, and made one last try at preserving a shred of self-respect. "The correct figure—"

"Excuse me," Wally said mildly, but it was the gesture with the Glock that cut Paul off. "I am not going to shoot you unless you absolutely insist. And I may work for you if we can agree on terms. But if you want to dick me around over *change*, I may be moved to pistol-whip you a little. Can we keep this friendly?"

"Sorry," Paul said. He turned to look at June. She felt his pain, like a blow to an already weary heart. His hand was limp in hers, now. "That's about everything we've got left," he said.

Technically he was lying; there were a few stashes here and there, though none easily accessible. But in another sense he was correct. There could be no more humiliating fate for a grifter than to have to pay the mark double. If they agreed to this—even if they swore Wally and Moira to secrecy—it would be the irrevocable end of both their careers. No one but the people in this room would ever know what a genius Paul Throtmanian was. She groped for words. As she did so, her eyes met his squarely for the first time since Wally and Moira had arrived . . . and she fell in.

"Yes, I will," she heard herself say.

He understood her perfectly and at once. His smile was a beautiful thing to see. "Then everything's okay, then."

"Yes, Paul," she said. Her pulse thundered in her ears.

"I was broke when I met you."

"So was I," she agreed. "Ow."

He eased his grip on her hand, *snap*ped their gaze-lock with a visible effort, and turned his smile-beam on their guests. "It's a deal. You'll want it up front." Both nodded firmly. "It'll probably involve a little pick and shovel work: the bastard burned my house down around it. But it should still be there, perfectly safe, untoasted and undiscovered, not far from a basement entrance I *know* survived. Best done in darkness; if we catch the next ferry the timing should work out." June had tuned out, distracted by the stunning awareness that she had somehow, despite a lifetime of wariness, become a fiancée. But her attention was caught again when Paul went on, "I guess the only thing left to be settled is whether you need to pistol-whip me before we can put the heat away and get this show on the road."

Moira visibly deferred to her husband. He considered the matter, frowning speculatively. "You're a prick," he said finally, "but I've worked for pricks without violence all my life. And for about twenty-four hours, there, I thought I'd saved John Lennon's life. Maybe that is worth what it cost me." He engaged the safety catch on his gun and put it in his lap. (Moira, startled, started to take her own safety *off* . . . then left it the way it was, and put the gun in her purse.)

June was so relieved she shamelessly allowed it to show.

Paul nodded. "In that case, I believe the moment has come when honor will permit me to apologize, to you and your wife, for what I did to you. I don't have any excuse, and I don't expect you to accept the apology, but I give it gladly."

No response.

"So do I," June said, largely to see if her numb lips could produce speech. "We're quitting the business."

"One last thing and then we can head for the ferry," Paul went on. "You're the first to know: we just got engaged."

Wally and Moira both raised their eyebrows and exchanged a glance. And began to smile.

"June," Moira said, "all your sins will be satisfactorily atoned for."

"You lucky duck," Wally added.

She found her cheeks were being squeezed up so tight by the corners of her mouth that water was threatening to leak from her eyes. "I hope we're as lucky as you two."

"Not a chance," Wally said. "But it's something to shoot for."

"Then I take it we're adjourned?" Paul asked.

"Just one thing," Wally said. "That PC I saw in the den—is that the one with the Pentium 133 chip?"

Moira smacked him on the shoulder. In spite of herself, June giggled. After a moment and a few blinks, so did Wally.

This might, June decided, just work out.

The ride to the ferry terminus in Wally and Moira's Toyota was undertaken in a slightly strained silence. All four knew that further discussion of the time traveler would be improper until the consultants had received their advance, and the only other interest they all seemed to have in common was the Beatles, which seemed inappropriate under the circumstances.

But by the time they shut off the engine at the

tail end of the lineup waiting for the next sailing (at this end of the trip, perhaps thirty whole vehicles—for which no accommodation whatsoever had been provided, stacked up in most of the downhill lane of "downtown" Snug Cove's "main street"), the women could stand it no longer. "How long have you and Wally—" June began, at the same instant Moira asked, "How long have you and Paul—" and everyone laughed, and that broke the ice. Then they swapped How We Met stories. June went first, and gave both the version they told people, and the truth. So Moira felt compelled to do the same when it was her turn. Sharing embarrassment forged another small bond. Yet another formed between Paul and Wally as each attempted and failed to edit his mate's account: that peculiar, wry late-twentieth-century brotherhood of shared public submission.

Whatever their business differences, it is difficult for really intelligent people not to enjoy each other's company. Each couple had good and recent reason to respect the other's intelligence. None of the four ever quite completely forgot that there were loaded firearms in the vehicle, or just where they were located; nonetheless they were all about as relaxed with each other as crime partners, for instance, ever get by the time the Queen of Something-or-Other snugged itself into its tire-studded berth, stuck out its steel tongue and began vomiting Jaguars, Ladas and 4X4s onto the land.

As Wally parked in the vehicle bay, they agreed they were all hungry, but not enough to eat ferry food. The two grifters went first up the steep narrow stairwell, out of an intuitive sense that they were still not fully trusted yet. The first time you climbed those stairs, you wondered why the handrails had studs along most of their length; halfway up you came to appreciate the pitons. June became slightly aware of Wally's nose only a few inches from her buttocks, and tried to climb as unprovocatively as possible. Apparently she succeeded; when they all sat together on a life-jacket locker outside on the upper passenger deck, Moira did not interpose herself between them.

It was quite pleasant on deck, no cooler or windier than they were dressed for. The rain had been over for so long it was not necessary to dry the surface of the locker before sitting on it. The sun was just settling toward the treetops, behind the ferry, crowning Bowen Island with glory. They were on the south or starboard side of the ship as it left Snug Cove and headed out into the bay; thunderheads comfortably far away on the horizon produced a Disney sunset. June mentioned that it reminded her a little of Key West; Moira said it reminded her of her and Wally's summer place in Nova Scotia. Paul observed that both couples seemed to look for similar sorts of things in a vacation home: remoteness, simple circumstances, few and tolerant neighbors. Wally suggested the needs of con organizers and con artists were not all that different—using the latter term somewhat shyly until he saw neither Paul or June took offense at it. Conversation became general; each of the four performed a few of their standard anecdotes, and was pleased with their reception. Wally beta-tested a new pun he was working up, to the effect that if the promised paperless digital world ever materialized, writers would all be The Artists Formerly Known In Prints. He lived; the only one armed besides himself within earshot had married him knowing of his affliction.

Shortly, the captain made a general announcement over the loudspeakers, and the four got up and joined ninety percent of the vessel's passengers on the north side to gawk in awe and inexplicable pleasure at a whale. A bitter argument broke out among several of their fellow passengers as to just which sort of whale it was. An elderly man loudly demanded to know why, for this kind of money, the captain couldn't for chrissake drive the damn boat closer so he (the jerk) could get some better shots of the fish. The air was cooler out of the cove, and the wind was from the south, so it was somewhat less nippy there on the port side; they remained by tacit mutual consent even after the whale had gone about its business, and most of the other passengers had gone back indoors to enjoy "food" or videogames or virtuously display their nonsmoking status.

It would not have made the slightest difference if they had remained where they'd started. The trackfly passed the ferry on the south side, no more than half a kilometer away at closest approach, but as stated, the wind was from that direction. The fly was not quite bright enough to change course to pass the ferry to leeward; in order to bring the search down to something manageable, it had been programmed to regard bodies of water as null areas, to be traversed as quickly as possible. Ignoring the can of pheromones downwind, it continued on a straight line toward Bowen Island.

If it had so much as glanced their way, even its rather poor vision might have picked out Paul's fuzzy skull, decided that it fit the parameters of a male head which had been bald three days ago, and vectored in for a quick sniff. If any of the

four had been scanning the right quarter of the
sky with good binoculars at precisely the right
instant, and known what to look for, they might
just have glimpsed the fly. They did, in fact, like
all the other passengers out on deck, hear a
muffled sound that might be termed a sonic poof,
and like everyone else dismissed it as some sort
of ferry noise, or perhaps a far-distant Canadian
Forces jet.

It was—as it had been at the very start—just
that tantalizingly close. But they were sailing to
Horseshoe Bay, not playing horseshoes, and so
again "close" was simply not good enough.

They ate in a *wonderful* place Wally and Moira
knew just outside Horseshoe Bay. (A law of nature
states that all sf fans know all superb and most
good restaurants within a fifty-kilometer radius of
their home. SMOFs generally at least double the
radius.) The food was so good that it was not until
the check was actually on the table that Paul
remembered to blush.

"Wally?" he said. "Are you familiar with a
condition called shellout falter?"

Wally's eyebrows rose sympathetically. "You suffer
from a reach impediment?"

"Well, it's been a hard week."

Wally waved a hand, and grinned. "Take it from
your mind. I cannot tell you how much you will
have improved this whole anecdote if you will
allow me to buy you dinner."

Paul and June considered that . . . and burst
out laughing.

Moira joined in too, but when the laughter had
subsided she said to June, "So you two took off
so fast you didn't have time to grab any cash?"

June nodded. "There are still a couple of small accounts around town we could tap in theory—but none I'd dare access until we settle this."

"So what were you going to do when O'Leary's fridge emptied out?"

"Pocket cash has never—" Paul began automatically, and then trailed off.

"What?" Moira said.

"Pardon me," he said slowly. "A phantom ache in an amputated limb. I said goodbye to my life out there on Bowen Island, but I'll be awhile unlearning old habits, I guess." He looked away.

June took his hand. "What Paul means," she said quietly, "is that he started to say cash has never been a problem for us, we'd just have worked some short con or other on some mark for operating capital. And then he remembered that we've retired, and there's no answer to your question anymore."

After an awkward silence, Moira spoke up. "You meant that about quitting your line of work?"

June nodded.

"*Why?*" In spite of herself she giggled. "I mean, you're *good* at it," she tried to explain. "That eye of power thing is awesome. And you had no way of knowing Wally and I were going to catch up with you. Why were you thinking about retiring?"

"To change your pattern, make it harder for the time traveler to track you?" Wally suggested.

Still looking at her fiancé's expressionless profile, June shook her head. "Basically," she said, "we woke up one day and found ourselves stinging nice people. People who we could have liked. We always swore we weren't going to. Maybe every grifter swears that, starting out—the good ones, anyway. Maybe not. But over the years, your standards slip, a centimeter at a time, while you aren't paying attention. Your partner's standards slip, too. Soon you're like two drunks trying to hold each other up, each certain you're sober. The next thing you know, you find you've written a truly brilliant new con . . . that only works on smart, kind people." She reached out and stroked Paul's cheek. "So you look back to see just where you lost control, and you can't pin it down. So maybe you've had it all wrong from the start, and *nobody* deserves to get stung."

"I'm not certain I agree with *that* part," Moira said. "There are bastards on this planet. Maybe you've just lost faith in your own wisdom to judge."

It was not said unkindly; June considered it, and shook her head. "My right to."

"It isn't right to be Simon Templar, and smite the Ungodly," Wally suggested, "unless you're in a book, where you don't make mistakes, and you can guarantee there won't be any innocent bystanders."

"Exactly," Paul said, and turned back to face the table. "There's a song James Taylor's brother Liv wrote, that goes, 'Life is good—when you're proud of what you do . . .'," he said to Wally. "Well, for a long time now, I've been trying to skate by on being proud of how I *do* it, instead. It just stopped being good enough."

"I see," Wally said.

"I mean, look at my masterpiece. My most brilliant artistic creation. Like June says, it only works on bright sensitive misfits with unusually flexible minds. I mean, it's pretty obvious who I'm really trying to sting, isn't it?"

"Your mother," June said.

He spun on her, thunderstruck, and started to cloud up—then his face went blank. "Good one," he said after a few seconds of thought. "I was going to say me, but that was infuriating enough to have some truth in it."

"Maybe some of both," she suggested.

"You two are going to be good at this marriage business," Moira said.

"And the rest will fall into place," Wally agreed. "It always does, if you've got the *basic* stuff covered."

June found herself smiling. "Well, if we don't get caught and killed, or shipped off to the Stone Age or something, I think we've got a shot. That's why I accepted his proposal."

"Oh, don't worry about that," Wally assured her. "I think we can deal with that."

Paul and June stared at him.

"Oh yeah," he said, somewhat abashed. "I worked it out on the way to the ferry. A plan, I mean. It needs a little polish, but it ought to work."

Moira's eyes were gleaming. "My heroin," she said in a swooning, theatrical voice.

Her husband smiled at her. "Aw, shocks."

The good fellowship that had grown up between the four of them made it sort of necessary for Wally to outline his idea then, even though he and Moira had not yet been paid their consulting fee. His scheme was not, at first, received with great enthusiasm, since it required large amounts of trust and faith and hope—ingredients Paul and June were mostly accustomed to selling to other people. But eventually they were forced to concede that their only other option was to cut their own throats, right now. June then spotted a potential hole in the scenario, but Moira was able to patch it brilliantly. They all left the restaurant feeling confident, and with that special warmth that comes from having made good new friends. Wally and Paul talked together in the front of the Camry, and Moira and June talked in the back, all the way back to Vancouver. When they reached the building behind Paul's former address, the ladies split the chore of keeping lookout—June in the parking garage, Moira on the other side of the burned-out property—while Paul and Wally excavated together, armed with a shovel and a good tire iron Wally kept in his trunk. Wally was poor at gruntwork, but turned out to be world-class at thinking of easier ways to do things.

The camaraderie thus engendered helped considerably to smooth over the awkward moment that arose when they reached the site of Paul's secret stash, and found only shrapnel.

After several minutes of silence, during which Paul considered using his swearing litany—after all, the house had already burned down—but couldn't work up the heart to begin, he felt Wally's pudgy hand on his bowed shoulder. In all the countless permutations of the English language, there was only one right thing Wally could possibly have said just then, and Paul was immensely gratified to hear him say it.

"You can owe us."

Too moved to speak, he nodded.

"Let's get our women and go to war," Wally said.

Paul nodded again, and they left.

Chapter 14
"... Danny Boy, this is a showdown ..."

Myrna and Johnson were alertly waiting—desperately hoping—for word of June Bellamy and Paul Throtmanian; indeed, they had done very little else in the thirty-six hours since they'd loosed the trackfly. It didn't help them much.

The one thing they'd thought they knew for sure about June and Paul's location was that it was *distant*. The fly had long since swept the entire Greater Vancouver area in a Drunkard's Walk pattern, conclusively reported null results, and expanded its search area to encompass all the inhabited islands nearby. It had scanned most of the small ones, was already halfway through the immense Vancouver Island. If it came up empty there as well, it would begin quartering the Lower Mainland and upper United States. The more infuriating minutes dragged by without news of success, the more distant became June and Paul's proved location. By now, it was certain they could not be within eighty kilometers of Pacific Spirit Park—or so the Lifehouse Keepers believed.

The truth came as a rude shock. A similar emotion might be experienced by a submarine skipper who—having lobbed a deckgun round through the night at a distant gunboat, and while waiting out the endless long seconds before he will know for sure whether or not he has scored a hit and is committed to battle, or has wasted a round but is still safe—feels the cold muzzle of a pistol against the back of his own personal neck, and hears the click of the hammer being cocked. By the time Myrna and Johnson's own personal alarms—which had seemed perfectly adequate for nearly a thousand years, and which had been tuned most carefully—sounded in their skulls, June was standing about half a kilometer from their home.

And about a hundred meters from the Lifehouse . . .

She got that far without being identified as more than just another passing hiker, biker or stroller because Myrna and Johnson's own sentries were nowhere near as sophisticated as the trackfly. A change of hair and eye color, cheek inserts and lifts sufficed to fool them on the physical level, as they would probably have fooled another human. They neither knew nor cared what she smelled like.

And she had obviously remembered her lost FM radio headphones, and somehow deduced what they could accomplish on the mental level.

The set she wore now had been altered to generate a much more powerful signal than usual. It did not merely mask, but completely shielded her thoughts. Indeed, what had finally triggered the alarm was the sentries' belated perception that a human-sized animal with a sentience level around that of a bluejay was probably a significant anomaly.

But Myrna and Johnson absorbed all this information *after* they perceived the message June meant them to get, so efficiently did she deliver it.

First, they saw the white flag she was waving in her right hand.

Next, they took in the modified cellular phone that hung from the belt of her jeans, to which she was speaking continuously.

And finally they noted the extra-extra-large black tee-shirt she was wearing, big enough to be a Rubenesque sf fan's convention souvenir. It was gathered and tucked in in back, so the white lettering just below her left breast could be clearly seen. It spelled out the simple words:

> *The Place*
> *because it's time*

She and Paul wanted to parley.

Knowing her as they did, they were at once dismally certain that she and her partner had rigged some sort of ingenious stalemate to protect themselves. The Lifehouse Keepers sent their awareness hurtling pessimistically out to trace it as far as they could.

Somewhat to their surprise, the cell phone's signal went less than a hundred meters, at first— to a phone Paul wore as a headset with a throat mike, very sophisticated gear indeed for a grifter. So was the high-powered rifle on a tripod, through whose sniperscope he was taking dead aim at the back of June's skull. (All the gear seemed brand-new; there was still a price tag on the tripod.)

But from there the phone signal went off on Hell's own journey. They followed it awhile, but gave up when it crossed its own trail for the third time in Singapore. The point was made: June and Paul had a third confederate Myrna and Johnson could not quickly affect, locate or identify save by overt telepathic conquest.

Worse: the existence of a third, combined with the fact that neither grifter had ever once been so much as indicted for any felony in any jurisdiction, strongly implied at least a fourth party as well. Both Paul and June were suspenders-and-belt types. Myrna herself was going to die because Paul's money stash had been doubly booby-trapped; he was clearly a man happiest with an ace up *both* sleeves at a minimum. He might, for all Myrna or Johnson knew, have enlisted an entire army of grifters, grafters, hucksters and dips, who could communicate in ways even a thousand-year-old layman could not hope to grasp.

This was very bad.

A Quaker watching her family tortured could not have felt more profoundly or primitively conflicted. Myrna had seen so much sorry death in her millenium of service that it had been centuries since she had even recreationally fantasized dealing it out to anyone as punishment for their silly human sins. Nonetheless she was a true descendant of a redhanded ape and his bloodthirsty mate, mortal as them now into the bargain, and to *hell* with the fate of all the sleeping dead and all reality: *these clowns were messing with her personal lifeboat*! If killing had been of the slightest use to her, she'd have used her teeth and fingernails.

Johnson, similarly, was descended from two million years of primates who had unanimously felt that anyone who killed their mate should be treated with great rudeness. Since his and Myrna's comment through the past thousand years, and not merely the last thirty-odd, he had been crafted with a normal amount of male dominance: he was not merely the titular but the effective leader of their team, and knew the ancient commander's desire to avenge his wounded as strongly as he knew the even more ancient protector's desire to avenge his mate.

Dealing with such emotional disturbances would never be impossible for either of them. At times it could be extremely difficult. Myrna, in particular, had lately had to do much more of that sort of thing than usual, as small bodily damages she was no longer able to heal sent chemical messages of unease to her alarm system. Emotional control was somewhat like a muscle that can be worn out to the point of spasm. She managed to master herself, now, but it cost her great effort.

And the shared knowledge made it that much harder for Johnson to do the same.

So it was that several seconds passed before they acted.

Then Johnson enveloped her in his field and flew them together like bullets, and at a similar velocity, through the forest toward June Bellamy.

There was no deceleration. Their velocity was simply canceled, at a point just out of sight and just out of earshot of June. As smoothly as children stepping off an escalator, they were walking hand in hand toward her at a slow pace, making no effort to muffle their footsteps in the (finally) drying underbrush. Their acute hearing picked up her muttered telephone monologue about the time she became aware they were approaching. They heard her alert Paul, and tell him to stand by.

"If I come, I die," she yelled then.

They had to admire the absolute absence of self-consciousness in her voice. She was stating a fact, and could not care less if some distant hiker thought she was kinky.

Johnson, who knew there was no other human within earshot, called back, "Understood," and he and Myrna kept walking.

They expected June to start visibly when she finally saw them. It was clear that she and Paul had *not* deduced their antagonists' cover identities, or they would have come directly to the park caretaker's cottage. Therefore, however she had been visualizing their pursuers, it could scarcely have been as a pair of snowcapped senior citizens.

But she betrayed no surprise. Professionally immune to surface appearances, she would not have lost her poker face if they had manifested hand in hand as Janis Joplin and Jimi Hendrix, on fire. Her only reaction was to give target coordinates to Paul, who shifted aim from the back of her head to Johnson's forehead the moment it entered his field of view.

Paul was largely visually concealed from them by undergrowth, though not of course from their sentries. He was a memorable sight. His headset phone sat atop a bright skull-hugging helmet of some sort of crinkly golden metal foil, almost a metal-maché, with small holes for eyes and mouth and absurd sculpted ears that came to Vulcan points (the phone's earbead cord disappeared into the one on his right), and to whose preposterous appearance he was plainly as indifferent as any holdup man in a Nixon mask. It shielded his thoughts even better than June's radio headphones did hers: the sentries rated him a rather bright shrub on the sentience scale. He seemed to sense that he was under remote surveillance of some kind—and didn't give a damn.

Johnson kept his own face blank, maintained his leisurely pace, and shifted their course slightly so that Paul could continue to track him without needing to move the tripod.

Myrna's grip was tight in his. They both knew a bad shot or a bad ricochet could kill her. They also knew if one did, it would be his immediate task—*before* he could so much as say goodbye— to try to reason with her killers.

They stepped out of the woods and onto the path together, stopped six meters from June, and perhaps ten meters from the great tree under which the Lifehouse lay hidden.

"I'll bet you can force your way through this," June said, pointing at her headset. "But I bet you can't take me over *instantly*." She pointed to the cell phone at her hip. "If anything makes Paul suspect a struggle for control of my mind is taking place, he will try to kill one of you, and failing that will take me out with the second slug."

Johnson nodded.

"If that happens," June went on quietly, "some- one else far from here—someone who *doesn't even know where he is himself*—will make a single mouse-click, and spam the planet with everything we know about you time travelers. Every science fiction or fantasy writer or fan, every scientist, science writer, news medium and national security agency with an Internet address will know every- thing we knew up to the moment of the mouse- click."

Determined to keep his features expressionless, Johnson found that his eyes had closed of their

own volition. It took immense effort to force
them open again. He did have the power to take
over the minds of both June and Paul by brute
force, despite radio headphones or metallic
masquerade masks, whenever he wanted to badly
enough to permanently lower their IQs by fifty
or sixty points—but no longer dared use it,
whatever the need. This was Armageddon. Here.
Now.

"You understand that would make a hole in
history too big to mend," he said softly. "Even if
not one person believed you."

It wasn't quite a question, but she nodded
superfluous agreement. "That's how little I'm
prepared to tolerate another hole in my mind."

"Do you have a proposal?" Myrna asked.

"Do we have a truce?"

Again, Johnson nearly showed surprise. "You will
accept our word?"

June nodded. "What choice do we have? If your
word is no good, there's no point in bargaining.
Besides, if you are time travelers without honor,
everything is already fucked . . . and the problems
of two little people don't amount to a hill of beans."

He exchanged a glance with Myrna. June was
emphatically not a science fiction reader, and Paul
only a recreational one, like a social drinker: that
last sentence was reasoning more sophisticated
than expected for either of them. At once the
Lifehouse Keepers began to suspect who the pair's
new allies might be. A pity that when they'd last
read June's mind, she had not then known the
specific names or addresses of the sf fans Paul
was about to sting—or that Paul had not left any
useful clues even in the encrypted partition of his
hard drive. If only the couple had trusted each

other a little more, been a little less paranoid by nature, the Keepers might now have a lead on their new antagonists.

The absurdity of that last thought caused them to spend a precious half-second smiling ruefully at each other. (Inside only.)

"We have a truce," Johnson said then.

June insisted on spelling it out. "You won't try to monkey with our memories any more?"

She was too good a liar to lie to. Johnson shrugged and spread his hands. "We *must* try, or die in the attempt. But we won't do it *now*. If this parley is unsuccessful, we'll give you an hour for a head start."

"A lot more than you needed the last time," Myrna pointed out. There was just a hint of an edge to her voice.

June nodded, and gave her just a touch of the eye of power in return. "If it goes that way, we'll suspend our upload for the same period." *Wanna play hardball, Granny?* said her gaze.

"Agreed," Johnson said. With eyes locked, both women said it together, and Paul's echo came in stereo, from June's hip and from a hundred meters away.

When he emerged from his place of concealment, his hands were empty, and he no longer wore the comedy space-monster mask. But his phone now rode directly on his own bristly scalp, and its circuit was still open. Johnson counted two hidden weapons (lethal to a human—such as his wife), and wondered how many he was overlooking.

Being impressed by an opponent was, for him, a novel and not utterly unpleasant sensation.

As Paul joined them there was a brief subtle dance that ended with the men confronting each other directly, each with his mate slightly behind him and to his left. Neither male consciously noticed it happen; neither female missed it.

"Had you actually already stung them?" Johnson asked.

Paul took his meaning at once, and if he found it an odd opening, he showed no surprise. "Yes," he said. "Ninety-eight thousand Canadian."

Johnson allowed his own surprise to show, in the form of a lifted eyebrow, and tried another gambit. "So that's, what, seventy-five in real money?"

Again Paul was impervious. "Call it seventy-three five American."

"Mr. Throtmanian, I am impressed. Even for you, conceiving of enlisting your victims as allies was uncharacteristically brilliant. Pulling it off was . . . As I say, I'm impressed."

"And I'm impressed by how well you know me, okay? As the saying goes, you must be reading my mail. Can we move on?"

"Certainly. My name is Johnson Stevens, and this is my wife Myrna. I'm afraid we don't *have* 'real names'—but we've been using those for nearly two centuries now."

June spoke up. "You're old: we get it." Her eyes were still locked on Myrna's. "We knew that anyway. We would not have gone to all this trouble if *we* were not impressed with *you*, alright?" She switched off her eye of power. "You're Myrna and Johnson; we're June and Paul. Like he said, can we move on now?"

Myrna blinked her own tired old eyes for the first time in a long while, and shivered slightly as if throwing off a chill. "Please go ahead, Paul," she said. The edge was gone from her voice now.

"In Minneapolis," Paul said, "in a joint called

Palmer's Bar, I heard a guy sing a verse once that stuck in my head. It went:

> *Very old man with money in his hand*
> *Lookin for a place to hide*
> *Along come a young man,*
>   *a gun in his hand*
> *They both sat down and cried*
> *Cryin all they had in this world*
>   *done gone."*

Johnson nodded. "Neither side in this matter much likes the role fate has cast them in. We don't want to edit your memories by force. You don't want to risk paradox to prevent us. Neither side can see a choice. But you did not come here to suggest we sit down and weep together, Paul."

"We came to see if there is any give in your position," Paul said.

"Is there any in yours?"

For the first time, Paul betrayed surprise.

"Can you conceive of circumstances under which you would consent to specifically limited memory-edit?"

"Cover me," Paul said softly, and closed his eyes to help him visualize. At the cue, June increased her own alertness, expanded her peripheral vision to encompass Johnson, and moved her right hand fractionally *away* from her own hidden weapon . . . presumably toward one the sentries could not detect.

"I can think of only one case," Paul said, reopening his eyes, "and it doesn't seem to pertain here. Can you conceive of circumstances under which you would consent to let us keep our present memories?"

"I'm afraid my answer is the same," Johnson

said, allowing as much of his own sadness as they would find credible to come through in his voice.

"Then we have two choices," Paul said. "Say goodbye now, and start fighting to the death in an hour . . . or try and persuade each other that the unique solution we each find imaginable might somehow be made to exist. I would prefer the latter. I assume you feel the same."

"Very well," Johnson said. "I will go first."

He held a hasty telepathic conference with Myrna. They had no contingency plan for negotiation; had not until this minute considered it a possibility. But their minimum requirements seemed clear—and highly unlikely to be acceptable. No point in pulling punches.

"I would let you and June and your allies walk the earth unedited under the following circumstances: you permit me to enter each of your minds, satisfy me that you will never voluntarily divulge any datum I label critical, to anyone under any circumstances, and permit me to insure you against drug or hypno interrogation. Not lethally— but any such attempt would leave you a very happy fellow with no memory of anything at all, for life. I realize that could be a significant hazard for you and June, given the nature of your profession, but after all you both *have* gone undetected by the authorities up to this—"

"That part's not a factor," Paul said. "My fiancée and I are retired. For good."

Johnson's face did not pale; it never did unless he told it to. But he was shocked. His superb and trusty Bullshit Detector told him Paul was not lying . . . but if this was a true statement, then he and Myrna did not know June or Paul nearly as well as they'd thought they did, could not hope to reliably predict what they might do. This might actually work! "Congratulations, twice," he said automatically, while his mind raced. "Then I see no problem. Our minimum requirements are, one, absolute assurance of your sincere will to be permanently discreet; two, assurance that you cannot be compelled to spill what you know of us against your own will; and three, your promise that when our business is concluded, you will never have anything to do with this park again as long as you live, or cause others to do so. We will trust you to keep the most important secret we know, our existence—*if* you will prove you can be trusted by opening your minds. In all candor, we might not require this of ordinary civilians . . . but I hope you'll take it as the compliment it's intended to be if I say that, for you two and your allies, nothing less will serve: you are two of the greatest liars we've ever encountered. Your turn."

Paul inclined his head. "Thank you. Coming from thieves of your caliber it is indeed flattering. I would permit you to enter my mind under the following conditions. One, you must first restore every second of the memories you stole from my fiancée."

Johnson nodded. "Acceptable." June had never learned anything more damaging than the simple fact that something was buried here.

"Two, you must give me your word that neither of you will ever use anything you learn from my mind in any way that, *in my opinion*, would harm me or anyone I care about. I don't have to define that any closer, because you'll *know*. And the same for the others."

Johnson nodded again.

"Three, it must be two-way."

"In what sense?"

"*I* get to walk around inside *your* head too."

Johnson shook his head sadly. "I'm sorry. That's impossible."

Paul's voice went flat. "Gosh, that's a real pity."

"*Please!*" Johnson said quickly. "I do not mean that word as a euphemism for 'unacceptable'—it literally is not possible."

Paul nodded. "I believe you. Like I said, a real pity. But a dealbreaker."

Johnson wondered why; was startled to hear himself ask, "Why?"

"Two reasons, either one sufficient. First, thanks to June here, and everything she has taught me in our time together about subordinating my precious ego, I am just barely willing to consider telepathy— *with an equal*. Wide-open two-way . . . or strictly limited on *both* sides. You want me to get naked in front of your brain, I'll consider it. But you don't get to keep *your* shorts on."

Johnson sighed. "I understand your position. And your second reason?"

"You want me to keep your dark secret for life. Only *I don't know shit*. All I know is, there's something from the future buried over there that's worth brain-rape to protect. Before I agree to keep my mouth shut about it, I have to know what it is, and why it's so important. For all I know, you came back here in your time machine to start the plague that'll solve your real estate problem. I have to be as sure of your sincerity as you are of mine."

Johnson knew more about serenity than most Zen masters. Nonetheless he was conscious of a powerful urge to bite himself on the small of the back. If any particle of him had believed in an external deity who was supposed to punish vice and reward virtue, he could have taken refuge in rage at that Being. Lacking this (expensive) luxury, he was instead so overwhelmingly sad it seemed his ancient heart might stop of it. There were very few bodily functions he could not control absolutely, but tears leaked against his will from his eyes as he said, "Paul, you break my heart. Everything you ask is perfectly reasonable, nothing more than you deserve, and the least I'd probably settle for in your shoes. And I wasn't lying—it just isn't possible. I'll be honest: I wouldn't do it if I could. But I can't."

"You want to amplify that a little?" Paul asked. "Or are we done here?"

As far as Johnson could tell, they were. But he did not want to admit it, even to himself, so he allowed himself a few more sentences, to buy time. "I can't drop my shields and let you in, because I can't do it partway. It's like being a little bit pregnant, or somewhat dead. You would get everything at once."

"Your point being?"

Johnson pointed at his own head. "This is not a brain like yours. It has been gathering memories more detailed and vivid than yours for a thousand years—and it was never really human by your definition to begin with. Furthermore, I am inextricably interwoven with Myrna: you'd get most of *her* thousand years, too. If I opened my mind to you, it might take you several seconds to actually hit the ground . . . but only because your knees would probably lock when the first seizure hit. Beyond doubt, what would finally fall to earth would be a vegetable with your face. A dying vegetable, too stupid to breathe."

Paul seemed to be listening to his earbead. "There *have* to be people trained to initiate new telepaths without burning out their brains," he said.

Damn. It would be one of the kibitzing fans who had realized that. "Yes," he agreed. "But none in this time. Nor would I be permitted to so initiate you, if I were able. Think it through. There would be no way but mindwipe to make you *unlearn* it again, afterward, and it would no longer be possible to mindwipe you."

As he had expected, the words "Think it through" shamed the unseen fans into silence again. It was June who spoke next. "Is that what you meant by, 'you wouldn't if you could'?"

He was tempted to agree just for the sake of simplicity, but something made him answer more honestly. "No. Forget telepathy for a moment. I would not even verbally *tell* you any more than you already know about our mission here."

"Then you better give me a better reason why not than, 'I might want to stop you if I knew,'" Paul said inexorably.

Fair enough. But *how*? "Paul, listen to me. I'll try to explain as much as I possibly can. The knowledge you want is knowledge that . . . that would change the coloration of every second of the rest of your life. It is a secret so . . . so precious, so *wonderful*, that a hundred times a day for the rest of your days you would be tempted to share it." He saw Paul's face twist into a grimace of insult, and went on hastily. "I am not disparaging your self-control! Please believe me—"

Myrna spoke. "Paul, we stipulate that you can hold out against needles under the fingernails. That's not what this is about. Knowing what you want to know would *change* you. In ways you would come to regret."

"Grandma knows best," Paul said flatly. Distant thunder was heard from the west, threatening rain.

"I will make one more try," Johnson said, "and then we'll give up and move on. Paul, by your standards I am not a human being. I was not born of woman. My personality was assembled from parts, and poured into a body whose DNA configuration had never existed before, designed for the occasion. The same is true of Myrna. A normal human given longevity and required to do our job would have gone insane about nine hundred years ago. Now that you are engaged, it may mean something if I tell you that I have been happily faithful to my wife for all that time. I was, if you will, *built* to accomplish one specific purpose: to preserve the secret you want to learn, for a thousand long, slow years." He met Paul's eyes squarely. "But *this* human I am: keeping that secret has been the hardest thing I've ever had to do. Even harder than the loneliness of being penned up inside a single skull."

"I promise you," Myrna said. "It would tear you apart. June too. The nicer a person you are, the worse it would tear you up."

"Cover me," Paul murmured again, and again went away inside to his thinking place. His features smoothed over. June's hand went this time toward the hidden weapon Johnson could identify, rather than away from it. Did that mean she was closer to attacking? Again, thunder rumbled faintly, to the north this time.

"The hell of it," Paul said finally, "is that I think I believe every word you say. But I cannot bet my species on it . . . and that's what you're asking me to do."

Johnson was in constant rapport with Myrna.

Nonetheless he turned his head toward her now, and used his mouth to say, "He's right," in mournful tones. Meanwhile his awareness was reaching out—

The trackfly had nearly succeeded in executing its new programming, by now—as he had known when he'd heard its thunder a few moments ago. It had returned from Vancouver Island, and located and identified both Wally and Moira; their brilliant antitelepath strategy of Moira driving Wally blindfolded to a location he himself did not know had not been of any help against a nano-dreadnought trackfly's hypersensitive nose. It was prepared to interdict and erase their Internet upload on command, and 100% confident of success. It was ready to help hold all four people immobile and helpless until the one-hour truce ran out, and Johnson could honorably begin mindwipe. There was only one . . . well, fly in the ointment: it reported that Moira seemed to be holding a *second* phone a bare half inch above its own cradle.

If forced to it, Johnson was barely able and barely willing to take over the minds of Paul, June, Wally and Moira at once—rendering them permanently autistic in the process. But even if he focused his full attention on Moira alone— allowed Paul to shoot Myrna dead, took the chance that a ricochet from his own body might kill one of them prematurely and ruin everything— he still could not seize control quickly and smoothly enough to prevent Moira from dropping that second phone, and thus hanging it up. If there were a *fifth* confederate somewhere, with a high-speed modem programmed to dial Moira's number continuously—and there was no way for even the trackfly to know where such a person might be—the instant it reported success, the fifth man could, and probably would, upload The End of Everything to the WorldWide Web. There was no way to stop him.

Yet Johnson knew if he did nothing, sometime in the next thirty seconds Paul Throtmanian was going to break the truce and try his best to kill him, fully expecting to die in the attempt but determined. Paul lied brilliantly in body language, but Johnson had been decoding that language for twenty lifetimes longer than Paul had been lying in it. He was going to have to risk everything whether he liked it or not, and there was nothing to be gained by letting Paul force his hand. He told the trackfly to hover, await his command, and then do its best to destroy Moira's second phone as she thrashed. He bade Myrna goodbye, and started the process of turning part of his consciousness into a long-distance sledgehammer—

"Wait," Myrna said, in his mind to him and aloud to all of them. "Don't just *do* something: stand there. All of you. I know one last thing I can try." She pulled her gaze from her husband's. "June—will you trust me, for about thirty seconds?"

June studied her for a long moment. "Give her thirty seconds," she said to Paul, not taking her eyes from Myrna's.

"Johnson, will you trust me?"

The question was so simple it confused him briefly. "With the universe," he said simply.

"Thank you, beloved." She turned back to the grifters, spoke slowly and calmly. "June, Paul, I'm going to cause a utensil to come to me. It will stop in midair, right in front of Johnson and me. After a few seconds, it will drop and bury itself in the soil. When that happens, we will all back away from the spot, and a time machine will appear on it. There'll be some special effects—but nothing that will hurt you, if you close your eyes when I tell you to. All right?"

"Go ahead, Myrna," Paul said. "I really hope you've got something."

"That's why I'm doing it," she said.

A chunk of quartz arrived from the house, took up station in front of her and Johnson. June and Paul regarded it with close interest, and Paul muttered a terse description of it to Wally.

Concealing her thought from Johnson for the first time in centuries, Myrna composed a message, impressed it into the quartz beacon, and planted it in the earth. They all backed away, Paul and June taking their cue from Myrna and Johnson as to how far away was far enough. "Here we go," Myrna said.

The air crackled. The scent of toasting basil and cinnamon stung their noses. A faint, high whine converged slowly from all directions at once. The temperature rose just perceptibly. The sound swelled and contracted, like an explosion played backwards—

"Close your eyes," Myrna called, and everyone but Johnson obeyed.

CRACK!

"Oh, shit," Johnson said, quite unable to help himself.

This time the Egg held a passenger.

It appeared to be the fetally curled corpse of a woman about twenty years older than June, with similar features and short thick chestnut hair, dressed in a white garment that somehow was able to suggest a hospital gown and still preserve dignity. At first blink the body was floating in a translucent fluid—then that was gone, and it slumped bonelessly to the bottom of the Egg. Inside his head, Johnson heard a sound very like the squeal of a modem connecting. For the first time ever, one of the buried Lifehouse's files was downloaded from it. Nearly at once the corpse stirred, lifted her head . . . glanced round and spotted her four observers. Her eyes locked on June.

June made a small sound in her throat, somewhere between a sob and a snarl.

The Egg sighed and vanished. The woman in white stood up. She turned slowly in a full circle, took in her surroundings, turned her attention to June again. Slowly she smiled, and started walking closer to June, who visibly turned to stone.

The wrinkles framing that smile were fake. That body had never been used before. Nevertheless it was somehow inexplicably and inescapably an *old* smile . . . and the brand-new body that bore it walked and carried itself as if it belonged to a woman in her fifties who had been ill recently and was still in recovery. She stopped before June, and put her hands on her own hips.

"You see, darling?" she said serenely. "I *told* you we were going to get it all said, some day."

Chapter 15
Call or Fold

June did not quite lose consciousness, merely misplaced it for a few moments. And she didn't quite go down, for Paul caught and steadied her. But for the longest interval in her life, perhaps ten whole seconds, she did not think anything whatsoever. Johnson could not have more effectively stunned her consciousness with his mental sledgehammer. Paul was somewhat less affected; his mind produced not only gestalts but words . . . but just the two, over and over: *Holy shit holy shit holy shit—*

By the time June was sentient again, she was in her mother's embrace, squeezing back fiercely. (She heard, but did not register, Paul behind her muttering, "Her fucking dead mother just showed up, okay, Wally? Shut up and stand by.")

This is a lie, was her first verbal construct. And then:

This is the most precious lie I have ever been told, and I must not waste a second of it!

She stepped back and looked.

It *had* to be a lie. It was just too perfect. Laura Bellamy in a brand-new replacement body, she might have been able to rationalize with Star Trek logic. The wasted, half-animate doll she had said goodbye to only days ago, she might also have accepted. But this Laura looked *precisely* the way she had in the childish wish-fulfillment fantasy June had been having repeatedly ever since her death: neither rejuvenated nor ruined, but partly recovered, as though her illness had miraculously remitted a week or two ago and she was nearly ready to be released. This was, at best, a very good model of Laura Bellamy, who was herself in fact dead.

Okay. Just now June was prepared to settle for even a fair model of her mother—gratefully. Any booby-prize is much better than total defeat. Too good to be true is the best kind of false.

"Are you all right?" she asked.

"Of course." A very good model. Even Disney's audioanimatronic boys couldn't have gotten that twinkle at such close range—much less the *scent*, the oldest and largest file in June's olfactory memory—or the skin temperature. "But you aren't. What's wrong, Junebug?"

"Don't *call* me th—" June automatically responded, and then caught herself and began to giggle.

Paul came up from behind her and put an arm around her, and that helped her stop and get her breath back. *Okay, I'm in the Twilight Zone. Time to stop acting like a protagonist, and go with it, then.* She came to a decision.

"Mom," she said, "this is Paul. We're retired, and engaged."

Her mother's smile nearly took her breath away again. "Oh, I'm *so* glad! Hello, Paul," Laura said, and embraced him. After a frozen second, he returned it. "Welcome to the family," she said. "Call me Laura."

"I'm . . . glad I got to meet you after all, Laura," he said gravely, and released her.

"Oh, so am I." She took both their hands in hers. "Now, what is wrong?"

"Well . . ." June gestured vaguely toward Myrna and Johnson, and Laura appeared to become aware of them for the first time. " . . . these are Myrna and Johnson Stevens. They're from the future. They say they *must* invade our minds—and will— but it won't hurt a bit, and they'd rather we let them. We say fine, let us into yours so we know we can trust you, and they say that's not possible, we'd go insane. We say, then at least tell us, in words, what you're doing here in our time, so we can be sure it's okay with us, and they say we'd be sorry if they told us and they can't anyway. They're at least as slick as I am, Mom, and I just can't tell if I can trust them."

Laura had nodded after the statement, "They're from the future," and continued to nod after each sentence to indicate that she was following the tale. After June stopped speaking, she nodded one more time, and then turned to face Myrna and Johnson.

"Mr. and Mrs. Stevens," she said, raising her voice but speaking in a polite, conversational tone, "from what I've read and been told by a dear friend of mine, I understand I am late for an appointment with a bright light at the end of a long tunnel, so I'll be brief. Are you conning my daughter?"

Myrna did not hesitate. "Yes, Mrs. Bellamy. We must."

"Is there no way you could tell them what they wish to know, and then, if they are indeed sorry to know it, cause them to forget it again, with their consent?"

"I'm sorry, ma'am," Johnson said. "At that point, the only thing that would serve would be to completely remove every memory they've formed in the last week—no, excuse me, the last several weeks. They would become different people than they are now. They've grown and changed a lot, in the last few days. Several weeks ago, for example, they were not retired. They would notice a memory gap that large, identify it as a wound, put their talented brains to vengeance, and sooner or later we'd be right back where we are now— at best. The only thing that will serve is for *that* Paul and June standing there beside you now— and all their friends listening in—to all agree to walk away and spend the rest of their lives knowing nothing more than they do right now. And we must be certain they mean it."

"But you state that if you could and did satisfy their curiosity, they would *ask* you to perform surgery to remove the knowledge again?"

"Yes," Myrna and Johnson said together.

"Thank you."

She turned back to her daughter and prospective son-in-law. She chose her words, and when she spoke her voice was firm and strong.

"Junebug, if you won't listen to your mother, listen to your great-great-grandchildren. Do what these people tell you. Walk away. You and Paul and whoever else is involved. They mean no harm, to you or anyone."

It never occurred to June to ask her how she knew. Her mother's people-radar had always been infallible. Instead she heard herself cry, "But how do I know you're not a hallucination?"

Laura Bellamy considered the question . . . and smiled. "How do I know *you're* not?" She thought about it some more, and her smile wavered. "This does seem an awful lot like the kind of dying fantasy I'd concoct. You're retired. And engaged. And only my wisdom from beyond the grave can save you." Her smile firmed again. "Only we both know it isn't a hallucination, don't we? We both know this is real, however it's happened. Just like we both somehow know I'm going to have to go again, soon. Tonto, our work here is done."

"*No!*" June cried.

Oh my God, she thought frantically, *I finally got one last chance to have that Last Conversation after all, without Daddy around . . . and just like last time, it's going to be over before I've even had a chance to remember all the things I needed to say, all the things I needed to ask—*

"Wait!"

"As long as I can, dear," her mother agreed, glancing at Myrna.

"Mom, you were wrong a minute ago. I *did* listen to you. Always. I know I gave you hell. I'm sorry. But I always listened. Hardest when I pretended to be deaf, maybe. You won The Fight, you know. Stubborn bitch that I am, I held out until the day after you died—but you won. I always knew you would. I just didn't want you to have the satisfaction."

"But I did know."

June blinked. Something knotted began to ease, deep within her. "Well, I'm sorry."

"I absolve you. Now ask the question you want to ask."

There's only one? she thought dizzily, and opened her mouth to let it emerge of its own accord. "How could you stay with Daddy, all those years?"

"It was my privilege," she said.

"Mom, forget the fact that on his best day, his brain was half as good as yours. The man is an emotional basket case. He needed round-the-clock care just to keep him functional, my whole life— hell, he managed to screw up your death scene! How could you waste a mind like yours on propping him up all those years?"

Laura took her time answering, seeking the right words. "June," she said finally, "you greatly underestimate my own selfishness. I got more from your father than I gave."

"But *what*?"

"The thing I married him for. The thing I never had much of myself, until he taught it to me. The thing I hope Frank and I together managed to pass on to you. His kindness. His clumsy warm never-failing kindness."

June stared. "But there's kindness everywhere," she protested. "The world is full of kindness."

"Oh, it certainly is," Laura agreed. "And most marriages still end in divorce. Most people can *be* kind, honey. Your father *is* kind. That's a different thing—and it's worth more than rubies." Seeing that her daughter still didn't get it, she went on. "Okay, yes: you have to hang a sign on a joke for Frank to recognize it. But dear, once you do, *he always laughs*, even if it's a poor joke. One time I'd gone with him to one of those awful sales conventions, and we were sitting in the most expensive restaurant in the convention complex, and by some accident they had a genuinely wonderful jazz combo playing. I looked up and saw a young couple we knew, a new salesman and his fiancée, standing in the entranceway, listening to the music and nodding. I started to wave and invite them to join us, quite automatically . . . and just as automatically, your father caught my hand and stopped me. 'But that's Jim and Shirley,' I said, 'You like them.' And Frank stopped and thought about it and said to me, 'Laura, look at the way they're dressed. Look at the way we're dressed. Why are they standing there in the doorway? If you wave to them, they're going to have to come in and sit down and blow half their weekend's budget on two drinks they don't want, just to hear the music for a few minutes. Kindest thing you can do just now is ignore them.' Once he explained it, I saw he was right, of course—but June, *he had to stop and think to explain it*. It's instinctive with him. If anyone in a room with him gets their feelings hurt, it's because his best wasn't enough to prevent it.

"Take the example you mentioned. Dear Frank tried to protect me from the terror of death. Clumsily, transparently, yes—and to the very best of his sweet ability. Even though it cost him his right to share his own crushing grief and loss with me. I had no choice but to let him think he was succeeding." She took June's hand again. "And in consequence, I could not allow myself to indulge in that terror. Do you see? For his sake, I kept whistling as I approached the graveyard—and so in the end he succeeded, and I died with as little fear as I could. Honestly, it wasn't nearly as hard as I'd thought it would be. All our married lives, he did things like that for me. Without him, I might have been you without Paul." She took his hand again as well, but kept speaking directly to June. "I approve of him as a son-in-law—but not because the boy is *clever*. Because I can tell he is kind."

"There are people who would disagree with you," Paul said softly. "Some of them are listening right now."

She met Paul's eyes. "Ah. I see. You were trying to unlearn the kindness . . . to impress June. She has always had enough mischief in her to get her boyfriends in trouble. Well, it didn't work this time . . . did it?" She watched his eyes, and nodded. "Kindness does you less credit than it does Frank, because you're smarter and more confident and less afraid: you can *afford* to be kind. But it's still a rare and sweet thing to be by nature. Teach her everything you know about it, teach her to respect her father and you . . . and forgive her what she finds hard to learn."

"I do," Paul said.

"I will," June said.

Laura smiled again—beamed, this time. "I now pronounce you man and wife," she said.

June felt herself beaming back, and burst into tears. "I love you, Mom."

"I love you, dear. And you too, son." She reached up, captured one of June's tears on her fingertip, and licked it. "We're done, aren't we?"

"Yes," June said in wonder, "I think we are."

At once her mother was gone. The pilot light went out behind her eyes, and as her vacated second body began to fall, it dissolved. There was no sound or heat. It was as though she simply turned to ash-laden smoke and blew away, like a digital special effect. In seconds, the last wisp was gone.

June kissed her fiancé firmly, and was kissed back. Then she pulled away and faced Myrna and Johnson.

"I'll never know for sure if that was real," she stated.

"That's right," Myrna said.

"I am in exactly the frame of mind a mark is just before I take 'em for everything they've got. Cold logic says I'm being set up, but I want to believe."

"I imagine so," Johnson agreed.

She squared her shoulders. "I'm wide open. Come on in."

Paul said nothing, very loudly.

"Sit down," Myrna said. "Since you are volunteering, it will not be necessary to invest you, the way we did Angel Gerhardt. There will be no orgasm involved. Or any other physical sensation."

June sat by the great ash tree, leaned back against it and relaxed utterly. "Go ahead."

"First, your stolen memories back," Johnson said.

There was a soundless explosion, an inertialess impact, and a vague inexpressible sense of relief, of healing from an unsuspected wound. She probed, and found that she had her missing minutes back. Quite dull and uninteresting minutes, really—but she cherished each one.

"That felt . . ." she murmured, "that felt like . . . like scratching an itch on a phantom limb I didn't know I had. Okay, I remember everything now. Scan away."

"It is done," Johnson said. "You are free to go."

She shook her head in awe, and got slowly to her feet. "So little," she said, "for all that trouble. Maybe I felt a tickle. Maybe I imagined it. I'm sure you didn't hurt anything. Paul?"

His voice was so well controlled that only his fiancée or a telepath could have detected the suggestion of a quiver in it. Wally probably never noticed. "I'm ready." He sat.

"It is done," Johnson said again. "Thank you. Mr. Kemp? I can hear you directly. . . ."

Suddenly, so could June—with crystal clarity, as though he were present. "Well, it's going to drive me nuts, that's for sure—but I'd like to put this whole thing behind me as quickly as possible. Moira and I have a convention to run in two weeks, and we've already lost about all the time we can afford. Go ahead: I'm dropping my shields."

"It is done. Thank you, Wally. Ms. Rogers?"

"The greatest puzzle of my life? And I can never ever know the answer? And never ever share it with anyone I haven't already? Johnson, you know more about what makes a SMOF tick than even Paul, there. Besides, I go anywhere Wallace goes. Make it so."

"Thank you, Moira. Mr. MacDougal?"

"You guys got a space program in the future?" Space Case asked.

Johnson seemed to grin in spite of himself. "At the time we left, pretty much anyone who wanted to had spent at least a decade or two off Saturn, in the Ring, just gawking."

"That's all I want to know. My lips are sealed, and I'm gonna die happy."

After a second, Johnson said, "I believe you will. Done."

June knew the meeting was over. She found herself reluctant to leave this place, this tranquil spot, these people she had wished dead for so many hunted days. Something wonderful was near here, and she would never know what it had been. "Will we ever see you again?" she asked Myrna and Johnson.

Myrna shook her snow-white head. "Not for a very long time," she said. "And not here."

"Is there anything you two need, that we can get you?" Paul asked.

June turned and looked at him with new and growing respect.

"One thing, perhaps," Johnson said. "And I'm afraid it's a dreadful cliché."

"Name it," Paul said.

"When you remember this—" he said.

"—and you will—" Myrna said.

"—think of us with kindness."

"We will," June said, and took Paul's hand, and they left Pacific Spirit Park without looking back, and with the firm resolve never to return.

They did, of course—but did not bring their bodies with them when they did, and never experienced a subjective instant of all the long years they spent there together in the Lifehouse. The answers they had wanted so badly would be granted them only in the next life—the longer and happier one. But their reward had already begun. For the remainder of their short first life together, they would display such uncanny talent at remaining married that their many close friends would often say it was as if they had been granted some secret knowledge no one else had.

Chapter 16
Dead Dog

Every *other* house on the south side of the block had a front balcony or deck on its upper story, facing north toward the harbor and North Vancouver on its far side and the magnificent mountains beyond. Paul or June could turn their heads and see all those decks and balconies, up and down this side of the street—all quite empty, at sunset after a sunny day.

To get the same view from Wally and Moira's house, one climbed out an upstairs bedroom window and stretched out on the sloping roof. The roof showed signs of hard use, and was extremely comfortable. There was, for instance, a nook sheltered from the rain, up against the house, in which stood a minifridge, thermal mugs, and a coffeemaker Wally had connected to the house wiring and water systems: one need only bring a basket of grounds, and remember to leave the carafe out for the rain to rinse afterward. The nook also held a large bottle of John Jameson's Irish whiskey, whose continued existence was in doubt, and the controls for a set of external speakers. At the moment they were rendering Don Ross's percussive acoustic guitar, an excellent choice for a sunset.

Early November is right at the end of Vancouver's six-month spring, and the beginning of its six-month fall; it was chilly enough for the Irish coffees to be welcome. Paul took a gulp of his, and felt warmth spread through him—especially to his scalp: though furthest to leeward of the four, he was still unused to being bald. "Wally," he said, "my hair's off to you. It worked like a Swiss watch. I'm not sure how far they got on their own—but I'm certain they never got a definite count of how many of us there were, let alone where we all were, until we let them in."

"I don't think they even got as far as me," Moira said, "and even if they had, they'd never have found Space Case."

"Not even if they'd taken over your mind," Paul agreed. "It was a sweet bit, and I could never have thought of it in a hundred years."

"Aw shucks," Wally said, and something in the tone of his voice made June recall her mother's words about her fiancé's kindness. She tightened the arm she had around Paul, and grinned fiercely at the sunset. "I think the alien mask worked good, too," she said. "Did you see them *frown* at that, Paul?"

"Well, I just had it lying around in my masquerade trunk, and I happened to think of it," Moira said, clearly as pleased as Wally. "So what will you and Paul do now, June?"

"Haven't the foggiest," she said happily, and took a swallow of Irish coffee. "Something good."

"Shouldn't be a problem," Paul said confidently. "Our requirements are modest. All we really need is identities, a house, a car, and a modest income, ideally in the next twenty-four hours. Oh, and one other detail: I owe a guy ninety-nine large."

"Aw Jeeze, look—" Wally began.

"Even worse," Paul went on, "the guy is a friend of mine, so I can't just weasel."

Wally subsided, but bit his lip.

"You can't go back to the Point Grey Road place?" Moira asked.

June shook her head. "We were going to have to leave there soon anyway. Any time now, the bank and the realtor are due to figure out the money we bought it with was imaginary. I don't even think it's safe to go back and get my dirty comic books."

Wally coughed, and bit his lip some more.

"But like I say, I'm in the mood to scale back a little," Paul said. "A Honda gets you the same place a Porsche does—cheaper—and you don't have to keep it locked up as tight. I don't need a really good house, like this one—I'd settle for one of those modern pieces of crap." He gestured casually to his right. "As for work, the first thing that occurs to me is that this is a big movie and TV town, and June and I both have relevant skills."

"WOW!" Wally cried, loud enough to startle Paul and June.

Moira merely turned to him and raised an eyebrow.

"I almost got it," he said excitedly. "Help me, spice!"

Moira nodded, and he turned to present the back of his head to her. She quickly surveyed the tools available to her, finished her coffee in a long draught, and used the soft thermal plastic mug to whack her husband solidly on the occiput.

He caught his glasses as they flew off, and put them back on. "Got it—thanks," he said, and turned to Paul, who was regarding him with a strange expression. "You *are* both excellent actors," he stated.

"Well, actually, when I said 'relevant skills' I meant bullshitting—and I was thinking of bullshitting on a more serious scale than mere acting," Paul began. "I was thinking producer, or—"

"I have two jobs for you," Wally said. "I would also take both of them as personal favors. The first one requires acting—*and* bullshitting: specifically, writing."

Paul pursed his lips. "Well . . . I believe Heinlein said the difference between a writer and a con man was, the writer could work in bed and use his right name if he happened to feel like it. What did you have in mind?"

"Remember the story we gave the Net to track you down?" Wally said. "If Moira and I don't want to have to waste a whole lot of the precious two weeks left before the con doing a lot of fast talking, *somebody* is going to have to write and produce a play called 'Data Takes A Dump,' that stars a guy who looks like Jean-Luc Picard."

In spite of himself, Paul smiled. "Well, it's a little out of our line."

June was smiling too. "What the hell. Dad'll let us use the barn; I can sew costumes—"

"Wait," Wally said. "You haven't heard the second job. It goes along with the first. Both or no deal."

"Go ahead," Paul said.

"That house you just pointed to next door belongs to a life-form named Gorsky. He's the one you bought your magnesium from, and he's the one who gave you up as Metkiewicz."

"Oh, really?" Paul said, turning to look more

closely at the Gorsky home. His smile had become faintly feral.

"He's also sued Moira and me half a dozen times in eight years. Now I realize that you are both retired. But if you're willing to skirt grey areas like movie producers . . . would you be willing to lecture other citizens on the tricks of your former trade? Could you, for instance, explain to me how an unscrupulous enough individual could con, say, someone who lived on a block like this out of their house and land?"

Paul looked at June; she looked back. "You want him in jail?"

"No. Just somewhere else. And I want that property."

Paul's smile became positively vulpine.

"If you and June will do those two jobs for me," Wally said, "I will pay you ninety-nine thousand dollars Canadian, and lifetime free rent in that house—on the condition that you plant crabgrass."

"And we'll throw in free room and board here, until both jobs are done," Moira said. "Paul, you know what our guest room is like."

Paul and June exchanged another glance, finished their coffees, put their cups down, and stuck out their hands.

More coffee was poured, considerably more whiskey was poured, and the sunset was roundly toasted. As the sky darkened, conversation became general, veered around for awhile, and inevitably wandered back to the events of the day just finished.

"You know," Paul said, "I almost wish there was some effective way they *could* have edited my memories, without leaving gaps too big to shrug off as a bender. I mean, in a way I'm almost glad I'm never going to know any more than I do right now . . . but at the same time, the little I *do* know is going to stick in my mind like a burr under my saddle for the rest of my life, and drive me crazy."

"Tell me about it," June said. "I *know* my mother was dead. But that was *her*, today. How do you make sense of something like that?"

Wally sent Moira a glance she could read even in the dark, that meant, *They haven't figured it out.*

She sent one back that meant, *That's good.*

He sent, *But knowing is going to drive us crazy!*

She sent back, *So who said life was fair?*

And both grinned.

Just then there came a faint crackling sound, and an odor of toasting basil and cinnamon.

Paul and June stirred in sudden alarm. Wally and Moira caught their alarm at once, and guessed its cause. Each of the four freed their right arm and reached for a weapon. "Double cross?" Paul wondered. A sound at the upper range of perception converged slowly from all directions at once. The temperature rose just perceptibly. Paul started to rise, and June restrained him. The sound swelled and congealed, like a Bronx cheer played backwards—

A small Egg sat on the roof, directly in front of Wally and Moira.

It was about the size of a volleyball, but otherwise identical to the one Paul and June had seen appear that afternoon: a perfect sphere of something more transparent than glass. Paul and Wally both had the same wild thought: that the little sphere would contain a miniature Laura Bellamy, something like Tinkerbell.

But its contents seemed far more mundane.

The Egg vanished like the soap bubble it resembled, and the item within dropped to the roof and began to slide. Wally reached out and stopped it with a foot, leaned forward and recovered it.

It was a compact disk. The caddy that held it had no front or back cover or liner notes, was simply a plastic box. The CD itself was almost equally featureless. No corporate or manufacturer's logo, no catalog data, no copyright warning, none of the standard commercial icons, no printing at all—not even the basic stuff found on a blank CD-ROM. Just a rectangular white block printed on its upper surface, within which someone with careful, Spenserian penmanship had written the words:

Free As A Bird
Real Love
(final versions and
original demos)

"What the hell do you suppose *that* means?" Wally asked.

Hard SF is Good to Find

CHARLES SHEFFIELD

Proteus Combined
Proteus in the Underworld
In the 22nd century, technology gives man the power to alter his shape at will. Behrooz Wolf invented the process—now he will have to tame it....

The Mind Pool
A revised and expanded version of the author's 1986 novel *The Nimrod Hunt*. "A considerable feat of both imagination and storytelling." —*Chicago Sun-Times*

Brother to Dragons
Sometimes one man *can* make a difference. A Dickensian novel of the near future by a master of hard SF.

Between the Strokes of Night
None dared challenge the Immortals' control of the galaxy—until one man learned their secret....

Dancing with Myself
Sheffield explains the universe in nonfiction and story.

ROBERT L. FORWARD

Rocheworld
"This superior hard-science novel of an interstellar expedition is a substantially revised and expanded version of *The Flight of the Dragonfly*.... Thoroughly recommended." —*Booklist*

Indistinguishable from Magic
A virtuoso mixture of science fiction and science fact, including: antigravity machines—six kinds! And all the known ways to build real starships.

→

DAVID WEBER

Honor Harrington *(cont.)*:

Field of Dishonor

Honor goes home to Manticore—and fights for her life on a battlefield she never trained for, in a private war that offers just two choices: death—or a "victory" that can end only in dishonor and the loss of all she loves....

Other novels by DAVID WEBER:

Mutineers' Moon

"...a good story...reminds me of 1950s Heinlein..."
—*BMP Bulletin*

The Armageddon Inheritance

Sequel to *Mutineers' Moon*.

Path of the Fury

"Excellent...a thinking person's Terminator."
—*Kliatt*

Oath of Swords

An epic fantasy.

with STEVE WHITE:

Insurrection

Crusade

Novels set in the world of the Starfire ™ game system.

And don't miss Steve White's solo novels,
***The Disinherited** and **Legacy**!*

continued ☞

WALPURGIS NIGHT WAS NOTHING COMPARED TO THIS

When Andy Westin became a security guard at Black Oak Mall he had no idea what he was getting into. During daylight hours the place seemed ordinary enough—although there *is* just the occasional flicker of motion from the corner of the eye to mark its strangeness—but at night, well, things can get pretty wild, what with elven princesses, rampaging brownies, intelligent security computers and all.

What happened was that this particular mall, one of the biggest in the world, was built on an elven power source, and not just a garden variety source either, but an actual gateway between Elfland and Earth. This has made it a source of conflict between some very heavy elven hitters.

The good guys are merely ruthless; the bad guys are evil incarnate and will have your eyeballs for breakfast if they get the chance. On the eve before May Day this battle will overflow the night into the day, and all that stands between thousands of innocent shoppers and the worst that Faery has to offer is one bemused security guard...if the elven princess doesn't get him first.

MALL PURCHASE NIGHT 72198-4 ♦ $4.99 ☐
